Postgraduate English Listening and Speaking
(Revised Edition)
Teacher's Book

研究生英语
听说教程（修订版）

系列教材

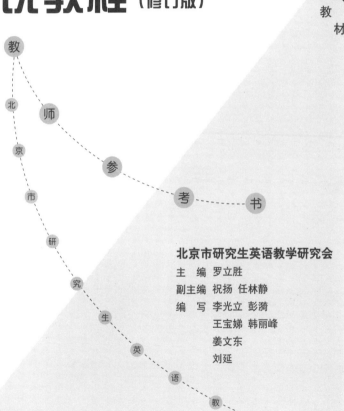

教 师 参 考 书

北 京 市 研 究 生 英 语 教 学 研 究 会

北京市研究生英语教学研究会

主　编　罗立胜
副主编　祝扬　任林静
编　写　李光立　彭漪
　　　　王宝娣　韩丽峰
　　　　姜文东
　　　　刘延

中国人民大学出版社

研究生英语系列教材编委会

罗舜泉　　（中国人民大学）
曹元寿　　（北京农业工程大学）
刘利君　　（北京理工大学）
胡德康　　（北京医科大学）
罗立胜　　（清华大学）
陆佑珊　　（国防大学）
金振东　　（北方交通大学）

出　版　说　明

　　1992 年 11 月,国家教委研究生工作办公室颁布了"关于印发《非英语专业研究生英语(第一外语)教学大纲(试行稿)》的通知"(以下简称《大纲》)。这个通知指出:"为了贯彻实施学位条例,保证研究生英语教学质量,提高研究生实际应用英语的水平,组织编写了《非英语专业研究生英语(第一外语)教学大纲(试行稿)》。"《大纲》颁布下达以后,从事研究生英语教学工作的教师们感到今后的教学工作有了基本法规,可以做到有章可循,同时又感到美中不足,即缺少一套能全面体现大纲精神的教材,供他们使用,俾能正确贯彻大纲精神,达到大纲要求。

　　北京市研究生英语教学研究会 1987 年成立伊始,即制定了北京地区研究生英语教学大纲,为全国编写统一的研究生英语教学大纲作出了自己的贡献。国家教委的《大纲》颁布后,我研究会多数成员要求研究会组织力量,尽快编写出一套完整的研究生英语系列教材,以实际行动促进研究生英语教学改革,贯彻《大纲》精神,不断提高教学质量和研究生实际应用英语的能力。

　　常务理事会根据大家的意见,成立了"研究生英语系列教材"编委会,负责策划、研究、统筹编写工作。编委会下成立了相应的教材编写组,具体编写《精读教程》、《泛读教程》、《听说教程》和《写译教程》,以及与之配套的辅助教材。我们希望,通过这套系列教材能比较全面地贯彻《大纲》的指导思想,充实研究生英语的教学内容。这套教材于 1994 年起由中国人民大学出版社陆续出版,使用几年来效果良好。

"研究生英语系列教材"（修订版）是在第一版的基础上，在广泛地征求使用单位的意见后，组织修订的。第一版教材在研究生英语教学及教学改革中起到了积极的作用，并产生了较好的影响。修订版保持了原有的特色及优点，加强了语言运用能力的培养，并修正了不足之处。修订版将会更好地满足研究生英语教学的需要。

本系列教材在编写、修订、出版过程中，除得到本研究会理事单位的全力支持外，还得到有关高校研究生院（部）领导和同仁的帮助和鼓励。特别是中国人民大学出版社的同志为本书的尽早出版做了大量的工作，在此我们一并表示衷心的感谢。

由于时间仓促，工作条件和物质条件等诸多限制，本系列教材的缺点和错误在所难免，敬请使用本书的教师和读者指正。

北京研究生英语
教学研究会
1999 年 1 月

修订版前言

《研究生英语听说教程》（修订版）是北京市研究生英语教学研究会委托北京市有关院校根据《研究生英语教学大纲》（试行稿）所编写的英语听说教科书，适用于高等院校文、理、工、医、农、林等各学科的非英语专业的硕士研究生。

《研究生英语听说教程》（修订版）是在较大范围征求了使用单位意见的基础上开始修订的。其修订指导思想是根据《研究生英语教学大纲》及《考试大纲》所确定的听力要求，进一步加强该教程的实用性和趣味性，同时尽可能满足当前听说教学的实际需要以及21世纪研究生英语教学发展的要求。

《研究生英语听说教程》（修订版）在保留第一版的优点和特色的基础上，作了以下修订：

1. 将《研究生英语听说教程》上下册合编为一本，使原来的四本书改为两本（学生用书和教师参考书各一本），学生用书改为16开本；可供两个学期使用。

2. 每个单元加入了新的听力材料，使其内容更加充实和丰富；新编了部分练习，从整体上增加了听说教程的难度。

3. 加强了口语实践的训练，每个单元增加了新的口语训练题。

4. 增加了研究生英语学位课考试听力部分的模拟练习题。

5. 改善了录音质量及磁带的清晰度，加快了录音的语速。

《研究生英语听说教程》（修订版）的安排基本上与第一版相同，每单元分为三个部分：1. 听力训练；2. 口语实践；3. 听力测试。修订版保留了第一版中的大部分素材，增加了新的听力材料及听力试题。全书共 30 单元，以听力技能训练为主，同时兼顾口语实践和学位课程考试听力部分的训练。

《研究生英语听说教程》（修订版）教师用书是配合学生用书编写的。书中提供了全部的录音书面材料以及答案，可供教师和学生参考。

《研究生英语听说教程》（修订版）由清华大学、中国人民大学、北京科技大学、中国政法大学、军事医学科学院和北方交通大学的教师编写；由金振东老师审校；澳大利亚英语教师 Mary Tarrant 通读了全稿并做了部分修改。

本书在修订过程中得到了北京市研究生英语教学研究会常务理事会、研究生英语系列教材编委会和部分兄弟院校有关教师的大力支持和帮助。他们对本教材提出了许多宝贵的意见，在此向他们表示感谢。

由于编写人员的水平有限，难免有不足之处，祈望使用本教程的教师和同学批评指正。

编 者

1999 年 1 月

CONTENTS

Unit One

Part I : Listening Practice

Section A: Taking a Photo
Exercise 1

Directions: The man is going to get a photo taken, but he does not know how to use a photo booth. Now listen to the conversation on the tape and then number the diagrams below in the order you hear the instructions.

M: Excuse me. Could you help me?

W: What's the matter?

M: I need a photograph, but I can't read English very well. How do I get a photo from this machine?

W: Oh, I see. Well, do you want color or black and white?

M: Color.

W: Right. So that's this booth. First of all, select your background.

M: Could you say that again please?

W: "Select". That means "choose" the curtain behind you. You see. Which color do you want?

M: Blue.

W: Adjust. Oh, move the stool to the correct height like this. Do you want one large or four small photos?

M: Four small.

W: So turn the dial to the four photos.

M: Dial?

W: Yes. That's the thing you turn. Yes, that's it. Right. Sit down and put your money in.

Have you got a pound?

M: Yes, two fifty pieces.

W: Don't put them in. It takes only pound coins.

M: Oh. Have you got one? Could I have it, please? Thank you.

W: Wait for the flash. Don't get up. It hasn't finished. Wait for four flashes, four photos. Ok.

That's it.

M: It's finished.

W: Yes, just wait for the photos to come out. It takes about five minutes. Would you mind moving please? I want to get some photos too.

Exercise 2

Directions: Listen to the conversation again and complete the following sentences. And then with your partner, put the instructions below in the same order as the dialogue.

Section B: About a Film
Exercise 1

Directions: Lynne is going to tell Steve about the film she saw last night. Listen to the cassette and then answer the questions.

Lynne: Steve, I went to see a fantastic film last night.

2

Steve: Which one?

Lynne: The Babysitter. It's brilliant.

Steve: What's it about?

Lynne: Well. There is the girl who is looking after a baby, and at the end of the film she is all alone in the big house, except the baby, of course. And there is a man outside. He is trying to get in. And well, she sees him and then she locks all the doors, but she forgets to lock the French windows.

Steve: Why doesn't she call the police?

Lynne: She tries, but the phone doesn't work.

Steve: Why doesn't she try to run away then?

Lynne: She can't, because she knows a man is outside.

Steve: Well, what happens the next?

Lynne: Well, the man gets in through the French windows and the girl rushes up the stairs. And he follows her, and she locks herself in the bathroom. Then the man is trying to break down the door. And then suddenly she remembers the baby is still in the bedroom. And the man...

Steve: Stop, stop. Don't tell me any more.

Lynne: Why? The next bit is the best bit.

Steve: Ok. But I don't want you to spoil the ending for me.

Exercise 2

Directions: Listen to the cassette again and rearrange the sentences below into the correct order.

Section C: Inviting Some People

Directions: You will hear someone inviting the people below to go somewhere. Check the correct item for each person, and then circle

3

it.

(1)

A: Well, thank goodness. It's Friday, huh, Jean?

B: Yes, it was a long week, Ken.

A: We should do something together this weekend. Got any plans yet?

B: No, not really.

A: How about going to a Yankee game or seeing a movie maybe?

B: Can you get tickets for a game? I haven't been to a baseball game in ages. Who are they playing?

A: The Blue Jays.

(2)

A: What are you going to do this weekend, Karen? Got any plans?

B: Want to see a movie? Flash-dance is on at the Marina.

B: Yeah, why not? The early or the late show?

A: Let's go to the late show, and we could do something afterward. Maybe go dancing or hear some music?

B: Sounds good. I really need to do something fun this weekend. I've had an awful week!

(3)

A: What are you and Joe doing this weekend, Michelle? Would you be free to come over for drinks after dinner sometime?

B: Hey, thank you, Pat, that sounds nice. I don't think we have made any plans yet, have we, Joe?

C: No, nothing I can remember. That'd be nice.

A: How about Saturday, about eight-thirty?

B: Great. Can I bring anything...?

4

(4)

A: How about going ice skating tomorrow night?

B: Gee. I'm not really too crazy about ice skating. But do you like roller skating?

A: Sure. Would you like to do that tomorrow?

B: Yeah, that'd be fun. But you know. I'm not very good at it.

A: Don't worry. Neither am I. But we'll have fun anyway.

(5)

A: Want to go to Annable's tomorrow night? They've got a new group playing.

B: You know, it's always so crowded there? There's never enough room to dance.

A: I guess so. Why don't we go to Spats? The music's always good there, and they've got a big dance floor.

B: Yeah, I haven't been there for a while.

Section D: Express Company

Directions: The following is an advertisement from Express Company in the United States. You may hear the advertisement twice. As you listen, complete the grid with the information you hear on the tape. Some of the information has been partly filled in for you.

This is the Express Company. We've recently expanded our business. The expanded business includes the three main services as follows:

The pre-paid express bag service. That means you buy the bags in advance and then just give us a call for a quick pick-up at any time. The delivery of a bag is made the next day to all major cities in the United States. The cost is $ 10 for a 3 kilo bag. That's $ 10 a bag.

The second one is the same day service. The Express can go to you, and deliver a letter or a small parcel within this city in the same day. The cost for the same day service delivery is $ 8.

For the large packages, we offer the express road service. We'll deliver to any town in the United States. Delivery time and cost depend on the distance and the weight of the package.

For further details of any of these services, call 33445656, and ask for the sales department. Remember, nothing is as speedy as Express.

Part Ⅲ: Listening Comprehension Test
Directions: In this part, you will hear 15 short conversations concerning different occupations. After you have heard each conversation, try to choose the best answer.

1. M: May I speak with Don Black, please?
   W: Sorry. He's out on his route delivering packages. He'll be back soon.
   Q: What does Don Black do?
2. M: Have a seat. What can I do for you? You look a little bit upset.
   W: I'd like to be an engineer, but now I can't decide. I need some advice.
   Q: What is the man's job?
3. M: Do your students study Japanese?
   W: No, but all of them are learning English. In this school

6

English is a compulsory subject.

Q: Who do you think the woman probably is?

4. M: What's wrong with your computer?

W: It doesn't work. Can I leave it here? But, I need it tomorrow.

Q: What is the man's probable occupation?

5. M: If you can make up your mind about the color, I can start to paint your house tomorrow.

W: Well, right now I like light blue for the wall, but I'll let you know this afternoon for sure.

Q: Who is the woman talking to?

6. M: We should get some one to mow the lawn and trim the trees in our garden.

W: Since we are both very busy, why don't we call Mr Davis?

Q: What is Mr Davis's occupation?

7. W: The drain is clogged again, and there's water all over the bathroom floor.

M: We'll have to call Mr Morris right away.

Q: What job does Mr Morris probably have?

8. W: Good morning. Your passport, please. Do you have anything to declare?

M: Only these two cartons of cigarettes, a bottle of brandy and some silver jewelry. That's all.

Q: Who do you think the woman is?

9. W: Hi, Mr Wood. Is my prescription ready? My name is Anne Emmet.

M: It's right here. Just follow these directions, and take one pill right after each meal.

Q: What is the man's occupation?

10. W: Can you make me a table three feet high and four feet wide?

M: Sure. How many drawers do you want?

Q: What most probably is the man's occupation?

11. M: How long have you been here? What is your subject?

W: Oh, I'm a freshman, and my major is chemistry.

Q: Who are these two speakers likely to be ?

12. W: Now, Sir. Just relax. I'm going to give you a little injection.

M: It's OK, Miss. I feel better now. The arm is in plaster.

Q: What's the woman's occupation?

13. W: What exactly are you looking for, professor?

M: I'm looking for any remains, any utensils, bones or buildings that will tell us something about the people who lived here 2,000 years ago.

Q: What is the man's profession?

14. W: The weather report says there will be sunshine tomorrow.

M: Good. The wheat is ready to cut. I hope it can stay bright and sunny for a few more days so that we can complete the harvest.

Q: What is the profession of the two speakers?

15. M: I must say, Miss, the food was great and I've never had such good service.

W: Well, thank you sir. I'll pass your compliments to the cook. And thank you too for the tip.

Q: What is the woman's occupation?

Unit   Two

Section A: Looking for a Flat

Directions: Joe is looking for a flat to rent. He is talking to the manager at the North London Accommodation Agency. Listen to the conversation and use the information to complete the following chart for Joe. You'll hear the piece twice.

Joe: Oh, Mr Berten.

Mr Berten: Take a seat. I think I've found something for you.

Joe: Oh, great.

Mr Berten: It's a one bedroom flat in Kanden.

Joe: Where is it?

Mr Berten: Thirty-four New Street.

Joe: Is that near the station?

Mr Berten: Yes, very close.

Joe: Oh, that's good, and how much is the rent?

Mr Berten: $ 75 a week, but that includes gas and electricity.

Joe: That's OK. Can you tell me about the flat?

Mr Berten: Well, it had central heating. There is a small kitchen
               and bathroom, and a washing machine.

Joe: Is there, what is it, a machine for drying clothes? a tumble

9

dryer?

Mr Berten: No. I'm afraid not.

Joe: Does the landlady live in the same building ?

Mr Berten: Yes. Mrs Green. She lives on the top floor, but I don't
see much of her.

Joe: Well, I quite like to see it. When can I go round?

Mr Berten: I can take you at 4 o'clock this afternoon if you like. Is
that all right?

Joe: Yes. That's fine. See you later then.

Section B: Finding out the House Rules

Directions: Now listen to the conversation twice and then make brief
notes of each rule.

Judy: Well, it's a lovely room. It's quite a nice size.

Landlord: Oh yes. It's a good-sized room and it's well-furnished.

Judy: Yes. I can see that. Erm... is there anything that I should
know?

Landlord: Well, I don't allow the cat to go upstairs at all.

Judy: Oh? Not at all.

Landlord: No, absolutely not. I don't like cats upstairs. And I
don't allow people to smoke in bedrooms.

Judy: Oh no, no, I agree with that. I don't smoke anyway.

Landlord: And... erm... I don't allow people to stick pictures upon the walls with sellotape. Well, you see, when you
take the picture down, the sellotape would leave... eum
a mark on the paper.

Judy: Oh, I see. Can I use blutack or something?

10

Landlord: Oh yes. Something like that is quite acceptable. And there are just two more things if you don't mind. If you go out, would you please remember to close the window?

Judy: Right, I'll do that.

Landlord: And there's the kettle here, as you can see, but when you boil the kettle could you please put it on the floor and not on the chest of drawers?

Judy: Yes, it would probably leave a mark.

Landlord: Is... is that all right?

Judy: Well, it sounds very fair. Thank you very much.

Landlord: Yes, all right. Good.

Section C: Apartments for Rent
Exercise 1

Directions: Betty and Paul are looking for an apartment to rent. Paul is checking through the newspaper. Which apartments does he talk about? Circle the advertisements.

Betty: Anything interesting in the paper today?

Paul: Let's have a look. Well, yeah, there are a few here that might interest us. Here's one for just under $400. It only has one bedroom but it sounds nice. Near a park. It'd be nice to live near a park.

Betty: Mmm, But you know, $390 seems expensive for just one bedroom.

Paul: Yes, you're right. Oh, here's one that's little cheaper, near University Avenue. It's $350.

Betty: How many bedrooms?

11

Paul: Just one again. That's not a very nice area.

Betty: No, it's pretty noisy. I'd prefer a larger place really.

Paul: Yeah. Let me see what the cheapest two bedroom apartments. Oh, here's real bargain. It's only 350. But it doesn't have any furniture.

Betty: No. You know how much it can cost to furnish an apartment?

Paul: Oh, here's another one for just over 400. This sounds very interesting. It's on Metcalf. That's a nice street.

Betty: Yes, it's quiet. Did you say two bedrooms?

Paul: Yes, at $415.

Betty: Why don't we go and have a look at it?

Paul: OK. I'll give them a call.

Exercise 2

Directions: Now listen again. Write the name of a street beside each statement.

Section D: Completing an Insurance Form

Directions: You will hear a conversation between a woman and employee of an insurance company. As you listen, complete the form with the information you hear. Some of the information has already been included in the form.

W: Good morning. I'd like to ask about an existing insurance policy, please?

E: What sort of insurance was it, madam? Home insurance, car insurance, home contents or life insurance?

W: Home contents insurance. I'd like to increase the insurance cover.

E: What's your policy number?

W: It begins with H. H3067B.

E: And what's your name?

W: Mrs Riley. That's RILEY.

E: I've got you on the computer. H3067B, Mrs Riley. Property, at 15th Cliff Street. Are you still at that address?

W: Yes. Number 15, Cliff Street.

E: Okay—well, you're currently insured for $50,000. How much would you like to raise it to?

W: $80,000. I'd like to insure some more items.

E: Right. What are they?

W: I've got a video camera worth $5,000 and a portable computer...

E: OK, let me get this down, A video camera valued at $5,000, and a portable computer, $4,000.

W: I've also got a diamond ring. It must be worth $20,000.

E: OK, then. let me run over these again. You want to raise the insurance to $80,000, and specify on the policy the video camera, the portable computer and the diamond ring.

W: Yes, that's right.

E: I'll get this out to you tomorrow.

W: Thank you very much.

E: Not a problem.

Part Ⅲ: Listening Comprehension Test

Directions: In this part, you will hear 15 short conversations concerning different relationships between the two speakers. After you

13

have heard each conversation, try to choose the best answer.

1. W: Would you like to see the menu, now?
   M: No, thanks. I already know what I'd like to order.
   Q: What is the relationship between these two people?
2. W: I'm terribly sorry. I really don't know what's wrong.
   M: You were speeding. May I have your driver's license?
   Q: What's the relationship between the man and the woman?
3. W: It's always hard to get this car into first gear, and now
      something seems wrong with the brake.
   M: If you leave it with me, I'll fix it for you this afternoon.
   Q: What's the probable relationship between the two speakers?
4. M: It was very nice to meet your family. I hope they enjoyed
      my company.
   W: Don't worry. My family approved of you.
   Q: What is the probable relationship between the man and the
      woman?
5. M: Could you please tell me at which stop I should get off for
      the City Council? Also, how much is the fare?
   W: Of course. You can get off at 72nd Street. I'll tell you
      when we get there. The fare is fifty cents, just put it in the
      box.
   Q: What is the probable relationship between these two people?
6. W: Go to bed early and get some rest, Peter. You have to get
      up early tomorrow.
   M: But I have to study. We're going to have a history test to-
      morrow morning. I failed the last test, so I must pass this
      one.

14

Q: What is the probable relationship between the two speakers?

7. W: Excuse me. Which way is it to the police station? I want to report that I have lost my wallet.

   M: Go up the high street and you'll see it on your left.

   Q: Who are these people?

8. W: I got a bad start in the last race. It was hard to catch up with others.

   M: We'll work on your start. The most important thing is concentration before a race starts.

   Q: What is the probable relationship between these two people?

9. M: Well, where are we going today and what time will we be back at the hotel?

   W: First I'll take you to one of the historical sites in the oldest part of the town, and then we'll go to the city park. We'll be back about 12 o'clock.

   Q: What is most probably the relationship between the two speakers?

10. M: When you saw the accident, did you ring us immediately?

    W: Yes. The first thing which struck me was to call the police.

    Q: From this conversation what is the probable relationship between the two speakers?

11. M: Excuse me. Do you have anything on the history of basketball?

    W: I believe so. Look in the card catalogue under sports and also under hobbies.

    Q: What is the probable relationship between the two speakers?

12. M: I'd like to return this jacket. I bought it for my brother yesterday, but he doesn't like the color.

W: We can't give you a refund, but you can exchange it.

Q: What are the two speakers?

13. W: I'd appreciate your professional opinion. Do you think that I should sue the company?

    M: Not really. I think we can settle this out of court.

    Q: What is the probable relationship between the two speakers?

14. M: Now. What's the trouble, Mrs Smith?

    W: I've been very dizzy lately and last night I had some chest pain.

    Q: What is the probable relationship between the two speakers?

15. M: Paul wants to move to California and find a job there.

    W: I hope he can work here in New York. He's our only child.

    Q: What is the probable relationship between the two speakers?

Unit Three

Section A: Describing Different People

Directions: James Pond, Agent 006, the famous British spy, is in Rome where he has to make contact with certain people. He is listening to descriptions of the people he has to meet. Complete his notes about each person, The first one has been partly started for you.

(1)

A: You'd better give me my instructions. I have to leave soon.

B: OK, 006. Listen carefully. You have to meet Agent X at the bus station at 7:00 this evening.

A: At the bus station? Fine. Now, what does Agent X look like?

B: She's about thirty-five, and she has long, black hair.

A: Thirty-five. Right, And... re... long, black hair?

B: That's right. Oh, yes. And she wears glasses.

A: Glasses. OK. And is she tall, short, or what?

B: About average height, I guess. And she'll be wearing a yellow flower in her hair.

A: A yellow flower? That should make it easier!

B: Good luck, 006.

(2)

17

A: Good luck, X. Thank you for your help. Now, tell me what A-gent Y looks like.

B: OK. Agent Y is an older man. I guess he's about seventy.

A: Mm-hmm. Gray hair I suppose?

B: Yes, gray and a mustache. I'll need a bit more than that.

B: Let's see. Well, he's kind of short. Only about five feet or five feet two, I'd say.

A: About five feet tall. And where do I meet him?

B: Meet him at the airport, at Gate 2, at 11: 00 tomorrow morn-ing. And one more thing, 006. He'll be wearing a white flower in his jacket.

A: A white flower? All right. I'll be there.

B: Good luck, 006.

(3)

A: OK, Y. What else do you have to tell me ?

B: One more thing. You have to meet Agent Z. Agent Z will be waiting for you outside the Gold Charge Building at 1:00 this af-ternoon.

A: The Gold Charge Building? Right. Now, tell me what you know about Agent Z. How do I recognize him?

B: Not him, 006, her! Agent Z is quite young, about thirty. And she's really tall.

A: Tall, about thirty.

B: And she has blond hair.

A: OK. And what about her flowers? Will she. . .

B: Oh yes, of course! She'll be carrying some red flowers.

A: Thanks, Y.

B: Sure. Good luck, 006.

18

(4)

A: I have to go now.

B: Just a minute, 006. I have a message for you. You have to meet the Boss, tonight.

A: Oh no! Not... the boss!

B: That's right, 006. He'll be in a disco called Mama Mia tonight at 10 o'clock.

A: In a disco? But... I've never met him! What does he look like?

B: Well. he's very tall, very tall, and he has very long, dark hair.

A: Long hair? How old is he?

B: Mm... About forty-five, I guess.

A: And what about a flower? Will he be wearing flower of any kind?

B: A flower? No. But he will be wearing a T-shirt saying "Bruce Springs is the Boss!"

A: A Bruce Spring T-shirt? All right, Z. And thanks!

B: Good luck, 006. And enjoy the disco!

Section B: At the Doctor's

Directions: Kevin is at the doctor's. He has the flu. Look at the pictures below, then listen to the conversation. What does the doctor tell Kevin to do? Circle the correct picture.

Doctor: Well, there's much you can do about the flu, you know. The best thing you can do is to stay home. It's best to stay away from other people, so why don't you take a couple of days off from work?

Kevin: Yes, I will. And do you think I should stay in bed and rest?

19

Doctor: It's not really necessary to go to bed. Just as long as you stay indoors and rest. You know, watch TV or read.

Kevin: I see. Nothing too active, huh? And is it a good idea to drink a lot?

Doctor: Yes, you need to drink lots of liquids. That'll help. Now you won't feel very hungry. But when you do eat, just a little. Don't have a big meal. That way, it'll be easier to rest.

Kevin: OK. Are you going to give me a prescription?

Doctor: No, I'm afraid there's no medicine for the flu. You just have to rest and wait for it to go away. Medicine won't really do any good.

Kevin: How about aspirin for the aches?

Doctor: Sure. Sometimes aspirin helps. Anyway, it can't do any harm. Take one every four hours.

Kevin: All right. Thank you, doctor.

Doctor: Call me in a few days if you don't feel better.

Kevin: I will. Bye.

Section C: Leaving a Message
Exercise 1

Directions: You are going to hear someone ringing up to leave a message. Read the questions below carefully. Then answer these questions in the space provided on the right after you have heard the conversation on the telephone.

Petty: Is Ann there?

Jenny: No. This is Jenny. I'm afraid she won't be in for another hour until 8 o'clock.

Petty: Could you give her a message from me. It's Petty.

Jenny: Yes. Just a moment... right, Okey.

Petty: Could you say I want to know if I can borrow her hairdryer. Every time I switch my own nothing happens. It must be broken. I don't know what's wrong with it.

Jenny: Oh, dear! That's annoying!

Petty: Yes. Is it? Could you also ask her to get me a ring the moment she comes in. I would like her to do that straight away. I must talk to her. It's very important. If you could say that.

Jenny: Yes, the moment she..., very..., Yes.

Petty: And I had a letter. Could you tell her, from my cousin. He is not coming now until the end of May, not the end of April as I thought at first. She'll understand. I told her April originally.

Jenny: Yes. I'm just getting that down. May... not April..., Okey.

Petty: Oh, well. Thanks so much. Ah, yes. Could you say I've found the other shoe.

Jenny: What? I can't get that.

Petty: Shoe.

Jenny: Oh, yes.

Petty: It was under the wardrobe all the time. Is it silly? We looked everywhere. I don't know how we missed it.

Jenny: No. Well. I suppose it must have hidden itself.

Petty: Yes. Sorry? What was that?

Jenny: Nothing. Nothing important. Is that the lot?

Petty: Yes. That really is it. Thanks again. It's very kind of you to take. . .

Exercise 3

Directions: Read the following sentences carefully. Then listen to the cassette once more and number the nine sentences in their correct order in the conversation. Number 1 is done for you, and try to number the remaining boxes.

Part Ⅲ: Listening Comprehension Test

Directions: In this part, you will hear three short passages about lectures. At the end of each passage, there will be some questions. You will hear both the passages and the questions only once. After each question there will be a pause, you must choose the best answer from the four choices given by marking the corresponding letter (A, B, C or D).

Passage Ⅰ

I wonder how many of you would like to work in a very tall building without an elevator. Not many, I suppose. If elevators were not invented, tall buildings would be unusable. The first elevator was just a box suspended on a rope. A group of oxen or strong men would pull the rope and lift the box to a higher point. At that time, elevators were used only for heavy materials, not for passengers.

In 1853, Elisha Otis invented the first safe elevator. He showed his invention in New York. At an exhibition, Otis was lifted up in an open box that was attached to two guide rails. When he was above the audience, he gave the order to cut off the rope. To the amazement of the crowd, the box did not fall to the floor. Instead, it moved smoothly up and down. The demonstration worked well, and people have been riding as passengers in elevators ever since.

1. What is the main topic of this lecture?
2. What was the earliest elevator used for?
3. What happened to his invention at demonstration?

Passage II

Today, universities and colleges are almost in every city in the United States. In fact, the higher education started only about 120 years ago after the civil war. The first development happened in the field of technological and professional education. Many colleges were set up to meet the urgent demands of industry and society. These colleges included technology, engineering, law, medicine, etc. The second development was in graduate education. The universities such as Harvard, and Princeton, quickly took the lead in this field. The third development was the higher education for women. This included the establishment of new women's colleges. Then a large number of American women could enjoy education at universities or colleges as men. These developments began over a century ago and continued to this day.

4. What is the main topic of this lecture?
5. How many major educational developments did the speaker mention?
6. What is the second development about?

Passage Ⅲ

Good morning! As you know this is the course in beginning, Economics. We will meet each Monday, Wednesday and Friday at 9 o'clock for the next twelve weeks. Each Monday and Wednesday I'll give a lecture on the different concepts and thoughts in economics based on this book. I'll show you some cases and examples in this field. On Friday we'll have discussions on some special topics. As a requirement I would like you to write three papers on these topics. Your first paper should be finished within four weeks, and the other two have to be handed in one week before the end of this semester. Each paper should be two thousand words long and should be typed. There will be no exam, so I'll give the grades only on these papers and your participation in the discussion. Are there any questions?

7. How long does this course, Economics last?

8. What will they do on Friday morning?

9. When are the students expected to hand in the last two papers?

10. How many words are required for the paper?

Unit Four

Part I : Listening Practice

Section A: Telephoning about Jobs
Exercise 1

Directions: You will hear four people telephoning about jobs. Listen to the cassette and find out which jobs they talk about. Then number the pictures.

(1)

A: Power Record Store. Can I help you?

B: Yes, are you still looking for salespeople?

A: Yes, we are. It's a weekend job. Eight hours a day Saturday and Sunday. Do you want to leave your name? The store manager will call you back later.

B: Sure. My name's Kevin McCartney, that's M-C-C-A-R-T-N-E-Y, and my telephone number's 643-5123. When should I...

(2)

A: Ronny's Restaurant. Can I help you?

B: Yes. I'm calling about your advertisement. Are you still looking for people?

A: Yes, we are.

B: Oh, good. Is it full-time work?

A: Yes, it is. It's Tuesday through Sunday, from five until about twelve. And we need someone as soon as possible.

B: Oh, OK, And how much do you pay?

A: It's 3. 35 an hour, plus tips, of course. Do you have any experience?

B: Oh, sure. I worked as a waitress at Chez Michel, and Tony's Steak House, and...

(3)

B: Jack's Watering Hole.

A: OK, I'm calling about the ad for a bartender. Is that still available?

B: Yes, it is, What kind of experience do you have?

A: Well, I've worked in a number of hotels and bars around town.

B: Fine. OK, well, you'd be working nights, starting on Thursday, five or six days a week. Why don't you come in for an interview?

A: OK. My name's Phil Peter, that's P-E-T-E-R, and...

(4)

B: Queen's Hotel.

A: Hello. I'm calling about the receptionist's job.

B: OK.

A: Is that a full-time job?

B: No, it's just a weekend job, three evenings a week. I think the hours are five to midnight. Why don't you leave your name, and I'll ask the manager to call you back?

A: All right. My name's Dee Hilton, that's H-I-L-T-O-N, and my number's 876-0194.

Exercise 2

Directions: Listen to the cassette once again and then complete the following table with the necessary information about each job.

Section B: Talking about Jobs

Exercise 1

Directions: You will hear Diane, Tracy, Greg, and Joe talking about their jobs. What does each person do? Draw a line from each person's name to his or her job.

(1)

A: How's your job going, Diane?

B: Great! I'm enjoying it a lot. The restaurant's really busy. so the tips are pretty good. I get free Meals, too, which is nice. We have a great cook.

A: I should come down and have dinner some time.

B: Yes, why don't you? Really, the only problem I have here is that the food is so good, I eat too much. I'm getting really fat.

(2)

A: What's your new job, Tracy?

B: I'm a typist. But I don't think I'll be staying long.

A: Why not?

B: Well, the typing's fine—I really enjoy it. But the boss... He's awful! He's always asking me out. He thinks every woman in the office just can't wait to go out with him! Yuck! No thanks!

(3)

A: Selling many cars these days, Greg?

B: Oh, yeah, We're pretty busy. We've got a big sale on at the moment. We've got some great deals on Toyotas. Hey! Isn't it time you sold that old thing you're driving?

A: No way! My car and I are old friends! I'll never sell it.

(4)

A: Haven't seen you for a while, Joe. Been busy at work?

B: Yes, I've been looking for some new people to work in the office and it isn't easy! Some of these kids just out of school aren't as clever as they think they are!

A: Yes, I know what you mean! Hey, Let's meet for lunch sometime. Why don't you give me a call when you're free?

B: OK, What's your number?

A: It's 534 – 2323.

Exercise 2

Directions: Now listen again and tell if these statements are True of False.

Section C: Same Job or a New Job

Directions: You will hear people talking about their jobs. Check below if they have the same job or a new job.

(1)

A: And how are things going at the bank these days, Liza?

B: Oh, didn't I tell you? I'm working for Central Air-lines now.

A: I guess they found out about all that money you were taking home from the bank.

B: It was a pretty awful job actually. Boring! But it's great at Central. I get lots of free tickets, too!

A: Great! How about one for me!

28

(2)

A: So did you decide to take that new job, Tom?

B: Well, I thought about it, then I decided it was better to stay where I am. The manager's just offered me a raise, so I think I decided to stay with the bank a little longer.

A: Yeah, that sounds good.

(3)

A: So you finally decided to stop teaching, Brian?

B: Yes. It was driving me crazy!

A: So, how is everything in the real estate business? Have you sold any houses yet?

B: Mmm. That's the problem!

(4)

A: How is everything at Sater's?

B: Well, you know what? I was really bored, so I quit!

A: Really? So, Kay, what are you doing now?

B: I got a really good job with the bus company.

A: You don't look like a bus driver!

B: Well, maybe not, but that's what I'm doing now.

(5)

A: Are you still working at the university, Janice?

B: Yes, I am, but I got a new job as a secretary in the geography department.

A: Is that right? How do you like it?

B: Well, I'm learning a lot about geography!

Section D: Interview about a Job

Directions: You are going to hear a conversation between a man in an employment agency and a lady who has gone in to look for a job. First, study the form carefully. Now listen and fill in the information on the form.

M: Good morning. What can I do for you?

L: Well, yes, I hope so. I am wondering if you are still looking for a lab assistant.

M: Yes. Could I have your full name, please?

L: Yes, it's Jessica Richards. That's J-E-S-S-I-C-A, R-I-C-H-A-R-D-S.

M: Jessica Richards. And your address, Ms Richards?

L: Thirty, three, oh, Landseer Road. That's L-A-N-D-S-double-E-R. Landseer Road, Newtown.

M: Now, when were you born?

L: 19th March, 1980.

M: Mach 19th, 1980. Good. Now what about your education? And did you go to college or university?

L: You don't need all the schools, do you?

M: No, only secondary school.

L: I finished my education in the Newtown Secondary School in 1997.

M: Good. And I suppose you passed some "O" Levels. What subjects did you take?

L: English Language, Chemistry, Maths, French, Physics, and Biology.

M: Six, is that right? English, Chemistry, Maths, French, Physics, and Biology. And no degree or college diplomas or anything.

L: No.

M: What about interests? Hobbies, sports and so on.

L: Well, I enjoy playing the piano. I'm in a jazz band.

M: That's interesting. Any sport?

L: Yes, I'm keen on water-skiing.

M: Fine. Now what are you doing at the moment? As a job, I
   mean.

L: I was made redundant a month ago. I'm afraid. I was with quite
   a large chemical company as a lab assistant.

M: I see. Lab assistant in a chemical company. Do you know why
   they made you redundant?

L: No, except that it was a case of "last in, first out" when they
   had to cut back on the number of their employees. Since I was a
   recent addition, I had to go.

M: Yes. It's a common situation. Now the most important question
   of all. What are you looking for now? The same sort of job?

L: Yes, I like this kind of job.

M: But, it is not well paid, I'm afraid.

L: I really don't mind.

M: Well, we'll call you in one week. Thank you very much for
   coming.

L: Thank you, Good-bye.

M: Goodbye.

Part Ⅲ: Listening Comprehension Test

Directions: In this section, you will hear three passages concerning
short speeches. After you have heard the passages and the
questions, try to choose the best answer from the four choices given

31

by marking the corresponding letter (A, B, C or D).

Passage I

Let me be the first to welcome you to Middletown. I hope you have had a pleasant journey. If you have to change to another flight, an attendant at the gate will give you the departure gate number for your next flight. If Middletown is your destination, we thank you for traveling with us. As you leave the plane, walk to your right towards the baggage claim area. Your baggage will arrive in about 10 minutes. Airport transportation is available under the green signs after you have picked up your baggage. There are buses there that will take you into the center of Middletown. Taxis are also available in the blue parking area. Please stay in your seats until the captain has turned off the seat belt sign. Thank you.

1. To whom is this announcement most likely directed?
2. When they leave the plane, what should they do first?
3. Where can they find a taxi?

Passage II

Before I start with today's lecture on vegetation. I'd like to tell you about a summer camp. It is a science camp for one month. The purpose is to offer you a chance to study plants, trees and bushes in a mountain area. The camp will start in June 6, and we will take a train there. The cost will be partly covered by our department, and the rest will be paid by yourselves. I think that will be $ 200 altogether for you. You will get the chance to use some equipment for your observation, and meet some people from other universities. After the camp, we may travel to Washington for a few days, because that area is close to the capital, about only 100 kilometers apart. One more thing I have to mention is that summer camp is not a part of this course. So it's up to you to decide if you want to go or not. If you are interested, please see me, and sign your name here after the class.

4. Where is this speech most likely taking place?
5. What is the speaker telling the audience?
6. What would students do if they want to go?

Passage III

First of all, I'd like to welcome you for your first year at this college. My name is Jane Anderson, and I'm the vice dean of the college. This college was first established in 1925, and at that time it was a private college for science and physics. Later on, the college began to admit foreign students. You are the twentieth group. This morning there are several things I want to say. First our college is on the first and second floors where we have administrative offices, classrooms and a small library. On the first floor, you'll find advisors' rooms and my office. You are welcome to drop in with your problems. I usually work with my door open. But for some advisors, you have to make appointments to see them. Your classrooms are on the second floor, and the library is open to you from Monday to Saturday. You may read books, periodicals and reference books there. Finally I hope you'll enjoy your stay here.

7. Where is the speech made?
8. When was the college founded?
9. Where can the students find the speaker's office?
10. What would the students do if they want to see other advisors?

Unit Five

Part I : Listening Practice

Section A: Shopping
Exercise 1

Directions: Mrs Coleman is in a department store. She is asking the clerk about the prices of different things. Match each object and its correct price tag.

Clerk: Can I help you?

Mrs Coleman: Yes, I need something for my daughter. It's her birthday, so I want something special.

Clerk: Well, how much did you want to spend?

Mrs Coleman: Oh, money doesn't mater.

Clerk: Oh? Well, how about a nice ring?

Mrs Coleman: That's a good idea. Mmm... how much is this one?

Clerk: That's, er, $1,259.

Mrs Coleman: Oh, er, well, it's, er, not quite the right design for my daughter.

Clerk: Well, here's a beautiful bracelet. It's only $545. It's eighteen carat gold.

Mrs Coleman: Hmm. Well,... no, that's not quite right. I don't like the shape.

34

Clerk: I know. How about this gold pen? It's only 135, and it will last forever.

Mrs Coleman: Mmm, No, no. I don't think so. It's, oh dear, it's much too heavy.

Clerk: Too heavy? I see. Well, how about a watch?

Mrs Coleman: How much is your cheapest watch?

Clerk: Let's see. Oh, here's one for, er, 23. 75. That's twenty-three dollars and seventy-five cents.

Mrs Coleman: Ah, No, I don't think she would like that watch, its too big, Ah Ah. How about that calculator over there?

Clerk: The calculator? But I thought you wanted...

Mrs Coleman: Oh, it's beautiful! How much is it?

Clerk: It's, er, 7.85.

Mrs Coleman: It's perfect! I'll take it. She'll love it.

Exercise 2

Directions: Listen again. What does Mrs Coleman say is wrong with everything? Write the name of each item below.

Section B: Paying for the Things

Directions: Listen to these conversations. How do people pay for the things they buy? Check the correct answer.

(1)

A: I'd like this one, please.

B: OK. Cash or charge?

A: Well, do you take personal checks?

B: Only if it's a local check. Oh, and I'll need to see your driver's license, please.

A: Hmm, that'll take me a minute to find in this bag.

B: How about some other kind of ID? A credit card of something?

A: Ah, here it is. At last.

B: Good. Thank you.

(2)

A: Cash or charge?

B: I'll put it on my Best Card.

A: OK, Thank you. Could you sign here, please?

B: There you go.

A: Thank you. Here you are. Have a nice day.

(3)

A: That's $ 18.22, please.

B: Eighteen twenty-two. Thank you. Can I put that on my Gold Charge Card?

A: I'm sorry. We don't accept credit cards.

B: Oh, I see. Well, I'll just have to pay cash. That's ten, eleven, twelve, thirteen... oh, no. I don't have enough cash. I'll have to give you a check. Is that OK?

A: That's fine. It's a local check, isn't it?

B: Yes, it is.

(4)

A: That'll be, uh, $ 12.43 with tax.

B: Twelve forty-three?

A: That's right.

B: Can I give you a check?

A: Sure.

B: Oh,... I think I left my checkbook at home. I'll just pay cash.

(5)

A: I'll take this one, please.

B: OK. Thank you.

A: Can I pay by traveler's check?

B: Sure. Oh..., do you have anything smaller than a hundred? I can only accept traveler's checks up to fifty dollars.

A: Mmm. I don't think so. No, no. I'm afraid not. Well, I'll just pay cash. Oh, just a minute.
Here's a twenty.

B: OK. Could I see your passport or some kind of ID?

A: Sorry ?

B: You do have some kind of ID, don't you?

A: Yes, I think so. Yes, here's my passport.

B: Oh, Good. And could you please sign the check?

Section C: Discussing Plans for the Weekend

Directions: You will hear people discussing plans for the weekend. Circle the letter of the phrase that describes their plans.

(1)

A: Hi, Lisa.

B: Hi, Cathy.

A: Are you coming with us to the movies tonight?

B: Hope. Wait till you hear this, You know that blond guy we often see at the pool?

A: You mean Dick Stevens.

B: Yeah. Well, he asked me out!

A: You're kidding! What are you going to do?

B: We're going out to dinner.

A: Great. Well, have a great time.

(2)

A: You're going to come to the ball game on Saturday, aren't you, Kim?

B: Wish I could. But I've got friends here from out of town.

A: Why don't you bring them along?

B: Well, they're not really football fans. I think we'll just eat out somewhere.

(3)

A: You're going to Fred's place on Saturday, aren't you, Kate?

B: Yeah. Sounds like there'll be quite a crowd there.

A: Should be fun. The last party was great, wasn't it?

B: That's what I heard, but I wasn't there.

A: You weren't? Why didn't you go?

B: Oh, I was busy. I had to drive my parents to the airport.

A: Oh, yeah. Where did they go?

B: Hawaii.

(4)

A: What are you doing on Saturday night, Jeff? I suppose you're going to study as usual, huh?

B: I should, with exams only two weeks away. But I really want to see that Clint Eastwood movie.

A: Oh, yes. I hear it's a lot of fun. Let's go together.

B: Good idea.

(5)

A: What are you doing this weekend, Jenny?

B: Well, I've finally persuaded Tony to help me paint the kitchen.

38

A: What color are you going to paint it?

B: A sort of yellow color. I like a light kitchen, but I don't want anything too bright.

A: Yeah, know what you mean. Should look nice. Have fun.

(6)

A: Staying in town for a long weekend, Christy?

B: No, I'm going away.

A: How nice. Where are you going?

B: My cousins have a house in the country in Vermont. I'm going to spend the weekend with them.

A: Who are you going with?

B: With my sister.

A: Oh, that'll be nice.

Section D: Completing a Complaint Form

Directions: You are going to hear a conversation over the telephone. Listen to the cassette and complete the complaint form. You will hear the piece twice.

Service Dept: Hello. Johnson's Electric Service Department.

Andrew: Oh, Hello. They asked me in the Electric Department to ring you for details. It's about the electric fan my wife brought in this morning.

Service Dept: I don't think it's come up yet. Anyway. I'll just fill this form in. Right.

Andrew: I thought it was a large one, but I found the box and it's the medium one.

Service Dept: I see. Not the large one.

Andrew: The year of manufacture is 1985. And the number is BE

42703-02. Am I going too fast?

Service Dept: No, no. That's fine. And what exactly wrong with it?

Andrew: Well. It just won't work. You switch it on and nothing happens.

Service Dept: It could be the plug. Do you use a fuse plug?

Andrew: Yes. I don't think it. . .

Service Dept: Never mind. We'll check it out. Is it a red or green one?

Andrew: Blue. ·

Service Dept: And your name is. . . ?

Andrew: Andrew Emmett.

Service Dept: Is it one or two ms?

Andrew: It's E-M-M-E-T-T.

Service Dept: Eh, good.

Andrew: My address is 5 Rainbow Terrace West Old-Field Surrey.

Service Dept:. . . Rainbow. . . , Code?

Andrew: Oh, TP33.

Service Dept: Where can we reach you during the day-time.

Andrew: 77480.

Service Dept: Well. Mr Emmett. As soon as they come up it will be checked out.

Part Ⅲ: Listening Comprehension Test

Section A

Directions: In this section, you will hear nine short conversations between two speakers. At the end of each conversation a third voice

40

will ask a question about what was said. Both the conversations and the questions will be spoken only once. After each question there will be a pause. During the pause, you must choose the best answer from the four choices given by marking the corresponding letter (A, B, C or D).

1. M: Mary, would you please run through this essay for me, and tell me what you think of it?

   W: Leave it on the desk. I'll read it after dinner.

   Q: What does the man want the woman to do?

2. W: Anne missed class again, didn't she? I wonder why.

   M: Well, I called her this morning. Her brother and his family have been visiting her. That's all. They live in Mexico.

   Q: Why has Mary been absent from class?

3. W: Excuse me, do you have a copy of Decline and Fall?

   M: Yes, I'm sure we do. Have you checked the card index?

   Q: Where is this conversation most likely to be taking place?

4. W: Have you found anything wrong with my stomach?

   M: Not yet, I'm still examining. I'll let you know the result tomorrow.

   Q: What is the probable relationship between the man and woman?

5. W: Is today the 10th of June? How time flies!

   M: Yes, and I have one more lecture to give. It's a week from tomorrow.

   Q: When will the lecture be given?

6. M: Do you really have to go down to the river to get all your water?

W: Yes, but all things considered, life in the country is still much less complicated than life in the city.

Q: Where does the woman think life is complex?

7. W: This game is so exciting. What's the time?

M: It's 3:40. They've only got 20 minutes before it's finished.

Q: What time is the game due to finish?

8. M: Do you like this book?

W: I'm just reading it.

M: I heard that the newspaper gave that book a terrible review.

W: It depends on which newspaper you read.

Q: What does the woman mean?

9. W: I prefer the personal service in the smaller shops, besides it's nearer.

M: But the prices there are somewhat higher. So I do all my shopping at the supermarket.

W: But it's too far away!

M: It doesn't matter. If you drive you'll find it quite near.

Q: Where does the man usually do his shopping?

Section B

Directions: In this section, you will hear two short passages. At the end of each passages, there will be some questions. You willll hear both the passages and the questions only once. After each question there will be a pause. During the pause, you must choose the best answer from the four choices given by marking the corresponding letter (A, B, C or D).

Passage I

Before we get to the student's center, I'd like to show you Sherley's Hall, one of the five dining halls in the university for undergraduates. Since there are not enough kitchens in the dorms, most students have to buy meal contracts. There are 20 meals per week in a contract. The students who have the contract can take the meals at any of the five dining halls at the university. They just simply present their meal ticket at the door and go through the line and help themselves to as much food as they want. Many of our students say that the dining halls' food, like most of dorms' food, is not very satisfactory and leaves much to be desired. However, there are certain times, especially around Thanksgiving and Christmas, when the dining halls' staff will prepare a good meal such as steak or seafood for their dinners. On these occasions, the students are certainly happy. Well, let's move on to the students' center.

10. Why do most students have to buy meal contracts?
11. What does the student need in order to eat at a dining hall?
12. What do the students who eat in the dining hall usually complain about?

Passage II

These days in some American supermarkets, paying a bill takes only 20 seconds. An electronic system "reads" a small stamp of black and white lines on each item of goods such as a tin, box or bottle. These little lines give the computer all the information it needs — the kind of product, the price and the tax. The girl at the counter simply moves the groceries along in front of the eye of the machine and the bill is ready in no time.

Most people are very pleased with this new invention because it offers a quick service and saves a lot of time. And they don't make mistakes as people often do. Some shoppers, however, are complaining. They can't read the price of the food on a tin, or other container. All they can see is little black and white lines. The prices are on the shelves but they want them on each item. Many people aren't sure that machines are honest shopkeepers. But everyone in the end will be happy because this will bring food prices down.

13. Why is it very quick to pay a bill in some supermarkets?

14. What do people think of these new machines?

15. Why are some shoppers unhappy about it?

Unit Six

Part I : Listening Practice

Section A: Talking about One's Family
Exercise 1

Directions: You will hear four people talking about their families. Choose the picture that matches each description. Label the correct picture with the speaker's name: Tim, Mary, Jane, or David.

(1)

Tim: Hi, my name is Tim, Come from a pretty big family, I have three brothers: Ted, Bill, and Frank. I also have a sister, Pat. So there are five of us in my family, plus my parents, of course. I'm the oldest and my sister is the youngest; she plays the piano really well and wants to be a professional musician.

(2)

Mary: Hello. I'm Mary. I'm an only child, with no brothers or sisters. But we do have lots of pets — three dogs, two cats, a parrot, and a rabbit. My father loves animals. You never know what he's going to bring home. Yesterday he came home with a...

(3)

Jane: Hi, my name is Jane. We're all girls in my family — except for my father, of course. I have four sisters. The youngest Debbie, is only four, and the oldest, Diane, is twenty-four. We are really proud of Diane. She ran in the last marathon here and she finished in the first twenty. My two younger sisters, Karen and Michelle, are still at school.

(4)

David: Hi, I'm David. There are five people in my family altogether: My parents, my elder brother, my elder sister, and me. My sister, Susan, is a nurse. My grandmother lives with us too; she's incredible — she's eighty and still very healthy. She goes for a long walk every day. And that's not all. She also. . .

Exercise 2

Directions: Listen again and answer these questions below.

Section B: Exam Results

Exercise 1

Directions: You will hear an evening class teacher giving some of her students their exam results. Fill in the chart below with the results you have heard.

Teacher: Mr Jones. Excuse me for a moment please. Thank you. I have got your exam result.

Mr Jones: Oh, good I hope?

Teacher: Let's see. "A" yes, very good as usual. Lisa. Have you got a minute. I have got an exam result here for you.

Lisa: Oh, I don't think I want to hear of this.

46

Teacher: Well. I'm afraid you have got "F". That's fail, you know.

Lisa: I know.

Teacher: What's wrong? I thought my class might be a little bit easier.

Lisa: I know. It's as clear as mud to me. I never understand Italian.

Teacher: Oh, Mr Allen. I have got your exam result.

Mr Allen: Oh, good. What's it like?

Teacher: Well, it's very good an "A".

Mr Allen: That's good.

Teacher: Mrs Craven. I'd like to talk to you for a moment. I've got your result.

Mrs Craven: Yes.

Teacher: Er, I'm afraid you haven't done very well, an "E" I'm afraid.

Mrs Craven: Oh, dear. I suppose I'm not as clever as others, am I?

Teacher: Alex. Are you busy? I have got your result.

Alex: Oh. How have I done?

Teacher: You have got a "C", not bad, but you could do better you know. Oliver. Come here. I've got your result.

Oliver: Is it good?

Teacher: No. It's as poor as ever, only a "D". Why don't you try harder?

Oliver: I think it's boring, Ms.

Exercise 2

Directions: Listen to the cassette once again and then answer the

47

following questions.

Exercise 1

Directions: You will hear people making arrangements to do something over the telephone. Number the correct picture.

(1)

A: Are you nearly ready, Jan?

B: Yeah, Give me about twenty minutes. The party starts at eight, does't it?

A: No, Jim said to be there around eight-thirty.

B: OK. What are you taking?

A: Jim said to bring some music. There's going to be dancing, and so he needs a few more records. You have some good ones, don't you?

B: Oh, yeah. I've got a couple of Billy Ocean records. They're good, and the new Wham Album is great to dance to. I'll bring that, too.

A: Good. So listen, can you wait at the bus stop in front of your place? I'll be there in exactly an hour.

B: OK. See you there.

(2)

A: Why don't we just meet at the river. OK?

B: OK. When are you going to leave?

A: Well, we should go soon. let's say, well, I'll leave here in about fifteen minutes. That way I'll have time to make some sandwiches to bring along.

B: Good idea. I'll bring some drinks.

48

A: By the way, you have an extra fishing rod, don't you? Mine isn't very good.

B: Yes, I do, Want me to bring?

A: That would be great. I hope to catch some big ones.

B: Umm, me too. So see you there in about half an hour.

A: Yeah, bye.

(3)

A: I hope there'll be plenty to eat there. I'm starving.

B: Don't worry about that. She's a great cook. Did you ask her if we should bring anything?

A: Yeah. A bottle of wine. I got some white.

B: Why did you get white? Do you know what she's serving?

A: I think she said she's cooking fish.

B: Oh, that sounds good. Let's see. Do you want me to pick you up?

A: Well, when did she say, six-thirty or seven o'clock?

B: Seven.

A: Then I have time to walk, so let's just meet at Pat's house.

B: OK.

A: But could you give me a ride home after dinner?

B: Sure. No problem. See you there in about half an hour then.

(4)

A: You haven't forgotten about the picnic, have you?

B: No, I'm looking forward to it. What are you bringing?

A: I'm supposed to bring dessert. You're bringing something to drink, right?

B: That's right. I'm picking up some soda this afternoon.

A: Great. I think I'll make a chocolate cake. Nothing like chocolate cake at a picnic!

B: Ummm, I love your cake.

A: You want a ride? I could meet you in front of your house at two o'clock sharp, and we could go in my car.

B: Sounds good.

Exercise 2

Directions: Listen again and write under each picture what they will bring and where they will meet.

Section D: Murder in Heasden

Directions: A man's body was found in a pedestrian subway, and Detective Chief superintendent John Day explains what they know of the man's movements in the early hours of this morning. Fill in the information on this form while you listen to his explanation.

D: Well, what we have learned is the fact that he left the Level One Club, which is a drinking club about 1:30 a.m. , and we're trying to account for movements up till 2:15 , because it was about that time he was found by a member of the club, an employee. He was found in the underpass under the North Circular Road. Death was due to multiple head injuries. We understand that there may have been two girls and a man who was drunk near the entrance of the subway. They may have seen our man walking in that direction.

L: About what time would you think that they were there?

D: Just after half past one to a quarter to two.

L: Then in that case the gap you have is really quite short. It's only more or less half an hour or forty minutes.

D: In fact, yes, as short as that.

L: Any idea of what he was wearing?

D: Yes, he was wearing, a light colored raincoat, gray trousers, black shoes, pink tie, dark hair. 165cm.

L: Is there any speculation that the motive might have been robbery?

D: I don't think it is robbery in the circumstances. I'm more inclined to think there was another reason for him to have been attacked.

L: And how far away from the Heasden underpass was the drinking club?

D: Fifty meters.

L: And at that moment were there only the drunk man and the two women who were seen with him or near him?

D: Yes. The club closed at half past one and there may have been other people who left the club and went that way.

L: Well, thank you very much. That was Detective Superintendent John Day in North London for the murderer of a man in his forties whose body was found under the pedestrian subway.

Part Ⅲ: Listening Comprehension Test

Directions: In this section, you will hear 15 short conversations concerning different locations. After you have heard each conversation, try to choose the best answer.

1. M: Can I help you, miss?

W: Yes. I'd like you to fix my headlights. When I was driving on the highway last night, I couldn't see a thing and almost hit a tree.

Q: Where did this conversation most probably take place?

2. W: The admission price to the gallery is ten dollars per person. I think that's pretty expensive for a single exhibit.

M: But if we have student cards, we can get in for two dollars.

Q: Where is the conversation most probably taking place?

3. M: How should I pay the fee for the first visit?

W: No need now. Just sign here and we'll send you a bill later.

Q: Where is this conversation probably taking place?

4. M: We could go to the concert this evening, or would you rather eat in a restaurant and then see a movie?

W: To tell the truth, I really can't go anywhere because I'm expecting an important phone call from out of town.

Q: Where will the woman most probably spend the evening?

5. M: There's a limit of five books per person. You can't keep them longer than two weeks.

W: All right. I'll be certain to return them on time.

Q: Where did this conversation probably take place?

6. M: Wait a second. I like the sofa displayed in the window.

W: I like it, too. Let's go in and have a look.

Q: Where is this conversation probably taking place.

7. M: Do you want the same cut as the last time?

W: The same cut on the top, but I'd like it to be longer over the ears and in the back.

Q: Where does the conversation probably take place?

8. W: Excuse me, sir. Visiting hours are over now. I'm afraid

you must leave, so your wife can get some rest.

M: I'm sorry, nurse. I didn't hear the bell. I'm leaving right now.

Q: Where did this conversation most probably take place?

9. M: Excuse me, Madam. Are man's suits on the 7th floor?

W: No. They are here on the 6th. The 7th floor is for electric appliances.

Q: Where does the conversation probably take place?

10. M: Let's have a picnic this Sunday. Do you like the beach, the mountains, forests or where?

W: Well, I don't like sand around my food and I certainly don't like walking long. Let's just go where most people have picnics.

Q: Where might they decide to go for a picnic?

11. M: While you are out, I wish you'd get me some dinner rolls, cookies, and a chocolate cake.

W: Are you having a party? Have you invited your friends?

Q: In what sort of place would the woman find the food that the man needs?

12. M: I'm looking for canned apples and canned peaches. Can you tell me where to find them?

W: Go down to the next aisle and you'll see all the canned fruits there on the shelves.

Q: Where does this conversation take place?

13. M: I can rent you a pair of shoes and you can pick the right weight ball for yourself.

W: Fine. I'll take a size 5 in shoes, and this ball should be just right.

Q: Where did this conversation take place?

14. M: The plane was supposed to land at 10, and it's already 20 minutes late. I've got to get back to the office by 11 o'clock for an important meeting.

W: I'm going to be late, too. I'm getting tired of waiting. The bulletin board hasn't been changed either.

Q: Where are the two speakers now?

15. M: This room with all those bookshelves would be very useful. Can you show me the kitchen and the bedroom?

W: Yes. Here we are. This is the kitchen equipped with a built-in washer and dryer. That's the sink unit.

Q: Where are the two speakers?

Unit Seven

Part I : Listening Practice

Section A: Announcement
Exercise 1
Directions: You are going to hear a guide talking to a group of tourists. Then read two questions carefully. Write your answers to the questions in the space provided on the right after you have heard the announcement.

Guide: This morning we'll be walking first to the Town Hall. We shall look at it from the outside for a few minutes. And then I want to take you to the Toy Museum in the same part of the town. It's only a short walk. So we shall not need a coach. You shouldn't feel too tired. You have to pay to go in, but it's only 50p each. I'll collect that now before we start to save the trouble later.

Exercise 2
Directions: Read the statements below. Then listen to the guide again, and decide whether each statement is true or false by putting a tick under TRUE or a cross under FALSE.

Section B: Announcement for the Afternoon's Tour
Directions: You are going to hear the guide talking about the

afternoon's tour. Listen to the guide and complete the sentences.

Guide: This afternoon, ladies and gentlemen, we are going to visit the cathedral which was built in 1241, not long after the last part of the Great Walls. The cathedral was designed by Hugo Derash, who came from France with his brother. So naturally, it's completely Norman in appearance and details. The building is in the oldest part of the town which still has one or two remains to remind us of the days when the Romans were here, a part of the wall and a small statue beside the fountain. Though the fountain itself, as you notice, is very modern indeed. I'm afraid it won't please everybody. Anyway, it's in the market place where a regular Tuesday market is held. And in the summer there is a flower market every two weeks on Saturdays. The statue, by the way, is thought to represent Venus, the Roman Goddess of Love, but it's very worn and the detail isn't too good.

Man: Excuse me, can you drink the water?

Guide: You certainly can. The water in the fountain comes from the springs in the hills. It's crystal clear and it's one of the purest sources of drinking water in the whole area. Well, if you are all ready, I suggest we move off.

Section C: Library Regulations

Directions: You are going to hear a librarian talking to a group of students about some of the library regulations. Listen carefully and complete the chart below with the information you have heard.

Librarian: Good morning everybody, and I'd like to take this opportunity to introduce to you our library. Our library was set up in 1902, and now it has a collection of five million books. If you would like to join the library we need your identification card. Then you can get a library card from us. There is no charge for it. With this card you may borrow 5 books at a time, and you can keep them as long as three weeks. When the books are due, you have to come and renew them or make a telephone call to us. Otherwise you will be fined. A fine of each overdue book is 50p each day. If a book is damaged you have to pay for that, I'm afraid. Usually that depends on the value of a book.

Well, with this card, two magazines or periodicals can also be taken out, but not newspapers. They must be read in the library.

We also have a record library. Records are quite popular these days, and you have to pay £5 as a deposit in case you damage them. Two records can be taken out at a time. Cassettes, you have to pay a deposit too, are also available in our library. I think that's all and I hope you will like our library and thank you for listening.

Section D: A Dialogue about One's Vacation
Exercise 1
Directions: Julie has just come back from her vacation. You are going to hear a dialogue between Julie and her friend Paul. Now listen to the dialogue carefully and complete the following sentences according to what you hear.

Paul: Oh, Julie. Finally back from your vacation, I see.
Julie: What do you mean, "finally"? I feel like I've only been gone

for two days instead of two weeks.

Paul: Well, you know what they say — "Time flies when you're having fun." You did have fun, didn't you?

Julie: Oh, it was marvelous. It was so nice to get away from this cold, miserable weather. And those mountain views — they were absolutely breathtaking.

Paul: How was Vancouver?

Julie: Busy. So much to see and do there. It was nice to take an urban holiday for a change, although next year I'll be glad to go camping again.

Paul: So what did you all do?

Julie: Oh, we went to Stanley Park and the aquarium, up Grouse Mountain and to museums and galleries. All the usual touristy things.

Paul: Did you get over to the island? It's only two hours away by ferry, isn't it?

Julie: Yes, it was funny how on the ride over, everyone stayed out on the deck to enjoy the view, but on the way back, we just sat inside like seasoned travellers and read magazines.

Paul: Victoria is a city I've always wanted to visit. They say it's such an elegant city with a lot of British influence.

Julie: We liked Victoria so much that we stayed on a day longer than we had planned.

Paul: Oh, well, one of these days I'll get there myself. In the meantime, I better get back to work.

Julie: Before you go — I got you this pin for your collection.

Paul: A tiny totem pole! It's beautiful. Thank you very much.

Julie: You are welcome.

Exercise 2

Directions: Listen to the dialogue again and then try to answer the following questions. Write your answers in the space provided below.

1. What is the weather like in the city where Julie lives?
2. What kind of city is Victoria according to Paul?
3. What small gift did Julie give Paul?

Part Ⅲ: Listening Comprehension Test

Directions: In this section, you will hear 15 short conversations concerning calculations between two speakers. After you have heard each conversation, try to choose the best answer.

1. M: I ran all the way to the bus stop, but the man at the ticket counter told me the bus left only 5 minutes ago.

   W: That's too bad. Those buses leave only every 50 minutes.

   Q: How long does the man have to wait?

2. W: These are very nice shirts. How much are they?

   M: 10 dollars each. Two for 19 dollars. They are on sale.

   Q: How much do four shirts cost?

3. M: My son graduated from college in 1981. What about your son?

   W: He finished school a year after your son did.

   Q: When did the woman's son graduate?

4. M: How many years of science did you have in high school?

   W: I had only one year each of biology and chemistry.

   Q: How many science courses did the woman take in high school?

5. M: I would like to cash this check for $20. Small bills,

59

please.

W: Certainly, Sir. Here you are: three fives and five ones.

Q: How many bills did the customer receive?

6. W: I was hoping to get some bread from the bakery before it closes.

   M: My watch says 6:50, so we have around forty minutes left to get there.

   Q: What time does the bakery close?

7. M: These air mail envelopes cost 50 cents a dozen.

   W: A couple of dozen should certainly do.

   Q: How many envelopes will the man and the woman buy?

8. M: How far is it to the courthouse?

   W: Well, you go down this street for two more blocks, then turn left onto main and go four blocks, then right onto Oak Avenue for one block; it's right there on the corner; you can't miss it.

   Q: How many blocks will the man have to travel?

9. M: What time do you usually have breakfast?

   W: Around 7: 00, but lately I've been having trouble getting up in the morning, so I've been eating breakfast at 8:00, 9:00, even as late as 10:00.

   Q: What time does she usually have breakfast?

10. W: The shirt was a bargain. I got it for half the price.

    M: You mean you only paid $20 for it?

    Q: How much did the shirt cost originally?

11. W: How many students will take the exam?

    M: About 450, but only one third of them are able to pass the exam.

Q: How many students can pass the exam?

12. M: If Mr and Mrs Smith don't come to the party, we'll have 8.

W: Let's invite two more just in case.

Q: If everyone comes, how many will join the party?

13. W: I'll be out for 3 hours. What time is it now?

M: Half past eight.

Q: When will the woman be back?

14. W: You've borrowed so many books on the subject. Where did you get them?

M: I borrowed two from our library and three from the National Library of Beijing.

Q: How many books did the man borrow altogether?

15. M: Is everything ready? The meeting is supposed to start at two.

W: I have five minutes to clean the table. Afterwards we'll have five more minutes to arrange the chairs before the meeting begins.

Q: What time is it now?

Unit Eight

Section A: Story
Exercise 1
Directions: You are going to hear a story. Read the questions below carefully. Then answer these questions in the space provided on the right after you have heard the story.

Three men came to New York for a holiday. They came to a very large hotel and took a room there. Their room was on the forty-fifth floor.

In the evening the three men went to the theatre and came back to the hotel very late.

"I'm very sorry, " said the clerk of the hotel, "but our lifts do not work tonight. If you do not want to walk up to your room, we shall make beds for you in the hall. "

"No, no," said one of the three men, "no, thank you. We do not want to sleep in the hall. We shall walk up to our room. "

Then he turned to his two friends and said:

"It is not easy to walk up to the forty-fifth floor, but I think I know how to make it easier. On our way to the room I shall tell you some jokes; then you, Andy, will sing us some songs; then you,

62

Peter, will tell us some interesting stories."

So they began to walk up to their room. Tom told them many jokes; Andy sang some songs. At last they came to the thirty-fourth floor. They were tired and decided to have a rest.

"Well, " said Tom, "now it is your turn, Peter. After all those jokes we heard on our way here, tell us a long and interesting story with a sad ending."

"I shall tell you the sad story you ask me for, " said Peter. "It's not long, but it is sad enough. WE LEFT THE KEY TO OUR ROOM IN THE HALL. "

Exercise 2
Directions: Listen to the tape again and complete the sentences below.

Exercise 3
Directions: Read the following sentences carefully. Then listen to the cassette once more and judge whether the statements are true or false. Write a "T" for the true statement and an "F" for the false one.

Section B: Owning a Car
Exercise 1
Directions: You are going to hear a passage about the advantages and disadvantages of owning a car. Listen to the passage and then fill in the form with the information you hear from the tape.

Should a person own a car? This is an important question. In a

large urban area there are some good reasons for owning a car.
First, a car allows a person to move around freely. With a car there
is no need to check a bus schedule or wait for a train. Second, a car
is a comfortable way to travel, especially in the winter time. In bad
weather, the driver stays warm and dry, while the poor bus or train
rider is usually feeling cold and wet. Finally, a driver is usually safe
in a car at night. The bus rider might need to walk down a dark
street to get to a stop, or wait on a dark corner.

There are, on the other hand, many good reasons against owning a car. First, it can be very expensive. The price of fuel contin-
ues to rise each year. In addition, it is expensive to maintain and repair a car. A simple repair can cost $100. In an urban area, it
might also be expensive to park the car. Second, owning a car can
cause worry and stress. It is exhausting to drive in heavy traffic. If
you leave your car on the street, it might get stolen. This is something else to worry about.

Exercise 2
Directions: Listen to the passage again and complete the following
sentences.

Section C: Dialogue
Exercise 1
Directions: You are going to listen to a dialogue between a customer
and a saleswoman at The Self Drive Car Hire Center. Listen carefully and then fill in the form with the information you hear.

Saleswoman: 773141.

Customer: Oh, hello, is that Self Drive Car Hire?

Saleswoman: Yes, speaking. Can I help you?

Customer: Oh, yes, please. Erm... I wanted to inquire about hiring a car for the weekend. Do you have special weekend rates?

Saleswoman:: Mm-mm. Yes.

Customer: What will be the best for a family of four... erm... plus space for camping equipment? We're going on a camping holiday.

Saleswoman: Yes, I would think you would need something like an Allegro or Marina Estate or perhaps a Maxi (I see). That would be best I think.

Customer: Yes, Erm... we'd be leaving on Friday, that's Friday, July 7th (Yes) and returning on the Monday (Yes) that's... that's July 10th.

Saleswoman: Yes, that's fine provided you pick up the car after 4 o'clock on the Friday and return it by 10 o'clock on the Monday.

Customer: Ah-hA. I have to pick it up after 4 on Friday but return it before 10 (That's right) on Monday. (Yes) I see. Erm... could you tell me the basic cost?

Saleswoman: It's £29.25 (Mm-Mm) and the first three hundred miles are free but after that you have to pay $5\frac{1}{2}$ p per mile.

Customer: So that's $5\frac{1}{2}$ p extra (Mm-Mm) after the first three hundred miles.

Saleswoman: Over three hundred miles yes (I see) and £29.25.

65

Customer: Right thank you. What about insurance? Is that included in the cost?

Saleswoman: Yes, yes, that's all included.

Customer: I see. OK, thank you very much indeed.

Saleswoman: OK. Pleasure.

Customer: Byebye.

Saleswoman: Byebye.

Exercise 2

Directions: Listen to the dialogue again. Decide whether each of the following statements is true or false. Put a T in the bracket at the end of the true statement and an F at the end of the false statement.

Part Ⅲ: Listening Comprehension Test

Directions: In this part, you will hear three short passages. After you have heard the passages and questions, choose the best answer from the four choices given by marking the corresponding letter (A, B, C or D).

Passage Ⅰ

A mild earthquake shook the northwestern coast of the United States Thursday, the earthquake observatory in San Francisco reported today. There are no immediate reports of injuries or damage. The observatory said the earthquake was felt over a range of about ten miles, along the coastline of the United States and probably originated about one hundred miles out in the Pacific Ocean, east of the island of Nimi. The observatory also reported that more earthquakes can be expected to occur in the San Francisco area in the next several months, although the intensity of the quakes can not be predicted.

1. Where did the earthquake originate according to the bulletin?
2. Which of the following is true of the earthquake described in the bulletin?
3. According to the bulletin what can be expected with regard to future earthquakes in the San Francisco area?

Passage Ⅱ

In the U. S., the usual charge for a local telephone call from a public booth is ten cents. Instructions for depositing the coins are posted on the telephone instrument; in some pay telephones, the money has to be deposited in advance, and in others the operator will tell the caller when to drop the coins in the slot. Calls made from private homes or from offices are charged to the resident. If the call is to another city, there is a special charge for it. Calls from hotel rooms are handled by the hotel switchboard operator, and the charges are added to the guest's bill.

4. Where can one find the instructions for depositing the coins?
5. What kind of telephone call usually costs ten cents in the U. S.?
6. How are calls from hotel rooms paid for?

Passage Ⅲ

People of the United States regard Abraham Lincoln as one of the greatest leaders in the history of their country. Every year many thousands of Americans visit the great white marble Lincoln Memorial in Washington, D. C. They put his likeness on their money and their stamps. Why does Lincoln continue to be thus honored so long after his death?

The origins of Abraham Lincoln were humble. He was born in the year 1809 in the American state of Kentucky. The place where he was born was on the American frontier, an underdeveloped area with few people, inhabited by many wild animals. Living conditions were dangerous and difficult. Schools were few and generally bad.

Lincoln was born into a family of poor farmers. Every one worked hard just to obtain the necessities of life. Lincoln himself did manual labor on the family farm until he was a young man of 22 years. When it was possible, however, the family sent young Abraham to a local school. During his whole life, however, he had less than one year of formal education. Yet, through natural ability, determination, and study at home, he became one of the most learned men in the world of his time.

7. Where do people put Lincoln's likeness in order to show their honor for him?
8. What were Lincoln's living conditions like when he was young?
9. How much formal education did Lincoln have?
10. What did Lincoln's father do in order to make a living?

Unit Nine

Section A: Plans for a Weekend

Directions: Look at the pictures below. You will hear six of these people talking about what they like doing in their free time. What does each person like doing? Listen to the conversations and write one of the following names under each picture: Jane, Sam, Ted, Mary, Pat or Jill.

(1)

A: So, what do you usually do on weekends, Jane?

B: Well, I'm starting to play tennis.

A: Oh, yeah? I play tennis, too. Would you like to play some-time?

B: Sure. But I'm really not good!

A: Well, I'm terrible! We should have a good time.

(2)

A: Do you go out much on weekends, Sam?

B: Not much really, I prefer just staying at home and relaxing. Watching a little TV, you know, being really lazy.

(3)

A: Are you interested in sports, Ted?

B: Yeah, I like sports a lot. Especially baseball. I play with a group

69

of guys every Saturday at the park.

A: Oh, yeah? I think baseball's the most boring game in the world. Have you ever played soccer? That's a great game!

(4)

A: What kind of music do you like, Mary?

B: Well, I guess I'm really into jazz. In fact, there's a free concert in the park tomorrow. Do you want to go?

A: Sure.

(5)

A: What do you do to keep in shape, Pat?

B: Well, try to swim three or four times a week. It's great exercise.

A: You must be quite a good swimmer.

B: Well, I don't know about that.

(6)

A: Is there anywhere in town where you can see old movies? Like from the thirties and forties?

B: Mmm. You know, Jill. I think they sometimes show old movies at the museum. On Sunday afternoons.

Section B: An Interview with a Scientist

Directions: Listen to this interview with the well-known scientist Lily Tarkis. What kind of lifestyle does she have? Put a tick under Always, Often, Sometimes, or Never for each activity. You will hear the piece twice.

Inter: So Lily, now that we've heard about your work, the listeners would like to know something about your life outside work.

Tell us about what you do on weekends — when you get up, what you have for breakfast, what you do for fun, things like that.

Lily: Well, I get up very early, around five o'clock, because. . .

Inter: Five o'clock? That is early ! Even on weekends? Do you do that often?

Lily: Oh, yes, nearly every weekend. I never sleep late. There is just too much to do. I hate waking up late. Even on weekends. And then I sometimes go for a long swim in my pool. When I don't go for a swim, I go for a run. Exercise is very important to me.

Inter: At five in the morning you go for a swim?

Lily: Yes, sometimes, or as I said, I sometimes go for a swim.

Inter: OK. . . and then?

Lily: Well, then I have breakfast, and after breakfast I get down to work.

Inter: Oh, you work on the weekends, too?

Lily: Oh yes, I always work on the weekends.

Inter: But don't you ever relax?

Lily: Relax?

Inter: You know, take the day off and have a good time, enjoy yourself? Go to a museum or to the park or some thing?

Lily: To the park? Oh no, I never go to the park. But I enjoy myself at work. I always enjoy myself at work.

Inter: Well, OK. Thank you, Lily Tarkis. It has been very interesting hearing about your work and your, uh, your uh, your work. And now for a word from. . .

Section C: Talking about what They Like Doing

Directions: Bill and Maggie have just met for the first time at a party. They have decided that they would like to see each other again. You will hear them talking about things they like doing. What does Bill like doing? What does Maggie like doing? Write B for Bill and M for Maggie.

Bill: Well, Maggie, it's really been interesting talking to you. It'd be fun to get together sometime.

Maggie: I'd like that, Bill. What did you have in mind?

Bill: Well, let's see. What kind of things do you like doing? Do you ever go hiking? There are some great trails around here, you know.

Maggie: Well no, I don't hike very much, but I do like getting out of the city when I can. You know what I really like? I try to get to the beach as often as possible during the summer. Do you enjoy the beach?

Bill: No, I just go to a pool. There's a big pool close to where I live. It takes so long to get to the beach, and it's always so crowded on the weekends. Hmm, well... What sports do you play? I play tennis. Do you?

Maggie: Well, er, I used to play tennis, but I don't anymore. I'm not really athletic, actually. I'm more into things like going to museums, concerts, and that kind of thing. Do you ever go to concerts? There are some good ones coming up.

Bill: No, not often really. But I go to the movies quite a lot.

Maggie: Do you? Me, too ! What kind of movies do you like?

Bill: Oh, let's see. I like westerns with lots of action. Like old John

Wayne movies, or Clint Eastwood movies. How about you?

Maggie: Hmm, no, I don't really like westerns. But I do like mysteries with a lot of action. Do you like mystery movies, you know, like spy stories?

Bill: Yeah, I love the James Bond films. There's one on in town, you know. Would you like to go? We could go tomorrow, maybe.

Maggie: Yeah, I know the one. That sounds good. I'd like that.

Bill: Great, so we do share a few interests after all. Shall I pick you up around seven o'clock?

Maggie: Great! See you tomorrow.

Bill: OK.

Section D: Things They Want to Do for Weekend
Exercise 1

Directions: You are going to hear a dialogue between Chris and Ann. They are talking about what they do on weekends. Listen to the dialogue carefully and answer the following questions. Write your answers on the space provided.

Chris: Thank Goodness it's Friday. I've been looking forward to the weekend since Monday.

Ann: Oh, Chris, I thought you enjoyed your work.

Chris: Of course I do. I mean it's not that bad. But I'm not a workaholic or anything. I really appreciate my time off.

Ann: I don't like weekends. First I run around like crazy trying to get the housework done. Then I lie around and veg to try to recuperate for Monday.

Chris: Yeah, it's rough. I try to get most of my chores done on

73

weeknights to leave the weekend free.

Ann: To do what?

Chris: Oh, different things. Right now I'm really into painting. I spend my Sundays in the country doing landscapes.

Ann: I didn't know you were an artist.

Chris: Calling my painting art is really stretching it. I just like to dabble in it. And I also try to get in some squash or tennis.

Ann: How do you find time for all of that?

Chris: Just takes a bit of organization. My leisure time is important to me, so I make time. And look at Greg — you know those ceramic pieces he's always making at home? Well, he sells them to a local handicrafts store. Fun and profit.

Ann: I'm afraid I'm all thumbs when it comes to things like that.

Chris: Do you have any hobbies?

Ann: Nothing I stick to. I used to play guitar when I was a kid. Last year I thought of taking up photography but the equipment can be so expensive.

Chris: But you could get into it gradually. No need to go overboard with fancy gadgets. You've got a pretty decent camera already and if you take a course at the community center you'll have access to their darkroom facilities.

Ann: Hmmm, that's true. Maybe I'll look into a course to get me started.

Questions:

1. Does Chris enjoy his work?
2. Does Ann like weekends? Why?
3. How can Chris leave the weekend free?
4. What suggestions does Chris offer Ann?

74

Part Ⅲ: Listening Comprehension Test
Section A
Directions: In this section, you will hear nine short conversations between two speakers. At the end of each conversation a third voice will ask a question about what was said. Both the conversations and the questions will be spoken only once. After each question there will be a pause. During the pause, you must choose the best answer from the four choices given by marking the corresponding letter (A, B, C or D).

1. W: I learned that only one person got a perfect grade on the term project. I am sure it wasn't mine.

   M: But it was.

   Q: What does the man mean?

2. M: I'm so confused by my notes from Professor Johnson's lectures.

   W: How about reviewing them now over a cup of coffee?

   Q: What does the woman suggest they do about the notes?

3. W: Are you sure you have corrected all the typing errors in this paper?

   M: Perhaps I'd better read it through again.

   Q: What is the man going to do?

4. M: Look, I'm sorry to bother you about this. But could you turn that music down?

   W: Sorry. I didn't realize you could hear it.

   Q: What will the woman probably do?

5. W: Hi, here is the check for this month's rent.

M: Wait a moment. I'll give you a receipt.

Q: What's the woman giving the man?

6. M: Paul said he doesn't like television.

   W: Yes, but he seems to spend a lot of time watching it, doesn't he?

   Q: What does the woman think of Paul?

7. W: How often should I take these pills and how many should I take?

   M: Take two pills every six hours.

   Q: How many pills should the woman take in twenty four hours?

8. W: How long can I keep these out?

   M: Two weeks. Then you will be fined for every day they are overdue.

   W: I think I'd better read fast.

   M: Yes, I think so. Remember "Two weeks".

   Q: Where does this conversation probably take place?

9. M: If you want a bargain you should buy this new color TV.

   W: I'd like to, but it's a bit expensive.

   M: You can pay for it by installments.

   W: Well, it will take 3 years to pay off. I don't like that.

   Q: What does the woman think about the new color TV set?

Section B

Directions: In this part, you will hear two short passages. At the end of each passage, there will be some questions. You will hear both the passages and the questions only once. After each question there will be a pause. During the pause, you must choose the best

76

answer from the four choices given by marking the corresponding letter (A, B, C or D).

Passage I

Every human society has rules covering marriage. In Britain it is illegal to marry under the age of 18 without your parents' permission and an offence to marry at all under the age of 16. It is also against the law to have more than one husband or wife at the same time. Anyone who breaks this law may go to prison. You may marry your first cousin but you cannot marry anyone who is closer relative than this.

In some societies the rules are stricter. There are places where the men must marry outside their family. For the Nuer Tribe in the Sudan this means that a man usually has to find a wife in a different village because the people in his village belongs to the same family. The Nuer say, "We marry those with whom we fight". In this way friendship is created between enemy villages.

Other societies have a rule which says that a man must marry a daughter of his mother's brother. Another common marriage custom says that a man is supposed to marry a cousin on his mother's side but he needn't if he doesn't want to. The Kachin who live in Northern Burma are an example of this practice. It is sometimes a serious offence, however, in this kind of society to marry a cousin on your father's side.

10. In Britain, under what age is it illegal to marry if one has not got his parents' permission?

11. Why does a man of a Nuer Tribe in the Sudan have to find a wife in a different village?

12. According to the passage, which one of the following is true about the Kachin who live in Northern Burma?

Passage Ⅱ

Few people know that the fate of the most precious document in the history of the United States — the Declaration of Independence — was once entirely in the hands of a young man and an old man. It happened during the war of 1812 when the British invaded Washington and burned the capital. Fearing for the safety of the priceless document, Secretary of State James Monroe gave it to a young man who worked as a clerk in his office. No doubt thinking that the British would never suspect that a harmless-looking man would ever be entrusted with the safety of such a great treasure. As he handed the bag with the important document in it to Stephen Pleasanton, for that was the young man's name, Secretary Monroe said: "I'm entrusting you with the most important document of the United States. It was for this that our brave men fought and died during the revolutionary war. The British must not get their hands on it."

Stephen thrust the pouch which contained the Declaration beneath his shirt for safe keeping and started out in the general direction of Leesburg, Virginia, driving a wagon and disguised as a peddler. The second day he had a narrow escape when he ran into a patrol of British soldiers who eyed him and his wagon with suspicion. The leader of the patrol was satisfied with Stephen's story of being a peddler hurrying home for his family and let him go on.

Few have heard of Stephen Pleasanton, but what he did will always be remembered.

Questions:

13. When did the true story take place?
14. Where did the young man hide the precious document?
15. Which of the following titles is best for the passage?

Unit   Ten

Part Ⅰ : Listening Practice

Section A: About Building a Shopping Centre
Exercise 1
Directions: Several people from the town of Welford are discussing plans to build a shopping centre on some open space. Now listen to the cassette and decide whether these statements are true or false.

Luce: Are we all here? Good. Well, I called this meeting to discuss the plans to build a shopping centre on St Mark's Playing Fields, the only open space in this part of town. What do you think?

Mr Boulter: Ah. . .

Luce: Mr Boulter.

Mr Boulter: Thank you, Luce. Well, I think a shopping centre is a good thing for elderly people like me. I mean I can't get to the big shops in the centre of the town, and everything here is, I'm sorry Mrs Singh, I know you sell a lot of things in your shop, but your prices are rather high.

Mrs Singh: I disagree, Mr Boulter. My shop is not expensive. I think. . .

Woman: I think we are getting to the most important question.

Luce: Oh, what's that?

Woman: No, it's not the price, is it? The important thing is that we are going to lose an open space——the Playing Fields, and it's the only place around here for children to play. My boys are at the age of 8 to 11. I don't want them to play in the street.

Mrs Singh: No, neither do I. I have been very annoyed with children recently. They stole... some children have taken things from my shop.

Woman: Are you saying that my children steal...

Luce: Please, can't we discuss this quietly?

Mr Boulter: Yes, I really think a shopping centre is necessary here.

Young Lady: I agree with Mr Boulter. This part of town is so quiet. People at my age don't need open spaces. We need shops, clubs and discos.

Mr Boulter: Oh, no. Not a disco. It's so loud.

Young Lady: Exeuse me, Mr Boulter. There're lots of young people here. I know the old... I mean the elderly people don't like discos. I think the young people need something to do in the evenings.

Woman: I disagree. They can catch a bus to the centre of town. It's not very far, anyway. My house is opposite of Playing Fields. The view is lovely.

Luce: I live there too, Ellis. I don't think the view is very important.

Exercise 2

Directions: Listen to the cassette again and write down their opin-

81

ions.

Section B: Accepting and Refusing Invitation
Exercise 1

Directions: Listen to people accepting and refusing invitations. Decide whether they are accepting or refusing. Check the column under the correct response.

(1)

A: So, anyway, I was wondering if you would like to go out to dinner tonight. I'd like to take you somewhere really special.

B: Oh, thanks, but... hm... maybe some other time. I've got so much work to do. I'll be working at the office late tonight.

(2)

A: Hello.

B: Hello. Can I speak to Terry?

C: Oh, yes, just a moment. Terry, it's for you. I think it's Brian.

B: Oh, not him again. Hello.

C: Hi, Terry.

B: Oh, hello, Brian.

C: How are things?

B: Fine, thanks.

C: I was calling about tonight. Pat's having a party. I was wondering if you'd like to go with me?

B: A party. Gee, I really can't. I'm going to a movie. That would have been nice, sorry.

C: Oh, OK. Maybe some other time. We should get together soon.

B: Sure. I'll give you a call.

82

(3)

A: John and I are going to the baseball game tomorrow. Wanna come?

B: Sure, why not?

(4)

A: We're having a few people over for dinner Saturday. We'd love to have you.

B: Oh, thank you. That would be great. What time should I come?

(5)

A: Have you tried that new pizza place yet on Washington? Why don't we go there tonight?

B: I'm really sorry, but... you see, I'm on a diet. I've got to lose at least ten pounds. And pizza is not on my diet.

(6)

A: Hey, why don't we go out and do something tonight. I feel kind of bored.

B: I wish I could. But I really have to stay in and write to my parents.

A: Oh, maybe some other time then. We should try and do something together soon.

B: That'd be nice.

(7)

A: Are you planning to go to the football game this weekend? We could go together.

B: Yeah, I never miss a game. You know me. What time do you want to meet?

A: Oh... about seven?

B: Fine.

Exercise 2

Directions: Listen again and write down what a person is invited to and the reasons that a person refuses the invitation.

Section C: An Invitation to Car Racing

Directions: Listen to a short dialogue and decide whether the following statements are true or false according to the tape.

Sue: (answering the phone) Hello?

Bill: Hello Sue. Bill here. How are you?

Sue: Hello Bill. Not bad, thanks. How are you?

Bill: Pretty well... you sound a bit fed-up.

Sue: I am. I had the flat painted last week, and the painters made a terrible mess. There's paint all over the place.

Bill: Oh, that's too bad. Perhaps I can cheer you up! I'm going to go to the car races on Sunday. Do you want to come?

Sue: Oh, that sounds wonderful Bill—exactly what I need, but Barbara is coming to lunch that day.

Bill: Why don't you ask her to come with us?

Sue: That's a good idea, but are you sure you don't mind?

Bill: Don't be silly, of course not.

Sue: That's very kind of you. I'm meeting her in about an hour. We're going to go shopping. Can I ring you back about six?

Bill: Sure, there's no hurry. I'm going to stay in this evening, there's a good programme on television. Ring when you like.

Sue: OK. Bill. Bye for now.

Bill: Bye.

Section D: Making Arrangements

When Sue met Barbara she told her that Bill had called and said he was going to go to the car races on Sunday. She told her that he had invited them to go with him. Barbara was very pleased and accepted the invitation. They put off their lunch. Then Sue gave Bill a ring.

Sue: Hello Bill, Sue here.

Bill: Hello Sue.

Sue: Well, I saw Barbara and she asked me to thank you very much for the invitation. She's very happy to go. She likes car racing almost as much as I do.

Bill: Good. I'm going to leave here about nine. That'll give us plenty of time. I'll pick you up first, then we'll pick up Barbara, if that's OK. with you.

Sue: She doesn't want you to pick her up, Bill. It's out of your way. She said she was going to meet us here.

Bill: I don't mind, you know. There won't be much traffic.

Sue: No, no. We can all meet here about a quarter past nine. Barbara insisted.

Bill: OK. . . . By the way, I'm going to ask Phil Stone to come to, if you don't mind.

Sue: I don't mind at all. It will be nice to see him again. . . I'm certainly looking forward to the racing.

Bill: I am too. I'm sure we'll enjoy ourselves. See you Sunday at your place about a quarter past nine then.

Sue: OK. Bill, bye.

Part Ⅲ: Listening Comprehension Test

Directions: In this part, you will hear 15 short conversations concerning suggestion, implication and agreement between the two speakers. After you have heard each conversation, try to choose the best answer.

1. M: I don't like this novel very much.

    W: Neither do I.

    Q: What does the woman mean?

2. W: I'm going to the post office, then to the bank, and after that I have to prepare a presentation for my geography seminar.

    M: I'd say you have a pretty busy morning.

    Q: What is the man suggesting about the woman?

3. M: Would it be better to buy a monthly meal ticket, or pay for each meal separately?

    W: What difference does it make, the price per meal is the same either way.

    Q: What does the woman mean?

4. W: Where can I have copies made of my application?

    M: Isn't there a photocopy machine in the library?

    Q: What does the man imply?

5. M: Mitchell is the most talented actor in our school's Drama Society.

    W: Isn't he, though?

    Q: What does the woman think about Mitchell?

6. W: Mind if I borrow your physics notes for a while?

    M: Not at all.

    Q: What does the man mean?

7. M: Do you think professor Simpson will cancel class on account of the special conference?

W: Not likely.

Q: What does the woman mean?

8. M: The doctor told me to quit drinking coffee.

   W: Shouldn't you quit drinking tea, too?

   Q: What does the woman suggest?

9. M: Do you mind if I turn the radio off?

   W: I'm in the middle of listening to a program.

   Q: What can be inferred from the woman's response?

10. M: It would be nice if these last few days of vacation were sunny and warm.

    W: But that's not what they forecast, is it?

    Q: What does the woman imply about the weather?

11. M: We got someone to take over Harry's job.

    W: Oh, so it has been taken care of.

    Q: What had the woman assumed?

12. W: I wonder who'd be willing to take up the work.

    M: Well, you know more about it than anyone.

    Q: What does the man mean?

13. W: I honestly don't want to paint the room this weekend.

    M: Neither do I, but I think we should get it over with.

    Q: What does the man suggest?

14. W: During intermission, let's change our seats.

    M: Hard to see from back here, isn't it?

    Q: What does the man imply?

15. M: From Daniel's letter, I guess he is upset with his living situation.

    W: I'm not sure. We may just be reading that into it.

    Q: What does the woman imply?

Unit Eleven

Part I : Listening Practice

Section A: Making Appointments
Exercise 1

Directions: You will hear people calling a doctor's office to make an appointment. Listen to their conversations with the receptionist and complete the appointment cards below.

(1)

A: Dr Johnson's office. Can I help you?

B: Yes, it's Mrs Simpson here. I'd like to see the doctor as soon as possible. I'm having trouble with my back again. It's just terrible at the moment. I can hardly sleep.

A: Oh, I'm sorry to hear that, Mrs Simpson. Let me see if I can get you in this afternoon. No, I'm sorry. It will have to be tomorrow, Tuesday the eleventh. I can give you an appointment at 10 A.M.

B: Hmmm. I did have other plans tomorrow... But, I guess I'll have to go to the doctor instead. I'll be there at 10: 00 tomorrow. Thank you.

(2)

A: Good morning, Dr Johnson's office.

B: Hello. This is Mrs Katzen. Something just awful has happened. My

88

little boy Stevie has swallowed a coin. One minute he was playing with it, then the next thing I knew, he had swallowed it.

A: Is he all right?

B: He seems to be. He didn't choke or anything. It just went straight down.

A: Was it a large coin, Mrs Katzen?

B: No, just a dime.

A: Well, I don't think there will be a problem. It will take care of itself in a day or two, I'm sure. But if you want the doctor to have a look at him you could bring him in tomorrow, Wednesday, let me see, at 3:30 in the afternoon.

B: Let me check my calendar. Let's see, Wednesday the twenty-third. Yes, 3:30 is good. You're sure it's all right to leave it till then?

A: Yes, these things happen all the time with children.

B: I see. OK. So, 3:30 tomorrow.

A: That's right.

Exercise 2

Directions: Listen again. What is each person's problem?

Section B: Making Reservations

Exercise 1

Directions: You will hear people telephoning Intercontinental Airlines to ask about flights and to make reservations. Circle the days that Intercontinental Airlines flies to each place, and also write down the date that each passenger books on.

(1)

A: Intercontinental Airlines.

B: Yes. I'd like to book a flight from Los Angeles to Sacramento, please.

A: What day would you like to fly?

B: Do you fly there every day?

A: No, we only go there three times a week. On Monday, Wednesday, and Saturday.

B: I see. And how much is a one-way coach ticket?

A: It's $ 79 on our economy flight on Wednesday and $ 99 on Monday and Saturday.

B: Good. Well, I'd like a flight on Wednesday the twenty-second, please.

A: Let me see if it's available. All right. That would be flight IC 35. It leaves at 11: 00 A.M. and arrives in Sacramento at 12:15.

B: Flight 35 did you say?

A: Yes. Leaving Los Angeles at 11:00 A.M. Now I need to know your name...

(2)

A: Intercontinental Airlines, Martha speaking. Can I help you?

B: Yes. I want to fly from Los Angeles to Mexico City, please.

A: Mexico City. Well, we have four flights a week, Sunday, Tuesday, Thursday, and Friday.

B: How much is a one-way ticket?

A: Coach fare?

B: Yes.

A: It's $ 275.

B: Good. Could you get me a ticket for Friday the fifteenth?

A: Let me check the computer. Yes, we have plenty of seats on that flight. It's flight number IC 64. It leaves at 12 o'clock and arrives in Mexico City at 4:15 A.M.

B: That sounds fine.

A: Could I have your name, please...

(3)

A: Intercontinental Airlines.

B: Uh, do you fly to Montreal from Los Angeles?

A: Yes, we do. We have a flight on Wednesday and one on Saturday.

B: And how much is your cheapest round-trip ticket?

A: We have a special fare this month of only $ 520 if you fly on our earliest morning flight.

B: That sounds good. Well, I guess I'd like a flight on Saturday the fifth, coming back on, hmm, let's see, Wednesday the sixteenth. Is that possible?

A: Certainly. Just a moment, please. Your name, please?

B: My name is Susan Santos.

A: Susan Santos. I've put you on flight IC256, Ms Santos. It leaves at 6:15 A.M. on Saturday, September 5, and arrives in Montreal at 3:30 P.M. Now your return flight...

Exercise 2

Directions: Listen again. Write the flight number, the departure time, and the arrival time of each passenger's flight.

Section C: Asking for Information
Exercise 1

Directions: You will hear people asking for information about the places below. Listen to their conversations and write down the opening and closing hours of each place.

(1)

A: Traffic Department.

B: Hello. I need to come in and take the test for my driving license. What hours are you open, please?

A: Our downtown office is open from 8:00 to 2:00 and you can take the test anytime between 8:00 and 2:00.

B: And it isn't possible to do it on the weekend, is it?

A: No, I'm sorry. We don't do any testing on the weekends.

(2)

A: Hay's Bookstore. Good morning.

B: Yes, what time are you open till today, please?

A: We're open from 10:00 in the morning until 9:30 every weekday, ma'am.

B: I see. I'd like to come in and pick up some books for children. You do sell children's book, don't you?

A: Of course, ma'am.

B: Good. And in case I can't get in today, are you open on the weekends at all?

A: Yes, ma'am. All our stores are open from 10:00 till 5:00 on Saturday, but we are closed on Sunday.

(3)

A: Science Museum.

B: Yes. I'm a teacher at Wesley High School, and I'd like to bring my class into the museum sometime next week. I was wondering what would be a good time.

A: Certainly. Well, we're open every day of the week. We open at

9:00 and close at 5:00 . We are also open on the weekends, but from 9:00 A.M. to 1:00P.M. Will this be a large group?

B: About twenty-five.

A: I'd suggest a weekday. Saturday is always a bit crowded.

B: All right. I think we'll come in on Tuesday then. Is that OK?

(4)

A: Tower Records. This is David. Can I help you?

B: Hello. What time do you close, please?

A: We close at 10:00 every day. And we open at 9:00 in the morning.

B: Oh, OK. And are you open on the weekends?

A: Same hours as on weekdays.

B: Wow. You guys never take a break! I want to come in and have a look at your sale. Your sale is still on, isn't it?

A: Yes, it runs till the end of the month. But things are clearing out fast.

B: OK, I'll come down tonight. Thanks.

A: Thank you for calling.

Section D: Completing a Questionnaire

Directions: Listen to the dialogue and complete the form with the information you hear.

(Doorbell rings)

(Door opens)

Woman: Yes?

Man: Oh, good morning, Madam. I'm from Pestaway Market Research. I'm doing consumer Research in this area. I

	wonder if you'd mind telling me — do you use Pestaway in your home?
Woman:	Pestaway? Oh — the insecticide thing. Well, yes, as a matter of fact, I do.
Man:	What do you use it for, Madam? Fleas, ants, cockroaches, woodworm?
Woman:	Oh, cockroaches in the kitchen. I tried scrubbing and disinfecting but it didn't seem to be much good, and then I heard a commercial about Pestaway, so I thought I'd try that.
Man:	Was that on TV?
Woman:	No, it was radio — one of those early morning shows.
Man:	You heard it advertised on the radio. Fine. And you say you use it in the kitchen. Do you use it anywhere else in the house? In the bathroom, say?
Woman:	Oh, no, we've never had any trouble anywhere else. We get the odd wasp in the summer sometimes, but I don't bother about them. It's the cockroaches I don't like — nasty, creepy-crawly things.
Man:	And you find Pestaway does the trick?
Woman:	Well, yes, it's quite good. It gets rid of most of them.
Man:	How long have you been using it, Madam?
Woman:	Oh, let's see — about two years now, I think.
Man:	About two years. And how often do you find you have to spray?
Woman:	Oh, I give the kitchen a good spray round the skirtings and under the stove — you know — about every six

94

weeks.

Man:	Every six weeks or so. I see. Where do you buy your Pestaway, Madam? Supermarket? Chemist?
Woman:	Oh, no. I get it at the little shop at the end of this street. They stock practically everything. It means taking a bus if I want to go to the supermarket.
Man:	Well, thank you very much, Madam. Oh, could I have your name please?
Woman:	Mrs Egerton, Mary Egerton, that's E-G-E-R-T-O-N.
Man:	E-G-E-R-T-O-N. And the address is 12, Holly Crescent, Peterford?
Woman:	That's right.
Man:	Might I ask your age, Madam?
Woman:	Oh — well — er — just put down I'm over fifty.
Man:	As you like, Mrs Egerton. And occupation — housewife?
Woman:	Well, I used to be a telephonist before I married. I had a very good job with the Post Office, but what with a husband to look after and four children to bring up, it doesn't leave you much time, does it?
Man:	Occupation — "housewife". Well, thank you very much for your time, Madam. You've been most helpful...

Part Ⅲ: Listening Comprehension Test

Directions: In this part, you will hear 10 short conversations about plans and actions. After you have heard each conversation, try to choose the best answer.

1. M: Can you tell me how to make moon cakes ?

   W: I have a recipe that my grandmother gave me.

   Q: What will the man probably do next?

2. M: I heard Susan's going to college. What's she studying?

   W: She's taking courses in grammar, reading, and literature.

   Q: What career does Susan probably plan to follow?

3. W: I need to talk with the PR manager immediately.

   M: Please wait a moment, ma'am. I'll have him notified that you're here.

   Q: What is the man going to do now ?

4. M: Does Tom know we are having a birthday party for him?

   W: No. He thinks we're giving a retirement party for the teacher.

   Q: What are the man and woman planning ?

5. M: I'll move the sofa and then the armchairs over next to the bookshelf.

   W: Let's move the other chairs and the coffee table in front of the sofa.

   Q: What are the two people doing?

6. W: Come to my house if you can be there before 11 o'clock, Tom. Otherwise I won't be able to see you until tomorrow.

   M: The reading room closes at 10 tonight, Nancy, so you can expect me to come by right after that.

   Q: What do Tom and Nancy plan to do?

7. M: Would you like to go to a park this week?

   W: Thanks, I'd like to. I haven't been to a park for ages because I have been busy with my work.

Q: What are the man and the woman going to do?

8. W: There is a small-craft warning on the radio this morning. Have you heard it?

M: Oh, that's disappointing. I guess we'll have to change our plans. Would you rather play golf or go fishing?

Q: What had the couple planned to do?

9. W: Do you plan on flying to the summer resort, Bob?

M: Yes, it costs so much, but the trains and buses don't run the day I'm going, so I have no choice.

Q: How about Bob's plan to the summer resort?

10. M: Let's go to the movie, Jane. There is a good picture at the "Princess".

W: I can't, I'm afraid. My sister is coming from New York to visit us. We haven't seen each other for a long time and I have to arrange a party in her honor.

Q: What is the woman going to do?

Unit Twelve

Part I : Listening Practice

Section A: Safari Tour
Exercise 1
Directions: You will hear a guide giving some safety instructions to tourists. Listen to the cassette and write down the four safety instructions in note form.

Guide: Right. Is everyone here? Good. Well, welcome to the Safari Tour. I'm your guide, Mike. This is our driver, Sue. The land-rover will be leaving in a few minutes. I just like to go over some of our safety instructions before we set off. Firstly, you mustn't get off the land-rover without my permission. Remember you are safe only inside the land-rover. If you get out on your own, you could be attacked. Secondly, we will be doing quite a lot of walking in the reserved area, and you must all stay close to me.

Woman: I'm sorry to interrupt. But, do we really have to stay together even in the reserved areas?

Guide: Yes, it could be very dangerous, you know. Now, thirdly, you all have to sign these insurance declarations, saying you'll take all responsibility for your own safety. That's a company regulation, I'm afraid. Just pass around for you. . .

Finally, I want to remind you that we are going to a nature reserve. All the animals are wild. They aren't as tame as they are in zoos. They don't like being disturbed. So when we're walking, we must keep as quiet as possible. Just use your common sense. Now any questions?

Woman: Yes, and how far are we going?

Guide: Oh, about 50 miles altogether. That's 80 kilometers.

Man: I'm a bit worried about insects.

Guide: Oh, you needn't worry about that. Sue has got plenty of insect repellent inside the land-rover.

Woman: What about food and drink?

Guide: We have got 15 liters of drinking water in the land-rover. We are providing a packed lunch. Oh, by the way, I've got plenty of rolls of 35mm film, in case anybody runs out. Most people take hundreds of photos.

Exercise 2

Directions: Listen to the cassette again and fill in the blanks in the following sentences with correct words or phrases.

Section B: Making a Visit to the Zoo
Exercise 1

Directions: A person is going to talk about how to make a visit to the New York Zoo. Decide whether the following statements are true or false.

The New York Zoo is one of the largest zoos in the country,

and it's open every day except national holidays such as Thanksgiving, Christmas Eve, Christmas Day, and New Year. Our business number is 24473110. The open hours are 9: 30 A. M. to 6: 00 P.M.

Our general admission ticket is five dollars for an adult, and two-fifty for a child under 11.

We also have group rates. Group rates are for 10 or more people. No reservations are needed unless there are over 500 people. The group rates are three dollars for adults and a dollar and half for children under 11.

Special discounts are offered on Saturdays and Sundays before 10 A.M. Admission to the Children's Zoo is fifty cents, and baby carriages may be rented at the entrance to the zoo. Refreshments and souvenirs are also available. We'll be pleased to welcome you to the zoo.

Exercise 2
Directions: Choose the best answer to complete the following statements.

Section C: A Dialogue
Directions: Listen to the following dialogue and then for each of the questions 1～5 circle the letter that gives the right answer.

George Barker: Hello, Jane, I didn't know you went in for jogging.

Jane Evans: Oh, yes, George, I've been doing it for over a month now — twice round the park before breakfast every day. It's amazing what it does for one.

	I feel fitter now than I've felt for years.
George Barker:	Hmm, well, it's all right, I suppose, so long as you don't overdo it. I find exercising LuLu is about as much as I can manage these days.
Jane Evans:	LuLu?
George Barker:	Well, she's the wife's really. She's over there chasing that Great Dane. She gets a bit overexcited when she sees something ten times her size. Still, the wife thinks it does her good. She's terribly overweight, you see.
Jane Evans:	Your wife? But last time I saw her, she said the doctor thought she was still a bit underweight after her operation.
George Barker:	Not my wife, the dog. The trouble is she overeats. She's got a positive passion for cream cakes and — I say, do you have to keep jogging up and down like that? You don't want to overstrain yourself, not at your time of life.
Jane Evans:	Oh, I don't think that's very likely. Still, perhaps I will sit down a moment and get my second wind. I am a bit out of breath. It's not that I'm not fit, it's just that we've had rather a rush on at work lately.
George Barker:	Been overworking, have you? Now, that's something I make a point of never doing. A man who's overtired doesn't do his work well. It affects his judgment; he gets things out of perspective.

101

Jane Evans: You may be right. I did find it rather an effort getting up early this morning.

George Barker: It's always an effort with me.

Section D: Unfamiliar Objects

Directions: Now listen to this dialogue between two young people walking home down a country road on a clear, still night. Note particularly the informal style and limited vocabulary of the speakers, which make it difficult for them to describe unfamiliar objects.

Annie: It's a super evening, isn't it?

Joe: I'll say. Sky's covered in stars. Looks like someone's left all the lights on. Shouldn't like to pay that electricity bill.

Annie: Well, I don't suppose you'll have to. Hey, what's that?

Joe: What's what?

Annie: That sort of big orange blob over there.

Joe: I can't see any orange blob.

Annie: Yes, you can. Look up there.

Joe: Oh, yes, now I've got it. That's not a blob. Looks more like a soup plate wrong way up, only it's got a kind of aerial or something sticking out of the top.

Annie: It looks ever so funny. What on earth can it be, Joe?

Joe: How should I know? Probably some new plane or other they're testing at the Research Centre. Whatever it is, it's not much to look at.

Annie: I think it's a bit scarey. It's all yellowy now. I think it's getting bigger. Oh Joe, do you — do you think it's one of

	those UFO things?
Joe:	What do you mean? A Flying Saucer? 'Caurse not. There's no such thing. Anyway, it's gone now.
Annie:	It must've landed or something behind those trees. It couldn't just — well — disappear, could it?
Joe:	Well, it's landed, you'd better look out. Any minute now we'll be surrounded by little green men with ray guns saying "Taking me to your Leader".
Annie:	Don't, Joe. I didn't like the look of it one little bit. I'm glad it's gone.
Voice:	Good evening. I am Oris. Would you be kind enough to take me to your Leader?

Part Ⅲ: Listening Comprehension Test

Directions: In this part, you will hear 10 short conversations concerning attitude and response. After you have heard each conversation, try to choose the best answer.

1. M: The room is filled with smoke. I can hardly breathe.
   W: I agree, smoking should not be permitted in this room at all.
   Q: What can be concluded from this conversation?
2. M: Wasn't that a good way to see the show?
   W: I think we could have had better seats.
   Q: Where were they?
3. W: You must take some rest. You've been working too hard.
   M: But how can I? I have to finish it by Friday.
   Q: What does the man mean?

4. M: But, doctor, if I give up cigarettes and I give up beer, life won't be worth living.

   W: If you don't give them up, you won't live anyway.

   Q: Is the man going to do what the woman says?

5. W: If it rains on Saturday, the party will be ruined.

   M: Oh, it doesn't matter. We can always hold it indoors.

   Q: What are the man and the woman hoping to do?

6. M: What a nice flat this is!

   W: It's only small, but it's central and it suits me very well.

   Q: What does the woman think of the flat?

7. W: Let's go in here and order some coffee while we look at your pictures.

   M: Good idea. We both like coffee.

   Q: What are they going to do?

8. M: You've been very busy this week.

   W: At least now, I'm up to date on all of my laboratory experiments.

   Q: What does the woman mean?

9. M: Greg is friendly, good-looking and talented.

   W: What he needs now is a change of luck.

   Q: What did the man say about Greg?

10. W: Wendy is pretty smart, don't you think?

    M: Pretty smart? She's practically a genius.

    Q: What does the man think about Wendy?

Unit Thirteen

Part I : Listening Practice

Section A: Making an Order

Directions: Listen to the conversation and then complete the order form below with the information you hear.

M: Harrison's.

W: Harrison's "THE" Caterers?

M: Yes.

W: Can you do a business lunch? This is William Martin & Sons. It's for Wednesday, the 18th. I'm afraid it's a rather short notice.

M: I'll just have a look. It's the 6th today, isn't it ? How many is it for?

W: It's for 25. Oh, and then it's myself and Mr Wallis. He is the new man. So that's 27. Hello, Hello, are you there?

M: Hello, sorry to keep you. Yes, we can manage that.

W: What sort of menu do you do ?

M: Oh, it's really up to you. How many courses do you want?

W: Well, the thing is. . . What is going. . . I mean. . . how. . .

M: How are the charges ? It's very reasonable, you'll find. The three course lunch costs £ 10 a head and the four course £ 15.

You'll also get cheese and coffee.

W: I see. I think we'd better have a cheaper one. What does the three course cost with coffee?

M: 11.

W: Gosh. One pound for a cup of coffee.

M: We usually allow enough for two and half cups each.

W: Small ones ?

M: Average small, yes.

W: Okay, then. What about wine ?

M: How much will you want ?

W: Oh, not too much.

M: Say half a bottle for a person.

W: Half a bottle. That's on the generous side. All right then. I suppose there is no harm.

M: Red or white or rosy ?

W: Not rosy. Red.

M: A house wine or something a little more. . . ?

W: No. That sounds fine.

M: Three courses plus coffee, wine. Let's see. We can do the whole thing for £ 13 a head.

W: That's each.

M: Yes. You won't be charged for any wine left over.

W: Well, no. If we don't drink it, we shouldn't have to pay for it.

M: That's OK. We'll see it that way, and we would expect £ 50 for deposit.

W: That will be all right. Just send us the bill. That's it then.

M: You want us to go ahead.

W: Oh, yes. You see the firm we booked originally has just gone

106

broke. That's why it's so urgent.

M: I understand. Just a couple of more things. We still haven't discussed the menu and the time.

W: Oh, yes. It's 1:15 and we don't mind about the menu, usual great food or "Beed a la" something will be fine.

M: Really, but we don't want to do the business badly.

W: All right. So what's on your menu?

M: As a matter of fact, it's great food followed by Beef-harrison, our own specialty and ice-cream, very original we feel.

W: The original menu in fact without cheese.

M: Yes. If you don't mind, I'll just read the details back. First of all, the date...

Section B: Filling in a Timetable

Directions: Listen to a short talk and then fill in the information you hear on the timetable below.

Good morning everybody, and may I take this opportunity of welcoming you to the Universal English College. As you probably know, English classes are held every morning between 9:30 and 1:00, then there is a lunch break until 2:00. In the afternoon a variety of visits and lectures have been arranged for you.

Now to the English lessons, Monday morning starts with intensive text study. Then there's a break from 10:45 to 11:00. From 11:00 to 12:00, that's the second period, there's grammar practice, followed by pronunciation and spelling practice until 1:00. For Tuesday we start with dialogue work from 9:30 to 10:45, then followed by extensive reading until 12:00, finishing with oral activity work. On Wednesday morning, intensive text study lasts until 12: 00 and then is followed by writing. Thursday morning is occupied by a listening class from 9: 30 to 10: 45 , then grammar practice. From 12:05 to 1:00 on Thursday there's a news broadcast for the study of the day's news. Finally, Friday's first period involves a test, 11: 00 to 12: 00 is role-play and the final period is given over to free oral activity work. That then is the complete week's timetable; I hope you will all enjoy the course. Thank you for your attention and good luck in your studies.

Section C: A Talk about Earthquakes

Directions: Listen to a short talk about earthquakes and then take down notes.

Scientists learn about the inside of the earth when there is an earthquake. Different kinds of waves, or vibrations, are sent out in all directions. Some of these earthquake waves travel through the crust of the earth. Some go through the deeper rocks. The speed of these waves and the path they take depend on the kinds of rocks they go through. Earthquake waves slow down greatly as they pass near the center of the earth. This may be because the rocks, they are very different from any in the earth's crust.

The rocks in the earth's crust are under stress like huge bent springs. The pressures inside the earth's crust may cause great breaks, or faults. Huge blocks, often miles long, slip past one another. They may move up, down, or sideways along the breaks, or faults, in the rock. Faults may be several hundred miles long. The movement at each shift is small, but it may continue for century after century along large faults.

The total movement may be thousands of feet.

Rocks are smoothed and polished as they slip past one another, or they are crushed and broken. As blocks of rock shift, several kinds of vibrations spread out in all directions. This is an earthquake.

Section D: Filling in a Form
Exercise 1:

Listen to the conversation and then fill in the form with the information you hear from the tape.

A: Professor Jones, may I see you for a moment ?

B: Of course, Judie. Come in and have a seat. I have about half an hour before my faculty meeting. Let me move this chair closer to my desk.

A: Thanks. I've come to talk to you about my grade on my last economics project. I want to know why I was given an "F".

B: Well, Judie, your approach was so similar to that of another student in the class that I seriously doubted that you'd done the calculations yourself.

A: I did work closely with my roommate Serry, but let me explain why. A week before the project was due, I was too sick to do my research. Serry agreed to help me with the project the night before it was due. We stayed up all night in order to finish it on time. The calculations were really my own.

B: Well, you'd been given a month to work on the project. Wouldn't it have been better to get a head start rather than to wait until the last minute ? Each student was supposed to prepare this project individually. I'm afraid that my decision remains the same. However, next week we will be studying the government's role in running the economy. If you're willing to make an oral presentation about the subject, I'll give you extra credit.

A: Thank you, Professor Jones. I'll have my oral report ready for class on Friday.

Part Ⅱ : Oral Practice

Listen to a short talk and then do the oral practice.

Today I'd like to talk to you about group discussions which, in an academic context, are usually known as "seminars" and "tutorials".

Firstly, then, let's look at the meaning of the terms "seminar" and "tutorial". Nowadays it's becoming more and more difficult to draw a precise distinction between the meaning of the two words that all lecturers would be willing to accept. The traditional differences which are still accepted by many lecturers are firstly the size of the group and secondly, and perhaps more importantly, their purpose. A tutorial was usually for a small number of students, say between two and five, whereas a seminar was attended by a larger group, say between ten and fifteen. In a tutorial a lecturer or tutor adopted the role of the expert and asked and answered questions related to his most recent lecture. Often a student had to submit an essay or a report which was discussed by the tutor and then by other members of the tutorial group. In short, the tutor took the lead; he in fact "tutored". The purpose of the seminar, on the other hand, was to provide an opportunity to discuss a previously arranged topic.

110

More than one member of the staff might be present and one of them would probably act as chairman. Often one student presented a paper, that is, gave a short talk which served as an introduction to a more general discussion. The other students may have been asked to read a number of chapters of a book, related to the talk, so as to be in a better position to participate in the discussion.

Part Ⅲ: Listening Comprehension Test

Directions: In this part, you will hear three passages concerning short speeches. After you have heard the passages and the questions, try to choose the best answer from the four choices given by marking the corresponding letter (A, B, C or D).

Passage Ⅰ

Today I'd like to mention an interesting television program that will be shown on October 10th. It's about the brain. It's a new public television show produced in New York City. The program will investigate how the brain functions and malfunctions. Some interesting topics that will be discussed are dreaming, memory, and depression. These topics will be illustrated by using a computer to make explanations easy to follow. The show is not for children, but don't worry, it's not intended for scientists either. I think the program will be very helpful with the work we're doing in class on the brain. I hope you'll watch it.

1. Who is the speaker?
2. What will be broadcast on television on October 10th?
3. What will be the main purpose of the show?
4. Why does the speaker recommend watching the program?

Passage Ⅱ

Everybody knows hamburger is a very popular American food. However, people in the United States learned to make hamburgers from Germans, and Germans got the idea from Russia.

In the thirteenth century the Tartar people from central Asia moved into Russia and parts of Europe. They fought the Russians and won. They ate something like hamburger meat but it was raw. This raw meat was beef, goat meat or horse meat. Soon the Russians started to eat raw meat too. Germans from Hamburg and other northern cities learned to eat this food from the Russians. However, they added pepper, a raw egg, and then cooked it.

Between 1830 and 1900, thousands of Germans went to live in the United States. They took the hamburger with them. People called it hamburger steak.

In 1904 at the World's Fair in St Louis, a city on the Mississippi River, a man from Texas sold hamburger steak in a roll. Then people could eat it with their hands, like a sandwich. This was the first real hamburger like the hamburgers we eat today.

Today some people still like to eat raw beef. They call it "steak tartar".

5. According to the passage, who first had the idea of making hamburgers?
6. The hamburger made by Germans is different from that by Russians. Why?
7. Who sold the first real hamburger?

Passage Ⅲ

Although I think the United States generally has an excellent

112

system of transportation, I do not think that it does a good job of transporting people between cities that are only a few hundred miles apart. A person commuting between Detroit and Chicago, or between San Francisco and Los Angeles may spend only a relatively short time in the air, while spending several hours getting to and from the airport. This situation makes flying almost as time-consuming as driving. Moreover, airplanes use a lot of their fuel just getting into the air. They simply are not fuel effective on short trips.

High speed trains may be an answer. One fairly new proposal for such trains is for something called a maglev, meaning a magnetically levitated train. Maglev will not actually ride on the tracks, but will fly above tracks that are magnetically activated. This will save wear and tear on the tracks. These trains will be able to go faster than 150 miles per hour. At this speed, conventional trains have trouble staying on the tracks.

As you can see, maglev offers exciting possibilities for the future.

8. What is the main topic of the talk?

9. When are airplanes not fuel effective?

10. How does a maglev operate?

Unit Fourteen

Part I : Listening Practice

Section A: Farming Methods
Exercise 1
Directions: Listen through to the end of the passage. Decide whether the following statements are true or false. Tick under T for true and F for false.

Before modern farming methods, farmers lost many crops to dry weather. Sometimes dry periods lasted for many years. In those days, a long dry period, or drought, often turned the land to dust. Then winds came along and blew the good land away. This happened year after year.

Farmers didn't understand how to plant and so they made the situation worse. Each year they planted the same crops. They never gave the land a rest. The land became poor from too much use. They always planted in long, straight rows. They broke the land into fine dust. They never planted trees to break the strength of the wind.

The worst dry period was the drought of the 1930's. Good farmland on the Western Plains became a Dust Bowl. Farmers had a very hard time until they started to use modern farming methods.

Now farmers plant a different crop every year. Some years they give part of their land a rest. The land stays healthy and rich. Modern farmers form rows in curving lines and plant trees to stop the wind. Modern crops are much larger and more dependable.

Dry land farming is both a science and an art. From the air, the farms look like pieces of modern art.

Exercise 2
Directions: Listen to the cassette again and then complete the following chart.

Section B: About Littering
Directions: You are going to listen to a passage about littering. Some words on the printed passage have been taken out. Listen carefully. Fill in the blanks with the words you hear on the tape.

Litter is garbage — like food, paper, and cans — on the ground or in the street. Where many people live together, litter is a problem. People don't always put their garbage in the garbage can. It's easier to drop a paper than to find a garbage can for it. But litter is ugly. It makes the city look dirty, and it spoils the view.

The wind blows papers far away. Often they are difficult to catch. When they blow against a fence, they stay there. This fence is a wall of garbage.

Litter is a health problem, too. Food and garbage bring animals, which sometimes carry disease.

Some people want to control litter. They never throw litter themselves, and sometimes they work together in groups to clean up the city. In most places littering is against the law. The law punishes people who throw garbage on the streets. They usually pay a fine, and occasionally they go to jail.

Two famous sayings in the United States are: "Don't be a litter-bug !" and "Every litter bit hurts !"

Section C: Noise Pollution
Exercise 1

Directions: You are going to listen to a passage about Noise Pollution. Listen carefully and then fill in the following table.

Noise Pollution

Sound is measured in units called "decibels". At a level of 140 decibels people feel pain in their ears. Automobiles, trucks, buses, motorcycles, airplanes, boats, factories, bands — all these things make noise. They bother not only our ears, but our minds and bodies as well.

Noise can be separated into a few general groups:

Occupational noise —Factory workers who always hear noise have poorer hearing than other groups.

Aircraft noise — Around airports or on air routes the noise of airplanes taking off and landing causes the greatest complaints.

Traffic noise —Away from the noise of planes, traffic sounds break in on our peace and quiet. Trucks and motorcycles cause the most problems.

Outdoor noise —For people in the city, noise of buildings going up and emergency automobiles are the greatest problems. In the suburbs, barking dogs, playing children, and lawn mowers cause the problems.

Indoor noise — Radios, record players, and TV, the sounds of plumbing, heating, and air conditioning are all noise to some people.

There are two ways to cut down on the harm caused by noise. One is to cut down on the amount of noise. The other is to protect ourselves against the noise we can't stop. Ways of making less noise are now being tested. There are groups for the prevention of noise in this country. There are even laws controlling noise.

We cannot return to the "good old days" of peace and quiet. But we can reduce noise — if we shout loudly enough about it.

Exercise 2

Directions: Listen again and then answer the following questions.

Part Ⅲ : Listening Comprehension Test

Directions: In this part, you will hear three short passages. At the end of each passage, there will be some questions. You will hear both the passages and the questions only once. After each question there will be a pause, you must choose the best answer from the four choices given by marking the corresponding letter (A, B, C, or D).

Passage Ⅰ

No matter what type of holiday you are looking for you will find the answer in Switzerland. There is really no other country quite like it, for here you have some of the finest and most beautiful scenery in the whole of Europe together with attractive hotels and the friendliest people you could wish to meet.

Think of the variety of attractions. You may seek outdoor sporting activities: walking, swimming, sailing and fishing are just a few of the many possibilities for enjoying your holiday. Then there is an infinite variety of trips by coach or railway, free afternoons on a lake steamer and, visits to historic cities, these are just a few more of the variety of interests for your holiday in Switzerland. In the evening music fills the air, whether it is the local village band or an all star variety show.

Questions:

1. What do Swiss people do in the evening?
2. Which of the following is mentioned as a possibility for outdoor sporting activities?
3. Which of the following is not mentioned in the passage?

Passage II

Rubber is a very useful vegetable product. More than nine-tenths of the world's supply of rubber comes from a tree known as the para rubber tree.

Rubber trees are grown from seeds. These seeds are planted in beds of specially prepared rich soil so that they will come up quickly. When the plants are a few inches tall, they are set out in new beds. Those trees which do not develop well are removed, and the healthy trees are grafted so that they will produce a larger amount of latex.

When the trees are between five and six years old, they are ready to be tapped. This means cutting the bark in a certain way to allow the latex to flow into a cup, which is attached to the tree trunk. Some trees are tapped every day, but most trees are tapped every other day. Tapping goes on all year long, except for the period when the tree changes its leaves.

A tree produces a few spoonfuls of latex each time it is tapped. In a year, one young tree produces about three pounds of rubber. Well-grafted trees may produce ten pounds of rubber in a year, while some exceptional trees yield as much as twenty-five pounds in a year.

Questions:

4. How often is a rubber tree tapped for the latex?
5. When is the rubber tree not tapped?
6. How many pounds of rubber does a young tree usually produce in a year?

Passage Ⅲ

Many substances that come into contact with the surface of the eye can cause chemical burns, allergic reactions or inflammations, or can even be absorbed through the eye. Whenever one of these types of substances does come into contact with someone's eye, the eye should be flushed out immediately with water. Lukewarm water should be poured gently into the inside corner of the eye from a container, two to three inches above the victim's eye. A water tap will do very nicely as it produces controllable pressure. The victim's head should be tilted so that the water will flow across the eyeball and off the face. This procedure should be followed for five to fifteen minutes, depending on the severity of the problem. Adults who are not otherwise incapacitated may use a shower to wash out the eyes. Urgency is the key word in treating eye problems of this sort. Wash out the affected eye immediately, and as soon as possible call a physician or a poison control center for additional advice.

Questions:
7. What is the topic of this talk?
8. How far from the victim's head should the water be poured?
9. What is the key word in the treatment of eye problems?
10. Why is the treatment of eye problems so important?

Unit Fifteen

Part Ⅰ : Listening Practice

Section A: Dreams
Exercise 1

Directions: You are going to hear a talk about dreams. Listen carefully, then fill in the form with the information you hear from the talk.

Psychologists believe that our dreams can often give us interesting information about ourselves, if we will take the time to look at them seriously. On the simplest level, dreams can make us aware of things we have missed during the day because we were too busy to notice them. For instance, if you dream of your teeth falling out, you may have unconsciously picked up signs of dental trouble, or if you dream of missing an important appointment, your dream may be trying to remind you of an engagement coming up that you have forgotten to write down.

On a deeper level, dreams can show us how we really feel about our relationships. For instance, a young woman who considered herself fairly happily married dreamed of angrily bashing her husband over the head with a vacuum cleaner. The dream was urging the woman to get in touch with her feelings of resentment toward her husband for insisting that she stay home instead of taking an interesting job.

Exercise 2
Directions: Listen to the tape again and answer the following questions.

Section B: About sleep
Exercise 1
Directions: You are going to hear a talk about sleep. Now read the following form carefully, then listen to the tape and complete the form.

After a hectic day of work and play, the body needs to rest. Sleep is necessary for good health. During this time, the body recovers from the activities of the previous day. The rest that you get while sleeping enables your body to prepare itself for the next day.

There are four levels of sleep, each being a little deeper than the one before. As you sleep, your muscles relax little by little. Your heart beats more slowly, and your brain slows down. After you reach the fourth level, your body shifts back and forth from one level of sleep to another.

Although your mind slows down, from time to time you will dream. Scientists who study sleep state that when dreaming occurs, your eyeballs begin to move more quickly (although your eyelids are closed). This stage of sleep is called REM, which stands for rapid eye movement.

If you have trouble falling asleep, some people recommend

breathing very slowly and very deeply. Other people believe that drinking warm milk will help make you drowsy. There is also an old suggestion that counting sheep will put you to sleep!

Exercise 2

Directions: Listen again and tell if the following statements are true or false (T/F)

Section C: "Why Older Is Better"

Directions: You are going to hear a talk about "Why older is better". Listen carefully and then catch the main idea of the five reasons supporting the viewpoint "Why older is better".

We have tended to regard each successive birthday after 30 as a harbinger of loss. But today's outlook on getting older is changing. In fact, experts are finding that getting older means getting better, in very real ways. Here's how.

1. You smarten up: Gray hair doesn't mean fuzzy thinking. Sigmund Freud published his first great work, The Interpretation of Dreams, at 44. Environmentalist and author Rachel Carson completed her classic, Silent Spring, at 55.

If you continue reading, thinking and creating all your life, the knowledge you gain improves your intelligence. As you age, the speed of reasoning and remembering may decrease, but not the quality.

2. You toughen up: Our psychological defense mechanism — ways of coping with difficult feelings — become healthier as we grow older. The young protect themselves with strategies such as denial and impulsive acting-out. The middle-aged rely far more on defenses

such as humor, altruism, and creativity. That's because you have been fired once, or gone through a divorce, or lost a loved one — and you've survived. Psychologically, you're tougher.

3. You feel your power: Most people in their middle years are at the peak of their working lives. This is the time of competence when people get a great deal of satisfaction and security out of realizing they have something to offer others.

4. Your love deepens: As you get older, you're more secure in your relationships. The longer you have been married, the more likely it is that you are going to stay married. And if you have a good marriage, the chances are it will be even better after the children leave the house.

5. You become more yourself: It takes a long time to become a person. The older you get, the more unique you become. You become clearer about what you think, what you like and don't like. You know what you are.

　　Listen again and then fill in the blanks.

Part II : Oral Practice
Exercise 2
Directions: Listen to a conversation and then answer the following questions.

M: I still don't understand what it is that you're talking about. What is feminism anyway ? Does it mean you don't want to marry me anymore?

W: I'm not sure I can give you a perfect dictionary definition, but I'll tell you how I feel. I want both of us to share all responsibilities equally. Both of us will contribute to the life that we share.

M: But I earn enough money for the both of us. And what about the home?

W: I want to contribute financially so that we can both pay our own way; both of us will clean the house; both of us will raise the children, and so on. It may not be exactly equal, but we can try.

M: I was raised to treat woman with a certain respect: to stand when they enter a room, to open car doors and front doors for them, to let them sit first and eat first.

W: I think those things are old-fashioned. I'm perfectly able to open doors for myself, and do all sorts of other things. And besides, it makes me feel uncomfortable when you treat me as though I were a china doll. I'm not more special than you: I'm your equal.

M: It sounds as though you think men and women — or in our case, boys and girls — can be friends just like two girls or two boys can.

W: I certainly do. And I think we'll all be better for it.

Part Ⅲ: Listening Comprehension Test

Section A

Directions: In this section, you will hear nine short conversations between two speakers. At the end of each conversation a third voice will ask a question about what was said. Both the conversations and the questions will be spoken only once. After each question there will be a pause. During the pause, you must choose the best answer from the four choices given by marking the corresponding letter (A, B, C, or D).

1. M: I can't get my work done because there are too many phone calls.

   W: Maybe you should disconnect the phone.

   Q: Why is the man angry?

2. W: There's no room in the bookcase for this book.

   M: Just put it on the floor for now. I'll put it away later.

   Q: Where does the man say to put the book?

3. M: I'm having dinner with John and the boss tonight.

   W: How could you do that ? Don't you remember Gail and Jane are coming over?

   Q: Who will the man have dinner with?

4. W: Hello, Mr Jones. This is Betty Smith. May I speak to my husband?

   M: John is in the lab now, Betty. And then he's going to eat lunch. I'll tell him to call you at home.

   Q: Where is the woman's husband?

5. M: I really like this black necktie.

   W: But the blue or gold one will look much nicer with your brown suit.

   Q: What color necktie does the man want?

6. M: Do you think Ed will get here on time?

   W: If Ed doesn't, nobody will.

   Q: What does the woman mean?

7. M: I am exhausted today. I was in the library all day doing re-search for my thesis. How was your day?

W: It was all right. I'm starving. Let's go to the cafeteria now.

Q: Where did this conversation most probably take place?

8. W: I heard that you took a tour around the Great Lakes. Is it beautiful?

M: Yes, but I thought that Lake Erie is so polluted that almost every living thing in it had died.

W: I was told that there was so much algae that the oxygen supply was practically used up.

M: That's true. There was really excessive growth of algae there.

Q: Where has the man been?

9. M: What is the easiest way to reach Grand Hotel from here?

W: A taxi might be most convenient.

M: Is it very far from here?

W: Oh, it's about two miles. You can take bus or subway.

Q: What would be the most convenient way to get to the hotel?

Section B

Directions: In this section, you will hear two short passages. At the end of each passage, there will be some questions. You will hear both the passages and the questions only once. After each question there will be a pause. During the pause, you must choose the best answer from the four choices given by marking the corresponding letter (A, B, C, or D).

Passage I

Trees are useful to Man in three very important ways: they provide him with wood and other products; they give him shade, and they help to prevent drought and floods.

Unfortunately, in many parts of the world, Man has not realized that the third of these services is the most important. In his eagerness to draw quick profit from trees, he has cut them down in large numbers, only to find that with them he has lost the best friends he had.

Two thousand years ago, a rich and powerful country cut down its trees to build warships, with which to gain itself an empire. It gained the empire but, without its trees, its soil became hard and poor. When the empire fell to pieces, the home country found itself faced with floods and starvation.

Even when a government realizes the importance of a plentiful supply of trees, it is difficult sometimes to make the people realize this. They cut down the trees but are too thoughtless to plant and look after new trees. So unless the government has a good system of control, or can educate the people, the forests slowly disappear.

This does not only mean that there will be fewer trees. The results are even more serious: for where there are trees their roots break up the soil — allowing the rain to sink in and also bind the soil. This prevents the soil from being washed away. But where there are no trees, the rain falls on hard ground and flows away on the surface, and this causes floods and the rain carries away the rich top-soil in which crops grow. When all the top-soil is gone, nothing remains but worthless desert.

10. Trees are useful to Man mainly in three ways, what is the most important one?

11. Why did a rich and powerful country meet with floods and starvation two thousand years ago?

12. When there is heavy rain, trees can help to prevent floods, Why?

Passage II

These days, people who do manual work often receive far more money than clerks who work in an office. People who work in offices are frequently refered to as "white collar workers" for the simple reason that they usually wear a tie to go to work. Such is human nature that a great many people are often willing to sacrifice higher pay for the privilege of becoming white collar workers. This can give rise to curious situations, as it did in the case of Alfred Bloggs who worked as a dustman for the Ellesmere Corporation.

When he got married, Alf was too embarrassed to say anything to his wife about his job. He simply told her that he worked for the Corporation. Every morning, he left home dressed in a fine black suit. He often changed into overalls and spent the next eight hours as a dustman. Before returning home at night, he took a shower and changed back into his suit. Alf did this for over two years and his fellow dustmen kept his secret. Alf's wife has never discovered that she married a dustman and she never will, for Alf has just found another job. He will soon be working in an office as a junior clerk. He will be earning only half as much as he used to, but he feels that his rise in status is well worth the loss of money. From now on, he will wear a suit all day and others will call him "Mr Bloggs", not "Alf".

13. What does the story of Alfred Bloggs show?
14. Why did Alfred Bloggs consider wearing a suit all day and being a junior clerk so important?
15. What did Alf's wife never discover?

Simulated Listening Test 1

Section A

Directions: In this section, you will hear nine short conversations between two speakers. At the end of each conversation a third voice will ask a question about what was said. Both the conversations and the questions will be spoken only once. After each question there will be a pause. During the pause, you must choose the best answer from the four choices given by marking the corresponding letter (A, B, C, or D).

1. W: It must have at least two bathrooms and a good kitchen.

   M: And a 2-car garage and a half-acre garden.

   Q: What are the two speakers probably discussing?

2. W: And after that program, we'll have Saturday's Feature Film and then the 10 o'clock news.

   M: Good evening, everybody. Tonight we start with the story about the Old Roman Village.

   Q: What is this?

3. W: The teacher recommended that I get some newly published books on computer science.

   M: Why don't we stop at a book store on the way to school?

   Q: What does the man suggest?

4. M: Make thirty copies for me and twenty copies for Mr Brown.

W: Certainly, sir. As soon as I finish this typing.

Q: What's the probable relationship between the man and the woman?

5. M: What are you working so hard on?

W: An editorial for the newspaper. If I miss the midnight deadline, it won't be printed until next week.

Q: What is the woman trying to do?

6. W: I'm going now. Anything I can do for you?

M: Yes. Get me some airmail stamps and aerograms. By the way, when will you be back?

Q: Where does the man expect the woman to go?

7. M: How much is the rent ?

W: It's three hundred dollars a month unfurnished, or three hundred and fifty dollars furnished. Facilities are forty dollars extra.

Q: How much will it cost the man to rent a furnished apartment, including facilities?

8. W: Well, you see it's so troublesome for me to carry these packages home.

M: If you'd like us to send the packages to you, Miss, they won't take long to arrive.

W: There is no rush. Could you please have them delivered this week?

M: Certainly.

Q: What does the woman mean?

9. W: I hear you went shopping this morning.

M: Yes, but I couldn't find the kind of jogging shoes I wanted anywhere in town.

131

W: Why not order them from a catalogue ? It's easier than running around town looking for them.

M: That's a good idea.

Q: What does the woman suggest that the man do?

Section B

Directions: In this section, you will hear two short passages. At the end of each passage, there'll be some questions. You will hear both the passages and the questions only once. After each question, there'll be a pause. During the pause, you must choose the best answer from the four choices given by marking the corresponding letter (A, B, C, or D).

Passage I

There are a huge variety of books on sale. Every year, thirty to forty thousand new books are published in Britain. But what makes a book a best seller ? What makes people choose the books they buy?

Booksellers try to stock as many different books as possible, often a book will sell well because of a television programme. People buy books for pleasure to find out about particular things or places which interest them and to give as presents. As well as books by English speaking authors, many translations of foreign literature are on sale.

There are many people involved in the publishing business: authors, publishers, printers, booksellers, and of course, the people who buy books.

The publisher has to be the patron of the writer, that is, to pay the writer. So if a publisher decides to publish a book, he takes a risk. Some books become best sellers — like Angus Wilson's and Tom Sharp's books. Others just don't work out. But if a publisher gets about eighty percent right then he will "live to fight another day".

10. What can a television programme do?

11. What are the Angus Wilson's and Tom Sharp's books?

12. What does the sentence "others just don't work out" mean?

Passage II

Criticism of research lays a significant foundation for future investigative work, but when students begin their own projects, they are likely to find that the standards of validity in field work are considerably more rigorous than the standards for most library research. When students are faced with the concrete problem of proof by field demonstration, they usually discover that many of the "important relationships" they may have criticized other researchers for failing to demonstrate are very elusive indeed. They will find, if they submit an outline or questionnaire to their classmates for criticism, that other students make comments similar to some they themselves may have made in discussing previously published research. For example, student researchers are likely to begin with a general question but find themselves forced to narrow its focus. They may learn that questions whose meanings seem perfectly obvious to them are not clearly understood by others, or that questions which seemed entirely objective to them appear to be highly biased to someone else. They usually find that the formulation of good research questions is a much more subtle and frustrating task than is generally believed by those who have not actually attempted it.

13. What is one major criticism students often make of published research?

14. How do students in class often react to another student's research?

15. What do student researchers often learn when they discuss their work in class?

Simulated Listening Test 2

Section A

Directions: In this section, you will hear nine short conversations between two speakers. At the end of each conversation a third voice will ask a question about what was said. Both the conversations and the questions will be spoken only once. After each question there will be a pause. During the pause, you must choose the best answer from the four choices given by marking the corresponding letter (A, B, C, or D).

1. W: Bill certainly is in a good mood lately.
   M: I would say "yes".
   Q: What does the man mean?
2. W: I've got time to buy a magazine, haven't I?
   M: The train is about to leave.
   Q: What does the man mean?
3. W: I can't imagine what happened to Judy.
   M: Neither can I. I'm sure she planned to come to the party.
   Q: What can be concluded about Judy?
4. W: Do you think you could fix my television for me today?
   M: Sorry, I've got my hands full as it is.
   Q: What is the man's problem?

5. M: Laura's getting a part-time job next week.

W: Shouldn't she concentrate on doing her school work instead?

Q: What does the woman suggest?

6. M: I assumed you'd be in class until three o'clock today.

W: I usually am. Professor Smith let us out early.

Q: What do we learn from the conversation?

7. M: Sorry, I couldn't find the magazine you asked for.

W: Thanks anyway.

Q: What does the woman mean?

8. W: Did you go to see the school play last night?

M: Yes, I did.

W: Did you think it was a good play?

M: What I didn't understand was the very beginning.

Q: What does the man mean?

9. W: Bob has found a real challenging job.

M: I wonder if a job like that could be handled by him?

W: Well, if he can't handle it, no one can.

M: You seem so sure about it.

Q: What does the woman imply about the job?

Section B

Directions: In this section, you will hear two short passages. At the
end of each passage, there will be some questions. You will hear
both the passages and the questions only once. After each question
there will be a pause. During the pause, you must choose the best
answer from the four choices given by marking the corresponding
letter (A, B, C, or D).

Passage I

Here is the nine o'clock news.

Last night thieves stole a painting from the home of Lord Bonniford. The painting, a sixteenth-century master piece by Holbein, is said to be priceless. Lord Bonniford said he could hear noises in the middle of the night, but he paid no attention. The security guard, Mr Jane Potts, couldn't phone the police because he was tied hand and foot.

The thieves managed to get in and escape without setting off the security alarm by cutting off the electricity supply.

Andrew Garder, the man who had a liver, heart and kidney transplant, is doing well after his operations, say his doctors.

Andrew is able to sit up and feed himself. he can get out of bed but he can't walk yet, as he is still too weak. Doctors say he'll be able to go home in a few week's time.

10. What kind of painting is the one that is stolen?

11. Why couldn't the security guard phone the police?

12. How is Andrew Garder now?

Passage II

Archaeologist Malcom was inspecting the 300-year-old wreck of a ship when he discovered several small seeds. The seeds found were preserved in fresh water, and it was found that after the seeds had been in the fresh water a little over a week four of them sprouted. The sprouts then were planted in soil, and two of them started to grow.

David, a botanist, has studied the development of Malcom's plants. Indeed, it is very unusual for seeds to survive in salt water

137

and it is unheard of that they would sprout after 300 years.

David suggests these seeds have to have been in an environment where there was no salt water and probably no air. They might have been compressed into the tightly packed ballast taken on during the ship's last trip.

13. What was Malcom's profession according to the talk?
14. Where were these seeds found?
15. According to David's suggestion, why can seeds sprout after so many years?

Unit Sixteen

Part Ⅰ : Listening Practice

Section A: Listening for Gist
Exercise 1
Directions: You will hear ten people talking. Listen and write down what you think they are. You may read a list of words below the table which will give you some help with the exercise.

1. Good morning ladies and gentlemen. On behalf of Captain Kirk and the crew, welcome to this British Airways flight to New York. In accordance with international regulations, the cabin staff will now demonstrate safety procedures.
2. OK. Calm down everyone. Quiet please. That includes you, Matthew! Now first I'd like you to hand in last night's homework. Er, you'd better pass them down to the front. William! Will you stop that please and pay attention.
3. Right, Mr Baines. Now open up nice and wide. A bit wider. That's good. Now let's have a look. Hmm, the filling needs redoing. Right bottom three is chipped. Ah, there's a little piece of food trapped here. Yes. Now you were complaining of a pain here on the upper left. (Ow!) Sorry about that. Yes. I'm going to take an x-ray.

4. Yes, the trousers are a bit tighter, sir. Let me bring you a larger size to try on. Um, a 34 waist should do it. The jacket is a perfect fit, isn't? The dark blue really suits you. I'll just go and check if we have a larger size in stock. I won't be a minute.

5. Now ladies and gentlemen. Behind you is the Sheldonian Theatre, a magnificent building designed by Sir Christopher Wren who was actually a student here at Oxford. The theatre was built in the 17th century and is used for university ceremonies and concerts. In fact, it's never been used as a theatre.

6. A very good morning to you madam! I'm from International Cleaning Services. We're calling on selected households in this area to give a special demonstration of our new range of cleaning fluids. We're giving away a free carpet cleaner to every client who buys a giant bottle of Jiffy liquid. Now, if I could just come in and take up a few minutes of your time? I'd like to show you some of our excellent products.

7. Just love that record! A golden oldie from the 60's by "The Kinks". That one was specially for Tracey Rogers for her birthday from all her friends at Leicester Poly. Hope you enjoyed that one, Tracey, and you just have a WONDERFUL birthday OK! You're on Radio City 248 WHF.

8. Good morning madam. Did you realize your car is parked on a double yellow line? This is a no-parking area and you're disrupting the traffic. I'm afraid I'm going to have to give you a parking ticket.

9. Good evening sir, madam. here's the menu. May I recommend the chef's speciality: home-made onion soup and then to follow, Scottish salmon garnished with chef's own special dressing.

10. Nearly there, sir. It was Cricket Road, wasn't it? Here we are, number 27. I'll just park behind the lorry. Right, that'll be 6.50 please.

Exercise 2
Directions: Listen to the cassette once again. Then write down one or two important words which helped you decide.

Section B: Car Pool
Exercise 1
Directions: Listen to the dialogue and answer the following questions.

A: My goodness. We've been 20 minutes in this jam. Just look at the traffic! They should really do something about this. And it's so polluted.

B: Well, in New York a few years back, it was pretty bad too. But... er, they have taken some measures which have improved it quite a bit.

A: This is the state government?

B: The city. The city of New York. The geography helps. New York is an island. The main part of New York, I mean. You have to approach it either by tunnel or bridge. So you have a place where you can stop motorists and charge tolls.

A: That's Manhattan Island, right?

B: Manhattan, yeah. That's where most people are heading when they go to work in the morning. What they've basically done is to penalize those who use their cars. If you're travelling in a car with only one person, you pay a very high toll to get into Manhattan. If you've got a car with four people in it, you go free and you're in the express lane. The express lane is just for buses or for cars carrying four or more people. So you zip in free if you've got a lot of people. Now they've got into the habit of using car pools.

A: That's a good system.

B: And after you get in there-well, parking is so dreadfully expensive, most people think twice about bringing their cars into the city. What they've done is to provide free parking outside the city where you pick up public transport.

A: Look! We're moving at last.

Exercise 2

Directions: Listen to the dialogue once again and decide whether the information is true or false according to the speaker.

Section C: Energy and Environment
Exercise 1

Directions: Listen to the dialogue and answer the following questions.

A: The Energy Minister announced at a press conference yesterday the construction of three more nuclear power stations. These will form a vital part of the government's energy plans for the next two decades and are needed to satisfy the country's growing demands for electricity. The plans were strongly criticized by opposition MP's as well as antinuclear and environmentalist groups.

B: They must be absolutely mad. More nuclear power stations!

C: OK. Nigel. But we've got to get the energy from somewhere, haven't we? We can't just go on using oil and coal.

B: Look. The main point is they're just not safe. They're a real menace. Every one of these things is... an accident waiting to happen. Look at Chernobyl, for goodness' sake!

C: Yes, OK. I agree there's a risk. Of course there is. But it's minimal. With modern, er, technology, nuclear reactors are much safer.

B: Much safer! You must be joking. No. Just look at all that radioactive waste they're dumping into the sea and underground. They don't... I mean, nobody really knows what'll happen longterm.

C: That is a problem. Sure. But it's true that nuclear energy is cheap and can produce um, electricity very quickly. Lots of countries have no alternative. They don't have any oil, coal or anything. What are they supposed to do?

B: Oh, come on! There are lots of possibilities. Well, quite a few. We just haven't really looked at them seriously enough. There's um, solar energy, and wind power and, what's it called, wave power. We've still got a lot of coal.

C: Alright. But they'll all take time and money to develop. We need energy now and nuclear power is er, yes, the best alternative.

B: Oh, I don't believe this. I reckon it's just crazy.

Exercise 2
Directions: Listen to the cassette again and for each of the argument

in favour of nuclear energy note down the second speaker's response.

Section D: A Conversation between a Man and a Doctor

Directions: You are going to hear a conversation between a man and a doctor and then fill in the relevant information on the doctor's note-pad.

D: Good morning. Come in.

P: Good morning, doctor.

D: Take a seat, please. I haven't seen you before, have I?

P: No, you haven't. I'm here on a two-week holiday.

D: In that case, may I have your name, please?

P: John MacDonald.

D: John MacDonald. How do you spell MacDonald?

P: M-A-C capital D-O-N-A-L-D.

D: Capital D. thank you. And where are you staying?

P: At the "Seaview" Hotel.

D: Oh, the "Seaview". I know it. Good. Now what seems to be the trouble?

P: Well, I've had a very bad stomach-ache for two days, and I keep feeling sick and weak.

D: M-hm. But have you actually been sick?

P: No, I haven't.

D: Well, it sounds to me as if you've eaten something that doesn't agree with you.

P: You don't think it's food poisoning or anything like that?

D: Well, no, I don't think so. How long have you been here?

P: Four days. We arrived last Saturday.

D: In that case, I'm sure it's the change of diet, and the tempera-

144

ture. I'll give you something to calm your stomach.

P: Thank you, doctor.

D: This is a prescription for some medicine which you can get from the chemist's. There's one just round the corner.

P: And how often do I have to take it?

D: Three times a day, after meals. But try not to eat too much for a day or two, and drink plenty of orange juice. By the way, don't go out in the sun for a day or two, either. And if you don't feel any better by the end of the week, come back and see me again.

P: Thank you, doctor.

Part Ⅲ: Listening Comprehension Test

Directions: In this part, you will hear ten short conversations about cause and effect. After you hear the question at the end of each conversation, choose the best answer from the four choices given by marking the corresponding letter (A, B, C or D).

1. W: I was surprised to see you and your family at the Shopping Mall yesterday.

   M: Our junior school was closed down because flu broke out.

   Q: Why could the man come to the Shopping Mall that day?

2. W: Did you see the late movie on TV last night?

   M: No, I intended to watch the football game, but slept through it.

   Q: Why did the man miss the TV program?

3. W: Where's that Italian restaurant that used to be here?

   M: It burned to the ground last December.

   Q: Why couldn't the woman find the restaurant?

4. W: I wonder why the electricity went out this morning.

   M: It happened because of an oversight on the part of the engineer.

   Q: Why did the electricity go out?

5. W: Did you sign up for a course that fits into your current schedule?

   M: Registration hasn't started yet.

   Q: Why didn't the woman sign up for a course?

6. W: Susan still hasn't gotten her research paper back.

   M: I know and she's really burned up at the professor.

   Q: Why is Susan burned up?

7. M: Sally, how are you getting along with the translation work?

   W: I have written and rewritten so much that I don't know if I'll ever get it finished.

   Q: How does Sally feel?

8. W: Hello, this is the lost and found.

   M: My name is Joe Peterson and I left my coat in Mr Johnson's Political Science Class this morning. Do you have it?

   W: I'm sorry. It hasn't been turned in yet.

   Q: What happened to Joe Peterson?

9. W: I hear the old Delta Hotel has a new manager. Did you notice any change when you stayed there last week?

   M: The food was better than the meals they used to serve and the rooms were surprisingly clean for the Delta, I thought.

   Q: How is the hotel now?

10. W: Are you still teaching at the junior high school?

    M: Not since June. My brother and I went into business together as soon as he got out of the army.

    Q: What is the man doing now?

Unit Seventeen

Part I : Listening Practice

Section A: Guessing about the Situation and Speaker
Exercise 1
Directions: There are ten short passages. Listen and try to identify the situation which is taking place.

1. Now it's Robson for United. He passes to Strachan on the left. He beats the defender, oh and a beautiful cross to Whiteside! Lovely shot just over the bar. What a nice move by United!

2. ...and so members of the jury, we have heard the accused try to explain what he was doing on the afternoon of the robbery. However, we have to consider the evidence before the court which proves he was in possession of part of the stolen money.

3. Do you, Diana, take Jane to be your wedded husband, for better or worse, for richer or poorer, in sickness and in health and forsaking all others...

4. Right now Gerry. I want you to think very carefully before you answer. I know all the viewers out there are right behind you. Now Gerry, for the top prize of 10,000 can you tell me what the name of Napoleon's first wife was?

5. Attention please. Flight B. A. 324 for Rome is now boarding

at Gate 26. Will passengers for Flight B.A. 324 please proceed to Gate 26.

6. Tomorrow will start off bright and sunny but will cloud over later with some heavy rain in western areas by late afternoon and snow on higher ground.

7. Now Mr Baines. Just look at this little beauty here. Two years old, brand new engine, only 15,000 miles on the clock and in excellent condition. It's a real bargain at $2,400.

8. OK, Mrs Harris. Just drive straight on here please. Not too fast — we're in a 30 mile an hour limit. Good. That's better. Slow down for the traffic lights and then turn left and go on up the hill.

9. Ah, come in Nigel. Mrs Lacey asked me to speak to you about arriving late and failing to hand in any homework this term. Now, you know the rules as well as I do, so I'm afraid I shall have to speak to your parents.

10. Over there on your left you will see Buckingham Palace, one of the Queen's four official residences. To your right is the magnificent memorial to Queen Victoria, one of Britain's longest reigning monarchs, and over there on the right is St James's Park, one of London's many beautiful parks.

Exercise 2
Directions: Listen to the cassette once again. Then try to identify who is speaking.

Section B: Taking Messages
Exercise 1
Directions: Marcy has a telephone answering machine. She's not at home and has asked her roommate, Ellen, to listen to her messages.

Listen to each message on the machine. Then check the messages and make corrections if necessary.

1. Marcy, this is Stacey. Can you meet me at school at 4:30? I've told the others. Oh, and bring your volleyball. I've lost mine. And don't forget to bring the $ 10 you owe me, OK?
2. Marcy, this is Tim. Don't forget our date on Thursday night. Remember, we were going to have dinner and see a show. But can we meet at seven o'clock instead of six-thirty? I can't meet you earlier because I have to work overtime. I'll pick you up at your place and then we'll go straight to the restaurant.
3. This is Dr White's office. It's time for your six month dental check-up. We can give you an appointment next Thursday at 2:00 pm. If that time is not convenient, please call to arrange another time.
4. Marcy, this is Diane from the offece. Can you do me a favor? I promised to give Ruth Lee a ride to work tomorrow. But I have to go to the doctor and will be in late. Can you give her a ride? Please give her a call at 547 – 6892. Thanks.
5. This is Bob's Garage. Your car won't be ready till next Tuesday. Sorry, but it turned out to be quite a big job. We have replaced the battery but are still working on the starter. The bill will be about $ 350. You'll also need new snow tires.

Exercise 2
Directions: Listen to the cassette once again. Then put your correct messages on the lines provided.

Section C: What's Happening

Exercise 1

Directions: You will hear six short conversations. Where are the speakers? Write the number of the conversation beside each picture.

(1)

A: Wow! This place is awful! It's too crowded for me and. . .

B: Ummm. and the music's too loud! It's impossible to talk.

A: Yeah. It was terrible music, too.

B: Do you want to go somewhere quieter?

A: OK.

(2)

A: Hey! Did you see that? What a play!

B: Beautiful! Come on Raiders! They're going to win if they keep playing like this!

A: They sure are. This is a great game! You want some of this sandwich?

B: No. thanks.

(3)

A: Well, the food's OK, but I don't think I really want to come here again. The service is so slow. . .

B: Yeah. It's really expensive, too, isn't it?

A: Mmm. It's certainly not cheap!

(4)

A: It's a little slow, isn't it?

B: Mmm. What?

A: This is boring! The acting's terrible and the plot is bad. . .

B: Yeah, but nice photography.

A: I'm going to get some more popcorn and another soda. You want anything?

(5)

A: Oh, hello Margo, I didn't know you were taking Japanese Literature.

B: Well. I'm really only taking it because Dr Hari is such a good teacher.

A: Yeah. She's great, isn't she?

(6)

A: Some more, Ana?

B: Oh yes, thank you. It's delicious. It must have taken hours to prepare.

A: Well, thank you! It was really quite easy to make, as a matter of fact.

B: Mmm. I'd love to have the recipe.

A: I'm so glad you like it. I'll write it out for you later.

Exercise 2
Directions: Listen again and decide if the people like the activity or place. Write down your answer on the lines provided below.

Part Ⅲ: Listening Comprehension Test
Directions: In this part, you will hear three short passages. After you have heard the passges and the questions, try to choose the best answer from the four choices given by marking the corresponding letter (A, B, C, or D).

Passage Ⅰ

   Yesterday we discussed the problem of rising prices, or, in the economist's terms, inflation. We noted that, during periods of inflation, all prices and incomes do not rise at the same rate. Some incomes rise more slowly than the cost of living, and a few do not rise at all. Other incomes rise more rapidly than the cost of living.

We concluded that persons with fixed incomes, as for example, the elderly who depend upon pensions, and persons with slow-rising incomes as, for example, an employee with a salary agreed to in a long-term contract, will be most seriously affected by inflation. Please recall that while their dollar incomes stay the same, the cost of goods and services rises, and in effect, real income decreases; that is, they are able to purchase less with the same amount of money.

We also talked about the fact that stockholders and persons with business interests and investments would probably benefit most from inflation, since high prices would increase sales receipts, and profits would likely rise faster than the cost of living.

And now, before we begin today's lecture, are there any questions about the term, inflation or any of the examples given in our discussion so far?

1. What is the main purpose of the talk?
2. According to the lecture, what is inflation?
3. Who benefits most from inflation?

Passage II

W: I usually advise first-year students to take mathematics, chemistry, and an introductory engineering course the first quarter.

M: Oh. That's only three classes.

W: Yes. But I'm sure that you'll be busy. They're all five-hour courses, and you'll have to meet each class every day. The chemistry course has an additional two-hour laboratory.

M: So that would be seventeen hours of class a week.

W: That's right.

M: Okay. Which mathematics course do you think that I should take?

W: Have you taken very much math in high school?

M: Four years. I had algebra, geometry, trigonometry.

W: Good. Then I suggest that you take the math placement test. It's offered this Friday at nine o'clock in the morning in Tower Auditorium.

M: Do I need anything to be admitted? I mean a permission slip?

W: No. Just identification. A driver's license will be fine.

M: Do I take a chemistry test too?

W: No. Chemistry 100 is designed for students who have never taken a chemistry course, and Chemistry 200 is for students who have had chemistry in high school.

M: I've had two courses.

W: Then you should take Chemistry 200, Orientation to Engineering, and either Mathematics 130 or 135, depending on the result of your placement test. Come back Friday afternoon. I should have your score on the test by then and we can get you registered.

4. How many classes does the woman advise the man to take?

5. What does the man need to be admitted to the examination?

6. When will the man see his advisor again?

Passage Ⅲ

The cost is going up for just about everything, and college tuition is no exception. According to a nationwide survey published by the College Board's Scholarship Service, tuition at most American universities will be on an average of 9 percent higher this year than last.

The biggest increase will occur at private colleges. Public colleges, heavily subsidized by tax funds, will also increase their tuition, but the increase will be a few percentage points lower than their privately-sponsored neighbors.

As a follow up, the United Press International did their own study at Massachusetts Institute of Technology. At MIT advisors recommended that students have $9,000 available for one year's expenses, and $250 for books and supplies. Ten years ago the tuition was $2,000. To put that another way, the cost has climbed 150 percent in the last decade.

An additional burden is placed on out-of-state students who must pay extra charges ranging from $200 to $2,000, and foreign students who are not eligible for scholarships at state-funded universities.

On the brighter side, the survey revealed that college graduates are entering the best job market since the middle 1960s. Job offers are up 16 percent from last year, and salaries are good, at least for graduates in technical fields. For example, a recent graduate in petroleum engineering can expect to make as much as $20,000 per year. A student with a liberal arts degree might expect to make about half that salary.

7. What is the average increase in tuition expenses at American universities this year over last?

8. How much did tuition increase at MIT over a ten-year-period?

154

9. According to the reporter, what is a problem for foreign students at state universities?
10. What is the job market like for college graduates?

Unit Eighteen

Part I : Listening Practice

Section A: Listening for Specific Information
Exercise 1
Directions: Listen to the conversation and write down the topics being discussed, and the figure, date or amount that you hear.

(1)

A: Helen. You look great! You're much slimmer than the last time I saw you.

B: Well yes. Actually I've been on a diet and I've been doing a keep-fit class too.

A: Good for you! How much weight have you lost?

B: Have a guess.

A: I've no idea.

B: 13 pounds.

A: 13! That's amazing. Well done.

(2)

A: Um, yes. It's in pretty good condition really. I only use it to go to work and back.

B: Yes, but the body's rather rusty. Look at these bits here. It needs a lot of work.

A: Hmm. But it's got a new battery and um, three new tyres. Oh, and it's just had a service. The engine's almost perfect.

B: All right. I'll give you 650.

A: Oh no. It's worth a lot more.

B: 650 in cash. Take it or leave it.

A: Um, I'm sorry. I'd rather wait for a better offer.

B: OK. It's up to you.

(3)

A: Look. There's a machine over there.

B: Oh good. I'll get some money out and we can have a drink. Er...

A: What's up?

B: I can never remember my cash-card number.

A: Oh no.

B: Oh yes. Hang on. Let me think. I should have written it down. I think it's 8976.

A: Fingers crossed!

B: O. K. 8... 9... 7... 6. Great! It worked.

A: Lucky for us.

(4)

A: OK. Tony I'll see you next month to talk about the new contract.

B: Ah Stuart! Before you go let me give you our new fax number.

A: Oh good. That'll be useful. Just let me find a pen... Right. Fire away.

B: The, er, code is 440865 for Britain and Oxford.

A: 44... 0... 8... 6... 5.

B: And the fax number of the office is 593381. That's it.

(5)

A: Ah, Julia. Your check's ready.

B: Oh, great. I'm broke as usual.

A: We'll deposit it for you if you like.

B: OK.

A: What's your bank account number?

B: 60917718.

A: 6091... 7718.

B: That's right.

(6)

A: Good morning. I've come to pick up some foreign currency for a
holiday.

B: What currency did you order?

A: Mexican pesos. My name's Paul Allen.

B: Ah yes, Mr Allen. Here we are. 410,000 pesos.

A: Wow! What's the exchange rate?

B: 4,100 to the pound.

A: Right. Thank you very much.

(7)

A: More coffee?

B: Please darling. Well, Dave and Jane are in South America now.

A: Lucky things. I bet it's hot.

B: Let's look in the paper.

A: Here we are. Buenos Aires, 83 degrees Fahrenheit!

(8)

A: OK. It's my turn. Three. One... two... three.

B: History. Here we are. Ready?

A: More or less.

B: Right. When was the battle of Waterloo? 1805, 1815 or 1825?

A: Waterloo. Hmm, 1815?

B: Correct. Well done!

Exercise 2

Directions: Listen to the conversations again and then answer the following questions.

Section B: A Lecture on Bridges
Exercise 1

Directions: Listen to the lecture, write out the names of the three basic structures of bridge and then match each structure with its correct picture below.

Today, We are going to talk about the history of bridges.

Nobody knows who first decided to lay a branch across a stream and then step across. This early adventurer was, however, one of the world's first civil engineers and the primitive bridge is considered one of our ancestors' most important early achievements.

Bridges are very convenient in that they save both time and money, but they require skill and imagination to build. Early bridge architecture was largely guided by the kinds of materials available in the immediate area. In areas where wood was plentiful, flat beam bridges were popular. Suspension bridges were first constructed in the jungle areas of Asia, where rope was made from vines and other plant fibers. The third major type of bridge design, the arch bridge, evolved from the primitive stone arch bridges built in Europe and the Near East.

Modern bridge architecture is directly related to these early structures, although the local availability of materials is no longer a consideration, Engineers still follow the three basic designs, or combinations of these. The materials which are used now, mainly steel and concrete, allow for much longer spans. The longest bridge in the world — the Verrazano Narrows Bridge in New York — has a main span of over 1,280 meters.

Once the construction of a bridge has been completed, it seems to become a part of the natural landscape, as if it has always belonged there. People depend on bridges daily, and they often forget what life was like without them. Bridges have a kind of silent power in their tremendous effect on the economy, and also in the inspiration they provide for works of art, stories, poetry, and songs.

Exercise 2
Directions: Listen to the cassette again and complete the following sentences with the words you have heard.

Section C: A Lecture on the Educational Systems of the U. S. and Great Britain

Exercise 1
Directions: Listen to a professor's lecture and take some notes about the two educational systems.

Professor: Let me begin by saying that... ah... the history and culture of these two countries... Great Britain and the United States... seem to be similar in many ways, but... ah... not in others. In the field of education, for example, the school systems of these two English-speaking countries are no more alike than... ah... than cricket and baseball.

Let's look at the matter of examinations... those terrible inventions that students all over the world fear and dread... In England they are standard. That is, students all over the country take the same examination. Most children begin school at five, you see... and study the basics for about eight years... then, if they decide to go on, they select certain subjects and study for these nation-wide standard exams. This process ends at about age 16, except for those who want to enter universities. These students must... uh, study for yet more difficult examinations, known in England as the "A Levels", or Advanced Level Examinations.

As you can see, these national examinations are very important to British students... but in the United States there are none... oh, of course we have other kinds of tests that are important... but I mean there are no nationally set examinations that determine whether students can graduate from our public schools. Each local school system has its own standards, and these are set by the local school boards. So a high school diploma from... ah... Oregon, for example, is not the same as one from ah... Florida, or Minnesota, or California.

Generally speaking, there are twelve grades in the American system... and these twelve are divided into two levels: elementary and secondary... the secondary one is known as "high school". Each grade takes one year, so children who begin the first grade at the age of six usually graduate when they are about seventeen. If they want to go on to college... they have to write and find out what the entrance requirements are, because each college and university is different.

Now, as for which system is better... the American or the British, I can only say that each one... (fade)

Exercise 2
Directions: Listen to the cassette again and decide which of the following statements is for America and which for Britain. Write A for American system and B for British.

Exercise 3
Directions: You may listen to the cassette once again and decide which information is not included in the lecture. Then put a "T" or "F" beside.

Section D: An Interview at Scotland Yard
Directions: You will hear an interview at Scotland Yard. A policeman is trying to find out some information about the bank robbery. You should fill in the four small boxes with the letter of the correct picture.

W: Good morning, sir. You've come to look at some pictures, have you?

M: Yes, in connection with the bank robbery recently. I saw a man hanging around near the bank the day before the robbery.

W: Right. Well, here are four of our villains. Have a look at these. What about this one — Babyface — with the scar and bushy eyebrows?

M: Huh, they're real villains, aren't they? No, that's not him.

W: What about this one with the beard — Harry the Horse?

162

M: Which one?

W: This one here.

M: Yes, but he wasn't bald, and anyway, he wasn't bearded.

W: The one you saw wasn't. Yes, I see. What about a moustched? This one? Bad Billy, he's called.

M: Yes, but he hadn't got a cleft chin.

W: I see. The wrong chin. Mmm. What about Mickey Mouse?

M: He looks a bit like the man I saw. He wasn't spotty but he had eyebrows.

W: Ah, I see. Well, that's about it, sir. Would you like to leave me your number? I'll just jot it down.

M: Yes, it's 224466

W: Yes, 224466. Any extension?

M: Yes, but you won't need it. And if I want to contact you?

W: I'll write it down for you. 224477, and C202. That's my police number. The extension is 0132.

M: Thank you.

W: It's my pleasure. I'll show you out.

Part Ⅲ: Listening Comprehension Test

Section A

Directions: In this section, you will hear nine short conversations between two speakers. At the end of each conversation a third voice will ask a question about what was said. Both the conversations and the questions will be spoken only once. After each question there will be a pause. During the pause, you must choose the best answer from the four choices given by marking the corresponding letter (A,

B, C, or D).

1. M: I'm still waiting for the clerk to come back and make some copies of this paper for me.

   W: Why bother him? I'll show you how easy it is to work the machine.

   Q: What does the woman mean?

2. M: The way Vincent speaks Italian, you'd think he's a native.

   W: That's probably because he is.

   Q: What do we know about Vincent?

3. W: Well, El, shall we take part in the concert in the park this evening?

   M: Great idea, provided we can do the grocery shopping first.

   Q: What does El suggest?

4. W: Chemistry 502 is really a hard course.

   M: So was Chemistry 402.

   Q: What do we learn from the conversation?

5. W: If I were you, I would take a plane instead of a bus. It will take you forever to get there.

   M: But flying makes me so nervous.

   Q: What does the man prefer to do?

6. M: While I am in Washington, I want to see the Capital Building.

   W: You will. It's only a stone's throw away from the train station.

   Q: What does the woman mean?

7. M: Did you say you were driving to town this morning?

   W: Yes, I have to get a check cashed to pay my book-store bill.

164

Q: What is the woman going to do in town?

8. M: I am not sure what the best way is to hang this picture without damaging the wall.

    W: Couldn't you use tape? It peels off easily.

    Q: What does the woman suggest?

9. W: These are very nice shirts. How much are they?

    M: 5 dollars each. For two, 9 dollars. They are on sale today.

    Q: How much does one shirt cost?

Section B

Directions: In this section, you will hear two short passages. At the end of each passages there will be some questions. You will hear both the passage and the questions only once. After each question there will be a pause. During the pause, you must choose the best answer from the four choices given by marking the corresponding letter (A, B, C or D).

Passage I

How much living space does a person need? What happens when his space requirements are not adequately met? Sociologists and psychologists are conducting experiments on rats to try to determine the effects of overcrowded conditions on man. Recent studies have shown that the behavior of rats is greatly affected by space. If their living conditions become too crowded their behavior patterns and even their health will change. They cannot sleep and eat well, and signs of fear and tension become obvious. The more crowded they are, the more they tend to bite each other and even kill each other. Thus for rats, population and violence are directly related. Is this a natural law for human society as well? Is adequate space not only desirable, but essential for human survival?

10. For what purpose did the scientists conduct the experiments on rats?

11. When the rats become overcrowded, which one of the behavior patterns is not shown in the experiment?

12. What did the experiments prove.

Passage II

One of the main complaints of city residents is the lack of parking. This problem is partly caused by all the abandoned cars on the streets. It has been estimated that over one million cars are abandoned on the streets each year. And one third of these cars are removed and destroyed. The rest of the cars take up a lot of parking space.

Boston is a city which spends a large amount of money on museums and libraries, does not have tax money to clean the abandoned cars off the streets. In this city, the problem has been dealt by an agency called Street Horizons, which uses the money from selling the abandoned cars to pay for the cost of removing them. The program carried out by Street Horizons in Boston sounds good because it helped clean the streets and save the parking space.

13. What is one of the problems which have brought about the lack of parking according to the passage?

14. How many cars are abandoned each year?

15. What is Street Horizons?

Unit Nineteen

Part I : Listening Practice

Section A: Listening for Main Ideas
Exercise 1
Directions: Listen to the messages and write down what you think is being advertised in each of the following extracts.

1. Why worry about traffic jams, difficult driving conditions, speed limits and expensive parking? Our intercity service will take you faster, more comfortably and without delays to your destination. British Rail — it makes a lot of sense.
2. Nothing attacks those ground-in stains and dirt better than Blanco. Blanco with its quick biological action leaves your clothes whiter than white! More and more housewives are changing to Blanco. Try it and you'll be amazed at the results.
3. There's one very important thing about Spendcard. It's accepted in more establishments in more countries than any other card. Spendcard offers its members a whole series of services and discounts. Open up a new world with Spen-dcard.
4. A: Oh Alison. I can't possibly go to the disco tonight.
   B: Why not?
   A: Just look at my hair. Greasy, dull and lifeless!

B: Hey! Why don't you try Shine? It's got a new formula conditioner. It worked for me.

A: Hmm. All right.

B: Kelly. You look great!

A: Yes. Thanks to Shine!

5. The new Puma took over 6 years to design, test and build. With
its 2 litre fuel-efficient engine, aerodynamic lines and luxury finish, it's in a class of its own. If you consider that the Puma has a
large boot and space for a family of five it's worth a second look.
Contact your local dealer for a test drive.

6. A: What's that you're eating?

B: A new Frolic bar.

A: Looks good!

B: Uh ha. It's got nuts, raisins, coconut...

A: Let's try a bit. Mmmm, delicious, biscuity.

B: Er, yes.

A: Superb toffee centre... scrumptious!

B: Yes. Isn't it!

A: Lovely! Must buy one.

B: Yes !!

7. Glengunnich Malt has a long tradition — over three hundred
years in fact. It's made using only the finest traditional ingredients: fresh spring water and the best Scottish barley to produce
the unmistakable flavour of Glengunnich. By leaving Glengunnich to mature in wooden barrels for 10 long years its taste is un-
equalled. Try it straight, with ice, tonic or soda. Glengunnich
Malt for every occasion!

8. A: You'd like to get wide, objective reporting on current issues?

B: Certainly.

A: Full coverage of foreign and domestic news, finance, sport, the arts and entertainment?

B: Oh yes!

A: Plus special features, a colour supplement and the chance to win thousands of pounds every week?

B: I sure would!

A: Then change to the Daily Herald tomorrow!

9. Hi. This is Linda Nightingale. In my profession I always need to look my best. Acting is very demanding and I'm constantly in the public eye. Studio lighting can easily affect my looks so that's why I use Petal. It's so soft and gentle on my skin, so creamy and smooth, it leaves my complexion looking fresh and natural.

10. These days it's difficult to know where to invest. What with changing interest rates, bank charges and different types of investment accounts it's all very confusing. So isn't it nice to know that at the Midwestern there is friendly, professional help available to make sure you make the right decisions about how to handle your money. We can also advise you on a whole range of matters such as insurance, mortgages and pensions. Pop into your local Midwestern branch. We'll be pleased to see you!

Exercise 2

Directions: Listen again and write down two or three words which helped you decide.

Section B: Radio Announcements
Exercise 1
Directions: You will hear four radio announcements. As you listen, find the picture that matches the announcement and write the day or days when the event will take place.

(1)

Interested in what was really going on in the sixties and seventies? You can find out at a midweek lecture next week at Johnson Hall on the university campus. Professor John Hoy will give his view of the last thirty years of American history next Wednesday night at 7:00pm. Admission is free.

(2)

Do you like modern jazz? Well, if you do, you're going to like the jazz piano of Andy Steel. You can see him this weekend at the New World Night Club. Andy Steel is playing two concerts on Friday and Saturday at 9: 00 pm. Cover charge is $10.

(3)

The Houston International Film Festival begins this Monday! Take this opportunity to see great movies from all over the world! The festival begins on Monday at the Academy of Arts and will continue through the week. Movies will be shown from 11:00 am to 10:00 pm every day this week. The festival ends Sunday, April 12. Tickets are only $ 2.50 for each film.

(4)

This Saturday is July 4 — Independence Day! And one thing you should not miss on Saturday is the Independence Day fireworks. The fireworks will begin this evening at 8: 30 in City Park. Admission is free! Hey! That sounds fun! Check it out! I think I will!

Exercise 2

Directions: Now listen again, and write the time of each event and the price of admission on the lines above.

Section C: Sunglow Tours
Exercise 1

Directions: Listen to the conversation and complete the booking form below. You may tick right items if necessary.

Woman: Good morning.

Travel agent: Oh. Good morning, Madam.

Woman: Um — I wonder if you can help me?

Travel agent: Yes, certainly.

Woman: I'm looking for a particular sort of holiday, uh.

Travel agent: Right.

Woman: Er, we want to visit particularly Vienna and Belgrade.

Travel agent: Have you any idea which way you want to travel, do you want to fly or er...

Woman: Well I... possibly to fly to start with then a... coach trip between...

Travel agent: Ah a coach trip. Yes, well, I think a Sunglow holiday would suit your purpose. Um er that's a... how many weeks by the way?

Woman: Well, two weeks.

Travel agent: Two weeks, um, so you'll be a week in one and a week in the other. And a week in the other, yes.

Now which way do you think you want to do it?

Woman: Oh, it doesn't really matter.

Travel agent: No.

Woman: No, it doesn't really matter.

Travel agent: I think the easiest way from our point of view would be Vienna first, followed by Belgrade.

Woman: Certainly, that's lovely.

Travel agent: Yes, which is, there's a £166 each all in. Yes. That includes the accommodation, um, so we'll put flight and coach.

Woman: Right.

Travel agent: OK. Now, perhaps I could have your full names — of everyone travelling, it's just the two of you, is it?

Woman: Yes, that's right.

Travel agent: Right.

Woman: My name is Julia Carter.

Travel agent: Julia Carter — right — and your husband?

Woman: My husband is Mark.

Travel agent: Mark Carter — good. And the address?

Woman: 32.

Travel agent: 32.

Woman: Alderley Avenue, that's A-L-D-E-R-L-E-Y, Alderley Avenue.

Travel agent: A-L-D-E-R-L-E-Y Avenue.

Woman: And that's Hayes.

Travel agent: Hayes, Middlesex. Now the accommodation required —I mean it'll be, um, sort of moderately priced hotels but that'll be included in the package and you'll get breakfast and, um, an evening meal.

Woman: And, er, that's all included?

Travel agent: That's included, the midday meal is an optional extra.

Woman: Yes, well we'd probably go out anyway.

Travel agent: Yes, well you'll be out and about and there are excursions and season tickets, um, you can decide that when you get there.

Woman: And we find out about those from the representative?

Travel agent: From the representative, I mean you can do museum trips and art galleries and so on under your own steam but there will be the guided. . .

Woman: Well that's the side we're more interested in, the sightseeing, now mm — we won't need visas or anything funny like that?

Travel agent: No, you won't need visas, no, but an up-to-date passport obviously.

Woman: Yes, of course.

Travel agent: Oh well that's fine.

Woman: Have you any idea how long it's going to take for you to find out the final details?

Travel agent: Well the final details, I mean, I should know within the next week or so, you know, once you're booked.

Woman: Well, the only other thing I wanted to ask about was insurance.

Travel agent: Yes.

Woman: Is that covered in the package or will we need to find out about. . .

Travel agent: No, the forms will come to you, it works out... it's quite cheap; it's something like-um-about £8.50 between the two of you.

Woman: And that covers the medical costs?

Travel agent: Medical costs, yes, and there are various clauses and of course mislaid luggage.

Woman: Yes, right. Well lovely, lovely.

Travel agent: OK then, well. I hope you have a nice holiday but I'll be seeing you before then.

Woman: OK. Thank you very much indeed.

Travel agent: Not at all.

Woman: Bye, bye.

Exercise 2

Directions: Listen again and decide whether the following statements are True or False.

Section D: Traveling with Your Pet
Exercise 1

Directions: Listen to the passage and answer the following questions.

Nowadays, people aren't willing to leave their pets at home when they travel. According to a Gallup poll, 34% of dog owners and 11% of cat owners say they take their vacations with their pets. With a little planning, you can too.

Before you decide to take your pet on the road, be sure he does not get car sick. Try short trips around the block to accustom your pet to the sensation of riding, then gradually increase the distance.

Once you know your pet is comfortable riding in a car, begin packing for the long trip. Your pet will need toiletries (medications, scooper, paper towels, sandwich bags for dog waste removal, and disposable litter pans for cats), necessities (leash, bedding, water and food dishes, food, a jug of water, and vaccination records), and entertainment (toys and chewies).

When in the car, secure your pet in a carrier or a seat belt made especially for pets. Even in a minor accident, an unsecured animal can be severely injured or killed. Always attach your pet's leash before opening the car door or window because, no matter how well trained, he could get excited in new surroundings and run away. You should also add a second ID tag to your pet's collar during the trip that has your beeper number, cellular phone number or a friend's phone number in case your pet gets lost.

Exercise 2
Directions: Listen to the passage again and give the information in detail.

Part Ⅲ: Listening Comprehension Test
Directions: In this part, you will hear 10 short conversations about comparisons. After you have heard each conversation, try to choose the best answer.

1. M: My coat is smaller than my brother's.
   W: Really? He always seems much shorter than you.
   Q: How does the man's coat compare to his brother's?

2. M: I gave the job to Mary because your prices are too high.

   W: I don't charge as much as John.

   Q: Who charges the second highest price?

3. W: This light shines more brightly than the one upstairs.

   M: It's the same wattage. It must be the color of the shade, then.

   Q: What makes the light seem brighter?

4. M: The mountain seems higher. It makes me dizzy to climb it this year, but it's worth it for the view.

   W: The mountain may not be higher, but we're older.

   Q: What has changed since last year?

5. W: Do you think this skirt goes well with this blouse?

   M: Yes, but I think your blue dress would be more elegant for the reception and I like it much better.

   Q: What does the man think of the woman's choice of clothing?

6. W: In this city there are many kinds of transportation available. Which do you use, Bob?

   M: The buses are so crowded, especially during the rush hour, so I usually take the subway. It's faster and there's less chance of a traffic jam.

   Q: Why does Bob prefer to take the subway?

7. M: I think this exercise program has made me stronger.

   W: You look better, and I'm sure you feel better.

   Q: What has the man been doing?

8. W: I'd like to exchange this dress for one a size larger.

   M: Yes, of course. Pick out another one. I'll put this one back.

   Q: Why did the customer return the dress?

9. W: Can you tell me the least expensive way to get to Chicago?

M: If you go by bus it's only $ 20. But if you go by train, it's almost twice that much. And if you go by taxi, it's $ 80.

Q: What does this man explain to the woman?

10. M: This is the longest play I've ever seen. It's 3 hours long now, and we have another act to go.

W: It's shorter than the 8-hour play we saw last year.

Q: How do the plays compare?

Unit   Twenty

Section A: Guessing the Meaning
Exercise 1
Directions: In each of the following, write down what he or she wants.

1. No. They're much too tight round the waist. Can I try a size 14 ? Oh, and have you got a pair in dark brown?
2. Good morning. I'd like a return ticket to Cambridge please. Second class.
3. A copy of The Times please and um, a packet of mints.
4. Oh, good afternoon. Do you have any tickets left for tonight's performance of Romeo and Juliet?
5. Two pints of bitter and a whisky and soda please.
6. Hello. We'd like to book two places on the coach trip to London please. Um, where will we stop for lunch?
7. I'd like it much shorter, especially round the ears. Er, can you leave it a bit longer at the back?
8. Um, I'll have soup of the day and the fried plaice please.
9. Hello. I booked a squash court for 6.30. The name's Smith.
10. Good afternoon. Could you recommend something for a cough

and sore throat?

Exercise 2
Directions: Listen again. Decide where the person is and then put your answer in the table.

Section B: News Report
Exercise 1
Directions: Listen to the news program. Draw a line between a newspaper headline and the place where the story happened.

Diane Martinet: Good afternoon. This is Diane Martinet with the midday news on KALF. Fires in California continue to burn out of control, and several small towns in the forests near San Francisco are still in danger. One of the greatest dangers to the 500 fire fighters, however, comes not from the fires, but from plants in the forest — poison ivy plants. Many fire fighters have had skin problems after touching the plants, and at least three have had to go to hospital for treatment for their skin problems.

Following recent airline hijackings, the International Airline Association, the IAA, has been meeting in Washington this week. The IAA has been discussing ways to improve security and has introduced several new measures. Beginning in January, improved security measures will include more armed security guards on international flights and special training for pilots.

NASA, the National Aeronautics and Space Agency, today announced in Florida that the next Space Shuttle mission has been canceled. The mission was scheduled for an 11:30 a.m. takeoff on

Tuesday. However, the flight has been canceled because of problems with the shuttle's central computer system. NASA technicians noticed the computer problems during last minute checks.

Seven teenage computer specialists have been arrested by police in New Jersey. After taking an advanced computer course at school, the seven boys, all from Princeton, New Jersey, learned how to obtain top secret information from government computers in Washington. They also started to use their home computers to make free long-distance telephone calls.

In New York the value of the dollar stayed the same today. But in Tokyo, the dollar fell dramatically. At the end of the day, it was worth 183 yen, compared to 195 yen yesterday.

Exercise 2
Directions: Read these statements. Listen to the news program again, and decide if the statements are True or False.

Section C: Short Speech
Exercise 1
Directions: Listen to the short speech and then fill in the blanks.

It gives me great pleasure today to say a few words in praise of a man we will all miss very much. To be honest, I can't imagine how we will do without him when he's gone.

Bill Masters almost single-handedly built up our sales force in the Houston area and developed the market position that we enjoy today. In only six years, he has brought the firm from a very low fifth position in regional sales to the point where we now outsell all but one of our competitors. Not only have we captured 37 per cent of the market under Bill's leadership, but also we are increasing our share with each passing month.

As you are all well aware, the company has moved Bill to northern California to work his sales magic in one of this company's most competitive regions. But we know that if anyone can do it, Bill Masters can, and I know you all join me in wishing him the best of luck in his new job.

Exercise 2
Directions: Listen to the tape again and then answer the following questions.

Section D: Only 9, 900 shopping days until Social Security can't meet all its obligations
Exercise 1
Directions: Listen to the tape and then fill in the blanks.

Long fus. Big bang.
Given the aging of the population and the consequent changing ratio of workers to beneficiaries, experts are predicting that in 2032 the funds Social Security takes in won't be sufficient to pay full benefits to recipients.

It's also a fact that the sooner lawmakers address this shortfall, the easier it will be to redress it.
The question is, how?
What steps to take now to put Social Security on a solid footing? Raise taxes? Cut benefits? Raise the retirement age? Invest

some of the funds in the stock market?

These are questions for the American people to answer.

Which is where you come in.

Americans Discuss Social Security is a non-partisan, non-advocacy initiative that aims to give you and your fellow citizens the information you need to understand the options and a chance to register your views with policy makers.

Call us, and we'll send you an easy-to-read booklet, " Making Sense of Social Security," that spells out the situation and possible reforms. We'll also give you a variety of ways to discuss your views and communicate them to Congress and the Administration. You can reach us, toll free, at (888) 735-2377 or on the World Wide Web at www. americansdiscuss. org.

Call now. And help shape a policy that urgently needs your attention. It's your money, after all. And your future.

Exercise 2

Directions: Read the statements. Listen to the tape again, and decide if the statements are True or False.

Part Ⅲ : Listening Comprehension Test

Directions: In this part, you will hear three short passages. After you have heard the passages and the questions, try to choose the best answer from the four choices given by marking the corresponding letter (A, B, C, or D).

Passage Ⅰ

I would like to greet you all and tell you how happy we are, at the Admissions Office, to have you at Glenville College's annual welcome meeting for international students. A representative from the Registrar's Office will be here later to answer any questions you might have regarding registration procedures. We are also very happy to have with us the International Student Advisor, who will speak to you about your special concerns today. He also conducts weekly question and answer sessions to help you with your future plans.

1. Who is the speaker?
2. What is the main topic of the talk?
3. Who will discuss special concerns?
4. What does the speaker say about registration questions?

Passage II

W: What topic did you finally choose for the term paper for your World Economics class?

M: After tossing around a few ideas, I finally settled on the difference between Japanese and American styles of management.

W: Hmm. Why did you choose a topic like that?

M: Well, I'm planning to study Business in graduate school next year. After that, I hope to start my own company.

W: Isn't that a coincidence! I'm doing a paper on how Japanese management styles are being adapted by American firms for my Comparative Cultures class.

M: Why don't we sit down and share some of our sources after we've each been to the library?

W: Great idea! Should we meet at the snack bar next Wednesday at this time?

M: That's fine with me. See you then.

5. What is the topic of this conversation?

6. What will they do next Wednesday?

7. What is the man planning to do next year?

Passage III

The American Humane Association (AHA) is dedicated to preventing cruelty toward animals. Founded in 1877 as the first national animal protection organization in the country, AHA today helps all animals, and especially animal shelters across the U. S. through programs to curb pet over-population, assist animals in natural disasters and strengthen anti-cruelty laws.

AHA founded Be Kind to Animals Week over 80 years ago to celebrate the joy animals bring to us and to help us remember our responsibilities to them. Call your local animal shelter for details on how you can join in local celebrations during this special week and throughout the year. And, tune in to the special programming on the Animal Planet television channel during Be Kind to Animals Week, May 3～9, 1998. For more information about Be Kind to Animals Week, visit our Web site at www. americanhumane. org.

For a free copy of AHA's magazine, ADVOCATE, contact AHA at 63 Inverness Drive East, Englewood, CO 80112 or call (303) 792-9900.

8. What is the purpose of the American Humane Association (AHA)?

9. When was the American Humane Association founded?

10. Why did AHA found Be Kind to Animals Week?

Unit   Twenty-one

Part I : Listening Practice

Section A: Listening for the Gist
Exercise 1
Directions: Listen to the cassette, and write down the topic being discussed either in English or in Chinese.

1. A: This is very nice. What a lovely lawn!
   B: Yes. We're very lucky. We've got some good-sized flower beds, but it's a lot of work keeping them free of weeds.
   A: I can imagine. Oh, you've got a nice shed too. That must be useful.
   B: Oh yes. Over here there's a vegetable patch. I've got potatoes, cabbages and onions. At the back next to the fence there are blackcurrants and rhubarb. Here we've got some raspberry bushes.
2. A: Damn. It's done it again!
   B: What happened?
   A: Oh. I put my 40P in and pressed the button for hot chocolate.
   B: And?
   A: Look! A cup of cold water. This thing is always going

185

wrong.

3. A: Ah! This is new.

   B: That's right. Just bought it actually.

   A: How good are these things?

   B: I think they're great. You can put some food in and it's cooked in no time at all.

   A: It seems to be easy to use.

   B: Yes. There's a timer and you use very little electricity so it's cheap too.

4. A: Hmm. It looks really complicated to me.

   B: Well it isn't. Anyone can use it. Believe me!

   A: What do I do then?

   B: First you switch it on here. OK? Then you load the disc here, press the space bar and the programme is ready to use for word-processing, or you can load the games disc and just play games on it.

   A: Great.

5. A: How do I look?

   B: Not bad. Do they fit all right?

   A: Er, they're a bit tight round here.

   B: I really like the color. Suits you.

   A: Hmm. The trouble is they'll shrink when they're washed and then I'll never get into them.

   B: Pity, as they're reduced in the sale.

   A: Oh never mind. Let's try somewhere else.

6. A: I've got one of these.

   B: They're good, aren't they? Really compact.

   A: And very powerful — 24 watts per speaker.

B: Yes, I like having the double cassette-player.

A: You know what the best thing was?

B: No.

A: Interest free credit!

7. A: What do you think of this one?

B: It's really not my cup of tea. Too modern and abstract.

A: But look at the colors and forms. Very imaginative.

B: Hmm, maybe. I prefer landscape or portraits myself.

A: Oh, you're so traditional!

8. A: I didn't think much of that.

B: No. It wasn't too hot. Pity, because they're a good group.

A: I couldn't hear the lead singer at all.

B: Me neither. The guitars and drums were too loud.

A: Still, it got better near the end.

B: I reckon they sound much better on their records.

9. A: How did you get on?

B: Don't ask!

A: You lost. Well, he's a good player.

B: You're telling me. His service is incredible.

A: So is his backhand. What was the score?

B: 6-0, 6-1.

A: Oh dear. Come on. I'll buy you a drink.

10. A: John. Welcome back! Oh, what a tan!

B: I was really lucky with the weather.

A: Good hotel?

B: Not too bad. Food was average, but we were right on the beach.

A: Hmm. We should have gone abroad too instead of camping

in Wales.

B: Do you want to see some photos?

A: Oh, yes!

Exercise 2

Directions: Listen again, and write down two or more words which helped you decide.

Section B: Investigation on Damage

Exercise 1

Directions: Listen to the conversation and answer the following questions.

A: Ah, good morning, Mr Miles.

B: Yes.

A: How do you do. Julian Allen from Sun Insurance. I've come to make a damage report on the house. I'm visiting quite a few houses in this area actually. The storm did a lot of damage.

B: Well, you have been quick. I only phoned two days ago.

A: I know. We like to try and settle claims as soon as possible.

A: Good. Let's start here at the front, shall we? Er, you've got a lot of tiles missing off the roof.

B: Yes, and the TV aerial's fallen down. Um, you can see the bedroom window on the left was smashed. I've just put some boards over it.

A: OK. Anything else?

B: Er, yes. The chimney was damaged as well. You can just about see if you look.

188

A: Ah, yes. Some of the bricks have blown off. Right, let's walk round to the back.

B: Here we are.

A: Goodness, that tree's fallen down right onto the fence!

B: Yes. It's a real pity. Lovely tree that was. The shed roof was damaged too, I'm afraid.

A: Oh yes. Well, that's also covered in your policy.

B: The, er, kitchen window on the right was broken and part of the garden wall collapsed too.

A: I see. OK. I've got all that.

B: Um, that's about it, I think.

A: Good. I'll write up my report and we'll let you have a cheque as soon as possible.

Exercise 2
Directions: Listen to the cassette again and write down what has been damaged.

Section C: Stock Report
Exercise 1
Directions: Listen to the following Stock Reports. Then write down the important information about metals and experts' prediction.

1. Here is the Stock Report for Monday, December 12th. The market remained steady last Friday, and at the end of the day prices for all metals were exactly £1.

   Our market expert predicts that there will be only small fluctuations, though there may be increased interest in gold. In

189

the long term, it looks as though silver and tin are very good buys. And that's all from today's Stock Report.

2. Here is the Stock Report for Tuesday, December 13th. Yesterday was quite a busy day at the Stock Exchange. Gold was very much in demand, and closed at £1.40. The Price of tin increased to £1.05, but there were falls in the prices of silver (to 83p), platinum (95p) and nickel (92p). Copper remained firm at £1.

Our market expert predicts continued increases in gold and tin, and it is thought that decline in the price of silver is only temporary. And that's it from the Stock Report.

3. Here is the Stock Report for Wednesday, December 14th. Prices of all metals except nickel and tin fell yesterday. Closing prices were gold £1.35, silver 79p, platinum 91p, copper 98p, nickel and tin £1.10.

Our expert predicts a good future for silver, and it looks as though nickel is on the way up, too. That's all from Stock Report today.

4. Here is the Stock Report for Thursday, December 15th. The market does seem to be strengthening somewhat. Silver recovered yesterday to £1.02, and there were rapid increases in nickel (£1.10) and tin (£1.18). Gold, platinum and copper all fell slightly, to £1.30, 87p, and 95p respectively.

Our market expert predicts considerable fluctuations in the prices of many metals, though it seems that silver and gold are the safest investments at present. And that's all from the Stock Report.

5. Here is the Stock Report for Friday, December 16th. As predict-

ed in yesterday's report, there were many dramatic changes in prices. Nickel soared to £1.60, while at the other end of the scale gold plummeted to a record low of 81p. Copper also fell sharply to 65p, while tin ended the day at £1.15. Platinum and silver remained steady at 87p and £1.02 respectively.

Our market expert predicts improved long term performance for all metals, though there may be a temporary decline in the price of tin.

And that's all from the Stock Exchange for this week. We hope you've all managed to make a fortune.

Exercise 2

Directions: Listen to the tape again and then answer the following questions.

Section D: Hot Cake
Exercise 1

Directions: Listen to the tape and then fill in the blanks.

Fears that a much-predicted surge in consumer spending this year would fail to materialise can now be dispelled. According to figures out on July 24th, retail sales volumes were 1.3% higher in June than in May, compare with a consensus forecast amongst economists in the City of London of 0.9%. The growth in retail sales in the year to June was 3.3% (compared with a consensus forecast of 2.4%), the fastest yearly rate since late 1994. Sales figures for previous months, suggesting only modest growth, were revised up by half a percentage point.

June's strong sales have largely silenced, at least for now, calls for Kenneth Clarke, the chancellor, to cut interest rates again. He has reduced them by $1\frac{1}{4}$ percentage points since last December — most recently in June, against the advice of Eddie George, governor of the Bank of England. Assuming that his main motivation is economics not politics, his focus henceforth should be on when, and by how much, to raise rates in order to prevent inflation picking up.

This is not merely because retail sales are soaring. Mr Clarke was worried by sterling's strengthening in late May, but it has since weakened again. Manufacturing output, flat for a year, may be reviving. The Confederation of British Industry's latest survey of industrial trends found that output rose in the four months to July, and expectations that output will rise in the next four months are the strongest since October 1988.

There is no automatic connection between faster growth and higher inflation. Indeed, the CBI survey expects a sharp fall in manufacturers' unit costs, which may reduce inflation in the short run. But history suggests that as the economy grows, the labour market will tighten, leading to wage inflation. And retailers, after years of facing customers wanting only bargains, will look for every opportunity to exploit renewed consumer confidence by pushing up prices.

Exercise 2

Directions: Read the statements. Listen to the tape again, and decide if the statements are True or False.

Part Ⅲ : Listening Comprehension Test

Section A

Directions: In this section, you will hear nine short conversations between two speakers. At the end of each conversation, a third voice will ask a question about what was said. Both the conversations and the questions will be spoken only once. After each question there will be a pause. During the pause, you must choose the best answer from the four choices given by marking the corresponding letter (A, B, C, or D).

1. W: What happened next?

    M: Next I dreamt that Brown and Smith merged into one person while Robinson split into two.

    Q: What is the man describing?

2. M: Did you enjoy your trip to China?

    W: The scenery was magnificent and people were very friendly, but I got very tired of the rain and dark skies.

    Q: What does the woman think of the trip?

3. M: Nancy, why isn't Susan working here this month?

    W: She can't. She was dismissed from her work.

    Q: What reason was given for Susan's not working?

4. W: Tom, how did your football team do in June and July?

    M: We won four times in June and twice in July, lost six times altogether, and tied three times in June and five times in July.

    Q: How many times did they tie altogether?

5. M: Do you think we should urge Betty to study French?

    W: We'll have to leave that decision up to her.

Q: What does the woman mean?

6. M: Your room has such a nice view of the river and the mountains.

   W: Yours does, too.

   Q: What can be inferred from the conversation?

7. M: What's happening to the new laboratory building?

   W: The work crew is just finishing it up.

   Q: What does the woman say about the laboratory building?

8. W: Bob, did you clean the bedroom?

   M: No, I got Mary to do it.

   Q: Who cleaned the bedroom?

9. M: How long will I have to stay out of school?

   W: That depends. You still have a fever. Let me take your pulse and blood pressure.

   Q: What is the woman's occupation?

Section B

Directions: In this section, you will hear two short passages. At the end of each passage, there will be some questions. You will hear both the passages and the questions only once. After each question there will be a pause. During the pause, you must choose the best answer from the four choices given by marking the corresponding letter (A, B, C, or D).

Passage I

Can you imagine how difficult life would become if all supplies of paper suddenly disappeared ? Banks and post offices, schools and colleges would be forced to close. Food manufacturers would be un-

194

able to pack or label their products. There would be no magazines, newspapers or books. And we would no longer be able to write to our friends and relations.

Those would be only a few of the troubles of paperless world. Everywhere we turn we find paper. Without it our modern world would come to a standstill. Paper is the lifeblood of industry, the bringer of news, and the distributor of knowledge. It wouldn't be much fun chipping out our letters on a tablet of stone, or writing up schoolwork on slates!

10. What will happen if ever a day comes when paper is in short supply?
11. What is paper regarded as according to the speaker?
12. The passage supports which of the following conclusions?

Passage II

" When I was a young student, people used to think that memory loss and dementia were a normal part of aging. Today we know that in many cases, the real cause is Alzheimer's disease. As a pharmaceutical company researcher, I am committed to finding ways of treating this disease."

"Currently, there are about 4 million people in the United States with Alzheimer's disease. Unfortunately, this number will dramatically increase as our population ages. My company is searching for treatments that might slow down, halt or maybe even reverse the progression of Alzheimer's."

"We think Alzheimer's disease has several different causes," says Axel Unterbeck, a pharmaceutical company researcher. "Some forms are genetic while others might involve additional factors. Because it affects memory and learning, it's one of the most complex diseases we know of." Unterbeck and his team of researchers are working on genes that are linked to Alzheimer's disease. "Four genes have been identified so far," Unterbeck says. "These gene discoveries give us, for the first time, a realistic hope to find a cure."

13. According to the passage, what is the real cause of memory loss in many cases?

14. What is the pharmaceutical company doing now?

15. What do these gene discoveries mean?

Unit Twenty-two

Part Ⅰ : **Listening Practice**

Section A: Listening for Descriptions
Exercise 1
Directions: Listen to the five descriptions of people or objects and i-
dentify who or what is being described in each case.

1. A: Where does Adrian live?
   B: In Rose Cottage.
   A: Which one's that?
   B: Oh, you know. Beautiful old place with a thatched roof, two
      chimneys and a hedge at the front.
   A: Ah yes. It's got the date it was built on the wall, right?
   B: That's it.
2. A: Hey, Julie's just got engaged!
   B: Um, I don't remember who she is.
   A: Yes, you do. She works in the office. Long wavy hair, big
      eyes, attractive-looking and quite slim.
   B: Does she wear glasses?
   A: Don't think so. No. She has those big earrings and usually
      wears a V-necked sweater. She's got freckles.

197

B: Hmm, I think I know who you mean.

3. A: Good morning madam.

   B: Morning I just came to see if anyone has handed in a bag I left on the number 52 bus last night.

   A: Can you give me a description?

   B: Of course. It's plain blue, quite large with a zip on top.

   A: OK.

   B: Um, there's a pocket on the outside and it's got a tear down one side.

   A: Right. I'll just check for you.

4. A: Um, can anyone lend me their bike for half an hour?

   B: Sure. You can take mine.

   A: Oh thanks, Paul.

   B: It's the red one with the racing saddle and bags at the back. It's got a little mirror. Here's the key to unlock it.

   A: Thanks a lot.

   B: Oh, one of the tyres is a bit flat. You may need to pump it up.

5. A: International Plastics. Good afternoon.

   B: Hi Connit. It's Geoff.

   A: Hello. What can I do for you?

   B: I think I may have left my raincoat there. It's a plastic one with a hood. Er, it's got black stripes on the sleeve and pockets.

   A: OK. I'll have a look for you.

   B: Thanks a lot.

Exercise 2

Directions: Listen to the cassette again and write down the words which helped you decide.

Section B: Wills
Exercise 1
Directions: Fill in the blanks with the words you hear from the tape.

Will in law is about disposition by an individual of his or her property, intended to take effect after death. A disposition of real property by will is termed a devise; a disposition of personal property by will is termed a bequest. The person making a will, called the testator, must have testamentary capacity, that is, must be of full age and sound mind and must act without undue influence by others.

By statute in the U. S. and in England, a will is required to be in writing, whether it disposes of real or personal property; a soldier or sailor in combat, however, may make a will orally. In a number of jurisdictions in the U. S., an oral will is also valid when made by a testator during sickness that terminates in death, but it must be made at a point when, because of the apparent imminence of death, neither time nor opportunity exists to make a written will. The law usually provides that the contents of an oral will must be reduced to writing within six days after it was declared in the presence of the statutory number of witnesses, usually three. Such oral wills are termed nuncupative wills and may dispose only of personal property. A written will that is entirely in the handwriting of the testator is termed a holographic will and may dispose of real or personal property, or both. The statutes of some states in the U. S. recognize such wills as valid without formal execution or attestation, if wholly written, dated, and signed by the testator's own hand. A holographic will is valid only if it complies literally with the controlling statute.

Exercise 2
Directions: Answer the following questions according to the tape.

Section C: Cryptography
Exercise 1
Directions: Listen to the talk and answer the following questions.

The word " cryptography " comes from Greek words that mean " hidden " and " writing ". Thus, it means simply " hidden writing " or " writing in secret codes ".

Cryptography has been used for thousands of years. One early example was found in H. Cliffix about 4,000-year-old Egyptian tomb.

Military generals have long made use of cryptography to exchange secret messages, as have kings, smugglers, authors and businessmen. Julius Caesar's method of cryptography was so simple that it was easy to decipher. Charlemagne had special alphabets prepared which his generals had to memorize. The tales of Edgar Allan Poe, Sir Arthur Conan Doyle, O. Henry and Jules Verne contain cryptographic material, and there are many others.

In the United States, during the Prohibition Era, smugglers of alcoholic beverages communicated from ship to shore using cryptographic wireless messages. Today, business is using cryptography in the form of cryptographic codes to guard information in computers. The security of information is very important to banks, for example, these need to keep secret, the confidential nature of certain cash transactions. Security systems using cryptography protect this type of information. Our security systems can also protect information by telecommunications.

Cryptography is an ancient art, but is taking on a new form for the 21st century.

Exercise 2
Directions: Listen to the tape again and complete the sentences below.

Section D: Mike and Pat
Exercise 1
Directions: Listen to the dialogue and answer the following questions.

Pat: Mike! Look at the floor!
Mike: What's wrong with it?
Pat: What's wrong with it ? It's filthy!
Mike: Oh. . .
Pat: It's filthy because you never wipe your shoes.
Mike: Sorry, love.
Pat: What are you looking for now?
Mike: My cigarettes.
Pat: Well, they are not here. They are in the dustbin.
Mike: In the dustbin! Why?

Pat: Because there's cigarette ash on every carpet in the house. Anyway, cigarettes are a waste of money.

Mike: Maybe they are, but I earn the money! It doesn't grow on trees, you know. I work eight hours a day, remember?

Pat: Well, what about my money then?

Mike: What do you mean " your money "? You don't go out to work, do you?

Pat: No, I don't go out to work. I work fifteen hours a day... here !

Mike: Well, housework is different...

Pat: Oh, I see... so housework is different, is it? Housework doesn't matter. Well, you do it then.

Mike: Hey, wait a minute, Pat. Pat...

Exercise 2
Directions: Listen to the dialogue once more and then judge for yourself and give the number under each name.

Part Ⅱ : Oral Practice
Exercise 1: Professor Pinkerton
Directions: Listen to the short passage and answer the questions.

Professor Pinkerton lived alone and was very absent-minded. He used to arrive at the college to give a lecture and find he had forgotten to bring his notes. Or he would lose his spectacles and be unable to see the blackboard. He could never find any chalk to write with, and he often forgot the time and would ramble on for hours because he had left his watch at home. But the most amazing thing about him was his appearance. His coat was rarely fastened, as most of the buttons were missing, and his shoes were usually untied because he had lost the laces. He must have lost his comb as well because his hair was always standing on end, that is unless he was wearing his battered old hat with the brim missing! His trousers were held up by an old tie instead of a belt, and cigarette ash was scattered liberally over his waistcoat.

Part Ⅲ: Listening Comprehension Test

Directions: In this part, you will hear 10 short conversations about conditionals. After you have heard each conversation, try to choose the best answer.

1. M: If I go to the store, will you make dinner for us tonight?
   W: Bring back enough food.
   Q: What happens if the man shops?

2. M: It would be easier to drive if there were no other cars on the road.
   W: Did you bring your licence this time?
   Q: What would the man prefer?

3. W: If you're going there anyway, would you change my travelers' checks at the bank?
   M: It depends on whether or not they'll accept my passport as identification.
   Q: Where is the man going?

4. M: A record crop depends on whether or not it rains in June and is dry in August.
   W: Can't they just harvest it in July?

Q: What are they referring to?

5. W: If you spill ink on the tablecloth, what then?

   M: I'll buy you another one.

   Q: What word describes the man?

6. M: If you don't wear a sweater when you go hiking, you will end up with a chill.

   W: My sweater is so thin and ugly, though.

   Q: What does the man want the woman to do?

7. W: I promise to bring my boss home for dinner if he gives me a raise this afternoon.

   M: Just let me know so I can be here when he comes.

   Q: What does the man plan to do?

8. M: The doctor said if I kept smoking, I would increase my chances of having a heart attack.

   W: Did he suggest losing some weight, too?

   Q: How does the woman perceive the man?

9. W: I promised my sister I would attend the show if I didn't have work due the next day.

   M: Why not take me along?

   Q: Why will the woman go to the show?

10. M: Next time I see George, I'll ask him if he's forgotten he owes me money.

    W: Why not just ask him to repay you?

    Q: What will the man do to George?

Unit   Twenty-three

Part I : Listening Practice

Section A: Understanding between Management and Workers
Exercise 1
Directions: You will hear an interview between Mr Marden and an interviewer. Listen to the conversation and then answer the following questions.

Interviewer: Do you know, for instance, most of your... your employees by their first name?

Mr Marden: Oh, yes. If I was to use their surnames, their second names, they would think that I was annoyed with them.

Interviewer: Hmm.

Mr Marden: One doesn't normally in a company of this size use surnames. Christian names are used when addressing anybody on the shop floor. Or anybody else.

Interviewer: Do you have a firm's canteen?

Mr Marden: Yes. We have a canteen, yes.

Interviewer: And do the managers eat in one canteen and the workers in another?

Mr Marden: Oh, no. Everybody eats in the same canteen, including my partner and I...

Interviewer: Hm... Hm..

Mr Marden: I also eat in there when we are eating here and we have our tea there.

Interviewer: In the same canteen with the workers?

Mr Marden: Oh, yes.

Interviewer: And this is, of course, one advantage with a small firm, isn't it?

Mr Marden: Oh, yes.

Interviewer: You wouldn't be able to do this in a large firm.

Mr Marden: Uh.

Interviewer: Doesn't it have...

Mr Marden: It does in some large firms, but most large firms do in fact, have separate canteens, yes.

Interviewer: Do you think this is a good idea?

Mr Marden: No, I think it's a bad idea.

Interviewer: Hm... hm... why?

Mr Marden: Well, I think that it fosters the feeling that there's between them and us.

Interviewer: Hm... hm...

Mr Marden: That the workers and the management are on two separate sides of a fence. In fact, of course, they're on the same side.

Interviewer: Hm.... hm...

Mr Marden: We all sink or swim together. We're all in the same boat, and I think that anything that fosters this impression is good.

Exercise 2

Directions: Listen to the cassette once more. Then write down your substitutions in column B which are closest in meaning to the sentences on column A.

Section B: Motivating Employees to Work Harder
Exercise 1

Directions: You will hear an interview between Professor Mark Sloan and Jackie Lippleton. As you listen to their conversation, fill in the missing parts of the following outline.

Jackie: Professor Sloan, in your book you say that increases in salary, more fringe benefits and promotions are no longer the things that people want most in their jobs. You say that these things don't really motivate people to work harder the way they did in the past. What sorts of things, then, do motivate workers these days? What can managers do to get employees to work harder?

Sloan: Workers today look for more personal satisfaction in a job. They want to enjoy their work and feel proud of what they do. They want their bosses to treat them better, and they want to participate more in management discussions. Motivating workers is no longer as simple as it was in the past. More money or more fringe benefits just isn't enough anymore. Some workers won't even accept promotions that are offered to them.

Jackie: Why wouldn't a person want to accept a promotion?

Sloan: Well, maybe they don't want all the problems and pressures of being a supervisor or a manager: Maybe they like what they are doing, and don't think they would be as happy in the new position. Or maybe a promotion means leaving a town and friends they like and don't want to leave. There are several reasons why a person might not accept a promotion. People today always think about what will make them happiest, not just what pays more.

Jackie: What has caused this change in the way people think and feel about their work?

Sloan: Two things: people have a higher level of education these days and enjoy a much higher standard of living than in the past. It's no longer as hard to survive in this society.

Almost everyone can find some kind of job. And nobody needs to worry about having food to eat or a place to sleep even if they're not working. Today, if a person doesn't like his job, he'll simply quit and try to find a better one. Workers these days want more than just money from a job. As I said before, they want some personal satisfaction.

Jackie: So how can managers get people to work harder and be more productive?

Sloan: One way is to give workers more of a chance to participate in management decisions that concern them.

Jackie: For example?

Sloan: For example, managers can ask employees to help plan the work schedule and when they will take vacations. Many companies are including workers in management discussions and asking them to help on planning committees, and an increasing number of companies offer employees at all levels a chance to participte in profit-sharing and stock dividend plans. All these things make the employees work harder, because they want to see their company do better.

Exercise 2
Directions: Listen to the cassette once more. Then answer the following questions.

Section C: Questionnaires and Opinion Surveys
Exercise 1
Directions: You will hear another interview between Professor Mark Sloan and Jackie Lippleton. Fill in the missing parts of the following outline as you listen to the conversation.

Jackie: What do you think about questionnaires and opinion surveys? I know some companies use questionnaires to give workers a chance to express their opinions. Do you think such surveys are useful?

Sloan: Well, they can be—it all depends. If you ask all the workers to answer a questionnaire, then they will expect some changes as a result of the survey. If management is not really willing to consider the opinions of the workers or make changes then it is useless. In fact, it is worse than useless. Workers will feel angry that their opinions are being ignored. Sometimes it's difficult or maybe even impossible for management to do what the workers want. For example, there was a shoe company in Maine where almost all the workers wrote on a questionnaire that they wanted an increase in

209

salary. They felt they were not being paid enough, and this caused a great deal of dissatisfaction. Actually the company simply couldn't afford to pay the workers there more money. Labor is so expensive in the U.S. compared to other countries that the shoe industry in New England was almost unable to compete with the prices of imported shoes. Many shoe companies in the U.S. went out of business in the 1970's because shoes were being made so much more cheaply in other countries and sold in stores for lower prices.

Jackie: So what happened to the shoe company in Maine?

Sloan: The management at that company did a very clever thing. They asked employees to participate in a committee to study the possibility of giving everyone an increase in salary. The committee compared the costs of producing shoes in several other countries with their own costs and the prices of imported shoes with the prices of shoes made in their company. They even traveled to Korea to see how cheaply shoes were being produced there. The committee came to the conclusion that it would be impossible for management to increase the salaries of employees and still stay open. In fact, the employees even volunteered to take a cut in pay because they were afraid their company might go out of business and they would lose their jobs. Can you believe it? This is what I mean by giving workers more of a chance to participate in management decisions that affect them. A greater spirit of cooperation is the final result.

Exercise 2

Directions: Listen to the cassette once more. Then answer the following questions.

Section D: Drunk Driving
Exercise 1
Directions: You will hear a short passage. As you listen to the passage, fill in the missing parts of the following outline.

The United States has one of the lowest rates of car accidents in the world. Yet, every year about 44,000people die on the highways in car accidents in the United States. Half of these deaths are caused by drunk drivers. Because of this, stricter laws have been passed recently. California has one of the strictest laws. This law states that if you kill someone while you are driving intoxicated, you will be considered a murderer in the eyes of the law. This is a story about what happened to a thirty-year-old man in California. One afternoon this man drank four bottles of beer at a bar. After finishing his drinks, he got into his car and drove off. He was speeding. He ran through a stop sign and crashed into another car crossing the intersection. He didn't have enough time to stop. The car that was struck was being driven by a mother; inside were her four children. All of the passengers were killed. However, the drunk driver wasn't injured at all. When the police arrived, they arrested the driver and brought him to court. There he was indicted for murder. After a two-month trial, he was found guilty of murder. He was sentenced to seventy-seven years in prison. While some feel his sentence was justified, others feel he was sentenced too harshly because he had not planned the accident. However, those in favor of the sentence said this was not the first time he had been arrested for drunk driving. Last time he had his driver's license suspended for six months. This time his license has been revoked for life.

Exercise 2
Directions: Listen to the cassette once more. Then answer the following questions.

Part Ⅲ : Listening Comprehension Test
Directions: In this part, you will hear three short passages. At the end of each passage, there will be some questions. You will hear both the passages and questions only once. After each question there will be a pause, you must choose the best answer from the four choices given by marking the corresponding letter (A, B, C or D).

Passage Ⅰ

This is a story about eighteen-year-old foreign student who didn't hear his alarm clock ring so he woke up an hour late for school. Because he was late, he just threw on some clothes and ran out of the house. What a terrible mood he was in! He really felt he had gotten up on the wrong side of the bed.

He ran down stairs onto the subway platform. While waiting for the train, he picked up a newspaper he saw lying on a bench. After a ten-minute wait, the train arrived at the station. He got onto the crowded train. While the train was speeding down the tracks, he felt a man bumping into him. He thought that same man had been watching him read his newspaper on the subway platform. All of a sudden, he felt afraid. He remembered how his family had warned him about how dangerous the United States was. He didn't

212

think he was being paranoid. He thought he was being robbed.

Sure enough, when the student put his hand inside his bag, his wallet was gone. Just then the train stopped. He saw the man getting off. The student shouted, "Stop! Thief! He stole my wallet!" Immediately, most of the passengers near the door grabbed onto the man's jacket. Just then the doors of the subway train shut. The man looked shocked as the passengers tore off his sleeve. As the train pulled out of the station, the young man broke down into tears about his lost wallet. Some of the passengers, feeling sorry for the bewildered student, took up small collection for him so that he could get to school. When the student arrived home that evening, he was too sad to think. As he walked toward his bed, he felt even sadder. There on the table near his bed, he saw his wallet. He couldn't believe what a terrible mistake he had made. Never again would he leave his house when he was in such a mood. What would he say if he ever saw that man standing at the subway station again?

1. Why was the student late for school?
2. Why did the student mistake the man for a thief?
3. What was the feeling the student did not have when he found he had made a terrible mistake?

Passage II

In a recent survey, Ralph Nader, a lawyer, came in sixth as the man whom people in the United States most admire. Who is Ralph Nader? Why do so many people look up to him?

He is a man whom General Motors wanted to destroy. After graduating from Harvard Law School, Nader started doing research on the automobile. While studying automobile safety and design,

213

Nader discovered how manufacturers, in their desire for profits, routinely marketed automobiles they knew to be unsafe. Because he felt it was necessary that the government regulate the automobile industry, he wrote a book called Unsafe at any Speed. In it, he described a design problem with the Corvair, a model manufactured by General Motors. This book exposed how dangerous the car was because of a defect in the steering wheel. Often when the driver turned a corner, the car would flip over. There were many injured people, some of whom died. Although General Motors denied Nader's findings, the book caused an uproar. In fact, after government officials read Nader's book, they decided to make General Motors recall its product. It was the first time that the government forced a company to recall a pro-duct. Also, his book raised the consciousness of the consumer to understand how not enough attention was being paid to what causes the deaths and injuries in automobile accidents.

4. What is Ralph Nader's profession?

5. What did he do after his graduation from Harvard Law School?

6. Why did General Motors want to destroy Ralph Nader?

Passage Ⅲ

The engine of Margret's car was not runing smoothly. The spark plugs needed cleaning. Margaret could have done the job herself, but garages have special equipment that does such things very thoroughly.

Like her father, Margret did not like being overcharged. She knew that garages do this sometimes. Sometimes they even charge for work they have never done. She told the repairman at the garage not to do any extra work, she wanted the spark plugs cleaned, and

214

nothing more. Then she left, saying she would be back in a little while.

When Margaret came back, the repairman handed her a bill for $ 10. Margaret knew this was more than it should cost to have the spark plugs cleaned. Then the repairman said he had put new ones in. Margaret decided she was not going to stand for this, and began to get angry.

"But the plugs were worn out; what else could I do? " the repairman protested. "How long should these new spark plugs last? More than a few months?" Margaret demanded. "Of course! Much longer than that! " the repairman said with great emphasis.

"Well then, put the old ones back in. I had new spark plugs put in only a few months ago and I had the job done here!" Margaret said.

7. Why didn't Margaret do the job herself?

8. What did Margaret tell the repairman to do?

9. What did Margaret find when she came back?

10. Why did Margaret tell the repairman to put the old plugs back in?

Unit Twenty-four

Part Ⅰ: Listening Practice

Section A: Civil Service Reform
Exercise 1
Directions: Listen to the talk carefully. Decide whether the following statements are true or false. Write T for true and F for false in the right spaces.

Today I am going to tell you something about President Chester Arthur and his civil service reform. Chester Arthur was elected vice-president of the United States in 1880. In the summer of 1881 President James Garfield was assassinated. A few hours after the President's death, Chester Arthur took the oath of office. President Arthur had been a successful lawyer and worked in politics for many years, but be had never held an elected office, so in the beginning, some Americans questioned his ability to serve in the White House. President Arthur surprised them; his success in the reform of the civil service system won him much support from the people.

In his first message to Congress President Arthur proposed a new civil service system that would let ability, not politics, decide who got government jobs. The Republican Party leaders opposed this proposal because the civil service system would stop them from

216

giving federal jobs to their supporters. It would destroy much of their power. These Republican leaders controlled the Congress. They refused to act on the civil service proposal.

New cases of dishonesty were discovered in government departments. The public began to demand laws to clean up the civil service. In 1882 a new Congress was elected. The new Congress was controlled by the Democratic Party. President Arthur again appealed for civil service reform. This time he got results. The new Congress passed the Civil Service Bill, which required 10 percent of all federal jobs to be filled through competitive examinations. This 10 percent included most workers at the Federal Customs Houses and half the officials in the Post Office Department.

Chester Arthur's efforts for honest government won him much support from the people, but he could not win the support of his own Republican Party. He failed to win the Presidential nomination in the Republican Nominating Convention in 1884.

Exercise 2
Directions: Listen to the talk again. Then answer the questions.

Section B: Electronic Observation
Exercise 1
Directions: Listen to the talk carefully. Then fill in the form to explain the following terms.

The International Labor Organization has studied reports on workers' privacy in nineteen industrial nations. The study shows that electronic observation is most common in the United States.

Many employers are using computers, cameras, listening devices and telephones to observe their workers. In the 300 businesses investigated in the US more than 20 percent said they search computer records and listen to voice mail or electronic mail of their employees. Voice mail is a system for recording messages. Electronic mail, also called E mail is messages sent between computers. About 20 million American workers, from factory workers to highly paid engineers, may be under electronic observation. This does not include employers who listen to people using telephones on their jobs. The ILO study says that electronic observation is especially common in some industries, such as telecommunications, insurance and banking. It also says the use of cameras is increasing in factories and stores in Japan and the use of technology to observe workers has grown rapidly in many other European industrial nations since 1985.

Workers and worker organizations have major objections to electronic observation. They say it violates human rights and destroys the feeling of trust between workers and employers, because some employers use it to punish workers without the workers' knowing the reason. They say it also makes it easier to learn private information about their workers, and employers even have greater powers than law enforcement agencies to observe people. For example, police need court orders to listen to the telephone calls of suspected criminals, but no such order is required for a business that wants to listen to the phone calls of one of its workers.

The United States Congress is considering a bill to restrict the uses of electronic observation in work places. Employers will be required to tell workers if they are being observed.

Exercise 2

Directions: Listen to the tape again and answer the following questions.

Section C: Domestic Violence against Women
Exercise 1

Directions: Listening to the talk carefully. Then fill in the blanks in note form with the information you get from the talk.

A trial has increased Americans' interest in the problem of violence against women. O. J. Simpson has been accused of killing his former wife. Mrs Simpson and a friend were stabbed to death outside her home in June, 1996. Reports say that Mrs Simpson had called the police for help several times in the past few years. She reported that her husband had beaten her and she was afraid he would kill her. A jury was chosen, but it decided Mr Simpson was not guilty.

Domestic violence against women, especially wife beating, is a social problem in the US. Medical experts say wife beating is the most serious health threat to American women. The government says more young American women have been injured by men they know than by strangers, and more women are injured in this way than in accidents. Experts say violence against women takes place in almost every social, economic, racial and religious group.

A federal crime study says that every year more than four million young American women are beaten severely. Most of the violence is done by their present or former husbands or by their boyfriends.

In the past, many women were afraid to discuss the problem. They did not want anybody to know they were beaten by their husbands or boyfriends. Police usually refused to arrest a man who beat his wife, and the court did not take the issue seriously. Wife beaters were rarely sent to jail. Many women refused to take action against their husbands or boyfriends because they knew they would face even greater violence if they did.

A serious movement against domestic violence began in the US in the mid 1970's. Many activists were women who had been beaten. Since then great progress has been made. Activists have formed hundreds of local groups and set up many temporary homes for victims and their children. Progress has also been made in the justice system. Police and the courts now deal with the problem more seriously. In 26 states the police must now arrest wife beaters even if the victim does not cooperate.

New legislation has been introduced to help stop violence against women. It became part of a new crime bill signed by President Clinton not long ago. It includes programs to improve law enforcement against such crime and training for police and judges, to set up more temporary housing for beaten women and their children, and to establish a special national telephone number to provide information and help to all victims of family violence.

Exercise 2

Directions: Listen to the talk again, then answer the following questions.

220

Section D: Running for Mayor
Exercise 1

Directions: You will hear a conversation between two speakers. After the conversation a third voice will ask a few questions. Write down the answers of the questions in the space given.

W: What is so funny in the news?

M: You know Jerry Ward, the rock musician?

W: Yeah, the one with the pink hair?

M: That's the guy. Remember the strike last year? He had that rally with the doctors and nurses.

W: Oh, yeah, the rally during the hospital strike. So what about Jerry Ward?

M: He's running for mayor. He wants to run the city.

W: Jerry Ward? You're kidding.

M: Look at the paper: "Rock Star Runs for Mayor". Now listen here:

And if things aren't already crazy enough in San Francisco, rock star Jerry Ward announced today that he is entering the race for mayor. Ward is best known for his loud music and his pink hair. He hopes to use his popularity and his well-known support of striking hospital workers to make up for his late start. Ward was active in the strike at city hospitals last year when he appeared with several hundred doctors, nurses, and other medical workers at a large rally. Ward knows he has to make up for his late start in the election. He says he knows what the people want, because rock is the music of the people. His campaign slogan is: "From the concert hall to City

Hall, Jerry's with you." Will the people of San Francisco agree?
We'll know in six months. That's when the election will be held.

Exercise 2
Directions: Listen to the conversation again and then decide
whether the following statements are true or false. Write T for true
and F for false in the space given.

Exercise 3
Directions: Write down Jerry Ward's campaign slogan and explain it
in your own words according to the information given in the conversation.

Part III: Listening Comprehension Test

Section A
Directions: In this section, you will hear nine short conversations
between two speakers. At the end of each conversation a third voice
will ask a question about what was said. Both the conversations and
the questions will be spoken only once. After each question there
will be a pause. During the pause, you must choose the best answer
from the four choices given by marking the corresponding letter (A,
B, C or D).

1. M: Let's see if the basketball game has started yet.
   W: Started? It must be clear who's winning by now.
   Q: What does the woman mean?
2. W: I'm thinking of taking five courses next semester.

222

M: Wouldn't four be wiser?

Q: What does the man imply about the courses?

3. M: Have you seen the author's latest best-seller?

W: I've just finished it. I'd really recommend it.

Q: What are the man and woman discussing?

4. M: We've sure been having a lot of rain lately.

W: Haven't we ever?

Q: What do we learn from the woman's response?

5. W: John, I'm sorry to be so late. Thank you for waiting.

M: Oh I didn't mind. I've only been here fifty minutes. You said that you might be as much as an hour late, so I just bought my newspaper and ordered myself a cup of coffee.

Q: How long has the man been waiting?

6. W: Why did Jim Drake lose his job?

M: I didn't say he had lost it. All I said was if he didn't get out and start selling a few cars instead of sitting around all day discussing politics, he might find himself looking for a new job.

Q: What can we learn about Jim Drake from this conversation?

7. M: Have you started writing your paper for history?

W: Not yet. I'm still writing up my laboratory assignments for chemistry and studying for my midterms in English and French.

Q: For which class must the woman begin to prepare?

8. W: The flowers were lovely, weren't they?

M: Next time I'll choose the place to eat. It hurts me to pay so much for so little food.

Q: Where have the people most probably been?

223

9. W: Do you think Professor Adam will give us a long term paper instead of giving us tests for the Medieval Lit course?

   M: I don't know. I am keeping my fingers crossed.

   Q: What does the man mean?

Section B

Directions: In this part, you will hear two short passages. At the end of each passage, there will be some questions. You will hear both the passages and the questions only once. After each question there will be a pause. During the pause, you must choose the best answer from the four choices given by marking the corresponding letter (A, B, C or D).

Passage I

I am a person who bears grudges and I have a lot against three of my children, Manuel, Robert and Consuelo. My body is becoming half-paralyzed from being so angry with these children of mine. I am ashamed to talk about it. It is hard for a father to have such sons. They turned out bad because of bad surroundings and bad companions. Their friends are doing these boys no good. It is a shame that I cannot do anything about it. In spite of my advice, they go the other way instead of taking the straight path.

There is nothing better in this world than upright work. I am a poor and humble person, but I try to do things the best way I can. They can't say their father came home drunk or abandoned them. An uncle of theirs just died of drink. It seems they take after their uncle more than they do me.

10. How does the narrator feel about his life?

11. What is the tone of the father's speech?
12. How does the passage end?

Passage Ⅱ

Eight people, three of them women, died after being trapped in an attic when fire destroyed their two storey terrace house yesterday.

In the tragedy, about thirty-six people were sleeping in the building when the fire, started by a short circuit, broke out. Most of them managed to rush out in time. One of the first to leave the building was Miss Poh, nineteen, a factory worker, who was awakened from her sleep by shouts of "Fire!" shortly after 3:00 a.m. She said: "I shouted to the other tenants to get out. By this time, the first floor was in flames and I could hear people crying and screaming. Someone brought a ladder and placed it against the wall, but it only went up as far as the first floor. There was no hope for those trapped in the attic."

One man who did escape from the attic told reporters that he could only save himself by going through the ventilation opening in the roof and climbing to an adjoining building.

Chin Meng, twenty, a fitter, wept as he recalled how he had to leave his parents behind. He said: "When I tried to return for my parents, I was driven back by the thick smoke and the heat."

Shortly after the blaze was spotted, three fire engines raced to the scene and by 4 a.m. had the fire under control. The MP for the area visited the scene and said: "The landlord was wrong to rent out rooms irresponsibly. He had not given due thought to the safety of his tenants."

13. How many males were killed in the fire?
14. Which of the following was responsible for the fire?
15. How long did it take the fire brigade to get the fire under control?

Unit Twenty-five

Part Ⅰ: Listening Practice

Section A: Edward Heath
Exercise 1

Directions: You will hear the interview between Edward Heath and Geoffrey Stern. Listen to the conversation and then fill in the missing words of the following outline.

Stern: Edward Heath, you seem to have had two consuming passions in your life, music and politics. Is it important for a leader to have an escape like music or art?

Heath: I don't regard it as an escape, but I think it's very important that leaders should have a wide variety of interests. If you are just a politician and nothing but a politician, you gradually drive yourself into the ground. You become very inward-looking, very narrow-minded and then you don't look after the electorate. But if you've got other interests, you come back to problems with a fresh mind and you can serve your electors much better than you could otherwise.

Stern: Where did this interest of yours come from? Was yours a musical family?

Heath: It wasn't musical in the sense that Mozart's father was a

227

professional musician and Bach had brothers and sons who were musicians. On the other hand, my mother and father both wanted to encourage me, and my brother as well in music. He became a violinist while I was a pianist.

Stern: What about politics? Was yours a political family?

Heath: It wasn't at all. My father, I think, would have described himself as a Liberal. We certainly had the News Chronicle as our paper, and a look of abhorrence would come over his face if anyone ever mentioned The Daily Mail. I became interested in politics at school, very largely through a debating society. I've always enjoyed debating and arguing with people.

Stern: It is one thing to be interested in politics: it is another to want a political career.

Heath: Well, I became seriously interested in politics towards the end of the war, not in a party sense but in a general sense: that we couldn't allow Europe to tear itself apart again. If we were going to survive then we ought to do something about it after the war.

Exercise 2

Directions: Listen to the cassette again. Then answer the following questions.

Section B: A Politician Becomes an Executive
Exercise 1

Directions: You will hear a conversation between John Clark and Jackie Lippleton. Fill in the missing parts of the following outline as you listen to the conversation.

Jackie: Mr Clark, let me begin by asking you why you left politics. You had an extremely successful career in government. You were elected to the House three times and the Senate once. You became Director of the office of Management and Budget and ambassador to the U. N. under Nixon, and later White House chief of staff and Secretary of the Treasury under Ford. Many people thought you would be chosen to run with Ford as the Vice-presidential candidate in 1976 against Carter and Mondale, and most Republicans say you had your best years as a politician still ahead of you. Why, then, did you decide to leave it all after Ford lost in 1976?

Clark: Well, Ms Lippleton, first I did not necessarily leave politics for good. I may once again re-enter politics and government service at some date, but for now I'm not really thinking about that. In January of 1977 I signed a seven year contract with Austin and Goodwin. It wasn't that I really needed the contract. I wanted to sign a contract in order to show the degree of my commitment, and make it absolutely clear that I would be with the company for at least seven years. Why? Well, two reasons. First, I wanted to see what it would be like. As president of a large corporation, I'm seeing government for the first time from the businessmen's point of view. (Jackie: It's quite a change.) My second reason for switching from politics to business was financial. I'm not saying I'm in it only for the money, but I'm being perfectly honest in telling you I wanted to provide my family with more financial security than we would ever have in government life.

Jackie: How do you feel about it now? Are you glad you did it?

Clark: I sure am. It was about the best thing I could have done. It was the kind of new challenge I was looking for. It was a healthy change at just the right time. My work at Austin and Goodwin's has given me a whole new perspective on both politics and business, and I have much better feel for and understanding now of what businessmen are talking about when they complain of burdensome government regulations and unnecessary intervention. I'm on the other side of the fence now, but if I ever do re-enter politics again, I'll be doing everything I can to fight for less government involvement in big business.

Exercise 2

Directions: Listen to the cassette once again. Then answer the following questions.

Section C: Differences Between Managing in Government and Managing in Business

Exercise 1

Directions: You will hear another conversation between John Clark and Jackie Lippleton. As you listen to the conversation, fill in the missing parts of the following outline.

Jackie: You probably are always asked this next question. But I'll ask it anyway. What's the main difference you see between managing in government and managing in business?

Clark: You're judged more on the basis of results in business than in government. In business, the success of an executive can be measured by the amount of profit. But how can you measure the success of a politician. The success of a politician is based on appearances which can be measured by public image. As long as a government official looks as he or she is trying hard and cares a lot, then people are generally satisfied. In fact, in business it's almost expected that you will delegate authority and responsibility. As an executive, you have much more time to think and study and plan, And if you make a mistake in business, you can correct it and continue on with your work in a new direction. In politics however if you make a mistake, you don't want people to know you make a mistake. So mistakes very often go uncorrected in government. Those are some of the main differences.

Jackie: Are there any similarities?

Clark: Yes, certainly there are. Running a large corporation and managing some part of the government are both jobs that involve a great deal of planning and budgeting. And in any large and complex organization it is very important for the person at the top to know what's really happening at the lower levels. It's important to hear what the employees think about new policies and new directions. In government the news media always keep you pretty well informed about what's going on and what people think about the way you are doing your job. But in a big business, it's not so easy. At Austin and Goodwin's I try to have lunch with salesmen and lab technicians and others from time to time to hear their ideas for improving the company. They are the people who are affected by changes in company policy and direction, and they very often know better than anyone about what is working out well and what isn't. To a large extent, input is very important. Well, you know, your interview with me today shows that I haven't really stopped being a part of political life. To answer your question, though, let me say that for right now I'm enjoying my work at Austin and Goodwin's very much. But who's to know how I'll feel in another few years. Let's just say I don't have any plans to re-enter politics when my contract is up. It will depend on a number of factors, and there's no way that I can reasonably speculate on such a possibility at this time.

Jackie: There. Now you're sounding like a politician again.

Clark: Well, I could have said "no comment".

Exercise 2

Directions: Listen to the cassette once again. Then answer the following questions.

Section D: Dropouts
Exercise 1

Directions: You will hear a short passage. As you listen to the passage, fill in the missing parts of the outline.

In West Virginia and in New York, one out of four students drops out of high school. In Washington, D. C. , the statistics are even worse. One half of all high school students never graduate. Nationwide, the overall dropout rate is 29 percent. Many say they drop out because they are bored. Because of this U. S. educators are trying to figure out a way to stop this disturbing trend. In Chicago, some schools are throwing pizza parties for potential dropouts. In Milwaukee, some schools are having lotteries for used cars for students who stay in school. In Philadelphia, at-risk students are being awarded after-school jobs and summer jobs for staying in school. But in a New Jersey high school, one principal is using money, not jobs as an incentive.

West Virginian educators, however, have taken a different approach. Instead of paying students, they have decided to revoke a student's driver's license when the student stops going to class. But this ruling is now being challenged by a sixteen-year-old boy. He said that he had to quit going to school because he got his fifteen-year-old girlfriend pregnant. To support his new wife, he said he needed to drive a car. Now the court is deciding what to do in this case. Meanwhile, other states have enacted similar laws. Proponents of these laws say that students cannot understand that dropping out of school means a low-paying job, but they can understand what it means not to be able to drive. However, opponents of this law feel that a school may succeed in getting students to stay in school but it cannot make them learn. If students are not interested in learning, they will not learn.

Exercise 2
Directions: Listen to the cassette again and then answer the following questions.

233

Part III : Listening Comprehension Test

Directions: In this part, you will hear three short passages about lectures. At the end of each passage, there will be some questions. You will hear both the passages and the questions only once. After each question there will be a pause, you must choose the best answer from the four choices given by marking the corresponding letter (A, B, C or D).

Passage I

One rainy day two women wanted to go shopping at Bloomingdale's. They lived on the Upper West side of Manhattan and were waiting for a bus to take them across the Central Park to the store. It was raining cats and dogs. The women knew it could be hard to get around the city on such a lousy day. So, when no bus came after a twenty-minute wait, they decided to hail a cab. They tried, but all the cabs were full. Finally, they saw an empty one. They both ran out to the street and waved furiously to make the cab stop. But the empty cab passed them by. They wondered why the cab hadn't stopped for them. Luckily, the light turned to red and the cab had to stop. The women ran to the cab, opened the door, and jumped in. The driver turned around and looked surprised. The women didn't understand why. Ignoring his surprised look, they told him to take them to Bloomingdale's.

Off he went. Like a madman, he drove to the Central Park with his foot all the way down on the accelerator. One woman told her friend how scared she was, but she didn't want to be a back-seat driver. The other bravely shouted "Would you mind slowing down?" She also told him that he was driving too dangerously. The driver told the women not to worry as he continued to race to the store. Also, he never put the meter on. The women didn't understand what was going on.

At last, they arrived at Bloomingdale's. Both women felt exhausted. Neither knew how much to pay. So, one of the women leaned forward and asked the driver how much they owed him. The driver calmly said, "Nothing, ladies. I just stole the cab."

Questions:

1. Where did the two women want to go?
2. The empty cab didn't stop until _____.
3. Why was the woman scared on the way to the store?
4. What did they learn from the driver after they got to the destination?

Passage II

Some people do not like anything to be out of place; they are never late for work. They return their books to the library on time; they remember people's birthdays; and they pay their bills as soon as they arrive. Mr Dodds is such a person.

Mr Dodds works in a bank, and lives by himself. The only family he has is in the next town: his sister lives there with her husband, and her son, Mark. Mr Dodds does not see his sister, or her family, from one year to the next, but he sends them Christmas cards, and he has not forgotten one of Mark's seventeen birthdays.

Last week Mr Dodds had quite a surprise. He drove home from his office at the usual time driving neither too slowly nor too fast: he parked his car where he always parked it, out of the way of other cars, and he went inside to make his evening meal. Straight away, there was a knock at the door. Mr Dodds opened the door. To find a policeman standing on the door-step.

"What have I done wrong?" Mr Dodds asked himself. "Have I driven on the wrong side of the road ? Have I forgotten to pay an important bill?"

"Hello, Uncle." Said the policeman. "My name's Mark."

5. Where does Mr Dodds work?
6. What does he always do at Christmas?
7. Why did the policeman come to Mr Dodds?

Passage Ⅲ

At 9:30A. M. on October 28 on Interstate 71 in Ohio, there was an accident. But it was the kind of accident which makes people believe in miracles. The expression "In America the roads are paved with gold" seemed to come true.

An armored truck carrying more than a million dollars was driving down the interstate highway. Suddenly, the back door of the truck flew open. The sacks holding the money bounced out and split open. The bills started to float in the air. Because the truck driver had no idea that he had lost his cargo, he kept on driving to the bank where he was supposed to deliver the money. Some of the motorists, thinking that the bills were maple leaves because it was fall, didn't stop driving either.

However, when the drivers realized that these were not leaves blowing in the wind, but dollars, they screeched to a halt. People who had CB radios reported the news. Soon, others from a nearby town came to join the crowd on the highway. Scooping up the money, women, men, and children stuffed it into their pockets. Some praised the Lord for their good fortune. Finally, the police arrived at the scene. Over two hundred people were milling about. Angry that the police had come, the crowd accused the officers of pocketing some of the dollars themselves. The miracle had come to an end.

The insurance company advertised that it would give a 10-percent reward to anyone returning the money. About thirty people returned the money. One telephone repairman who had dreamed of buying a tractor with the $57,000 he had scooped up was the first to give the money back. He said he would not have been able to sleep at night if he had kept the money. Most, however, didn't return what they had found. The mayor, embarrassed by the incident that occurred in his town, insisted that those thieves were not his constituents.

Questions:

8. At what time did the accident happen?
9. Why did some of the motorists think of the bills as maple leaves when the bills started to float in the air?
10. How many people returned the money after the accident?

Unit Twenty-six

Section A: About U. S. Presidents

Exercise 1

Directions: Listen to the following passage carefully, and then fill in the form with the information you have heard about the presidents.

According to the Constitution of the United States, the person elected to the office of president must be a native-born citizen of the United States, a U.S. resident for 14 years, and at least 35 years old. Thus, while it is true that most presidents held high elective office before assuming the presidency, there is no such legal requirement. Of the 40 men who have served as President, seven arrived at the White House without having first been elected to a high office.

George Washington was the chairman of the Constitutional Convention, but he was elected president principally because he had been the commander-in-chief during the American War of Independence. Zachary Taylor, the 12th man to hold the office of the presidency, was a military hero in War of 1812. Ulysses S. Grant, the 18th, was the commander of the Union armies during the Civil War. Chester Arthur, the 21st, was a famous antislavery lawyer. William Howard Taft, the 26th, was a cabinet officer in the admin-

238

istration of Theodore Roosevelt and the appointed governor of the Philippines and later of Cuba. Dwight D. Eisenhower, the 33rd, was supreme Allied commander in Europe during World War II.

Exercise 2

Directions: Listen to the tape again and fill in the blanks with the words you have heard on the tape.

Section B: Words that Get You Hired
Exercise 1

Directions: Listen to the tape and then fill in the form to show how to give right answers to the eight questions in a successful interview.

Among applicants of equal ability, what any successful interview ultimately comes down to is giving the right answers to the right questions. In talks with job interviewers we pin-pointed eight key questions that, in one form or another, almost every good interviewer asks:

1. "Who are you really?" That's what your questioner wants to know when he or she greets you with "Tell me about yourself". Now you have to make sure your first words impress favorably. In a concise, two-minute reply, you might talk aboutyour education and work experience, bridging into why you're right for the job.

2. "Why are you in the job market?" The interviewer will be alert for deceptions. Be direct and quick. A simple, straight-for-ward answer can work: "The job they put me in wasn't the one I was hired for."

3. "What can you do for us?" The interviewer is seeking evi-

dence that you researched his company. "Lack of knowledge about the company and industry" ranked with "arrogance/cockiness" and "poor oral communi-cation" as principal job-interview turnoffs.

It's easy to research a prospective employer. Discover your library and read, read, read. Librarians can point you to annual reports, directories and sometimes even computer data banks crammed with information on potential employers.

4. " What are your strengths?" High energy level? Enthusiasm? Assertiveness? Decisiveness? Maturity? Social sensitivity? Results? Toughmindedness ? Back your assertions with concrete examples from work or school. Don't say "I can do anything you need." The interviewer wants more focus. But don't define your scope too narrowly.

5. "What are your weaknesses ?" Probing for candor, honesty and good psychological balance, the interviewer often says, "Tell me about one of your failures." The wrong answer is: "I can't think of any." It's an unrealistic egocentric who is above flopping once in a while. But don't go to the opposite extreme. Safe ground is the "weakness" that is really overuse of a strength. For example: "Sometimes people mistake my decisiveness for impatience, but I have learned to watch how I express things."

6. "What type of boss do you like ?" The interviewer is probing for whether you're likely to have boss conflicts, so don't knock your last boss. Here's the ideal boss as defined by one successful executive: "A competent and strong leader I can learn from, who will let me take chances and coach me when I need it."

7. "What are your most significant accompli-shments?" Some bosses never hire anyone who can't list at least one outstanding

240

achievement. Write down what made you proudest in each of the past five years.

8. "What salary are you looking for?" Don't bring up pay in an initial interview. If pressed, give a range, such as, "I'm considering opportunities between $45,000 and $60,000 ."

Exercise 2:
Directions: Listen again and then answer the questions.

Section C: Court Case
Exercise 1
Directions: Listen to the dialogue and answer the following questions.

The Magistrate's Court

Magistrate: Next case.
Clerk: William Black.
Clerk: Are you William Black ?
William: Yes, sir.
Clerk: You are charged with going on the fifteenth of this month into Smith's, the shoeshop, buying a pair of football boots and paying for them with a worth-less cheque. Do you plead guilty or not guilty?
William: Guilty, sir, but I thought it was all right.
Clerk: Wait——you will be able to give your explanation and speak for yourself later. Police Constable James Brown.

P. C. Brown:	Here, sir.
Clerk:	Take the oath.
P. C. Brown:	I swear to tell the truth, the whole truth and nothing but the truth. James Brown, Police Constable X51.
Clerk:	Give your evidence.
P. C. Brown:	Acting under instructions, I went to Smith's shoeshop and was there shown a cheque which they said had been given in payment for a pair of football boots. The cheque had been signed by William Black and had been returned by the bank. The people in the shop had the boy's address.
Magistrate:	Oh, they had, had they?
P. C. Brown:	Yes, sir. The assistant had thought the boy rather young to have a banking account and had asked him for his address, which he had given. I took the cheque to the address given. The boy was out, but the father was in. I ordered him to bring the boy up before you today.
Magistrate:	(to William) Why did you sign your name to a cheque when you had no banking account?
William:	I thought the cheque was all right, sir. I took it from my father's cheque book, and he always pays his bills with cheques out of it: he had recently shown me how to write a cheque.
Magistrate:	And is that all he told you about cheques? Didn't he tell you any more?

William:	He was going to, sir, but a visitor came in.
Magistrate:	We had better hear what the father has to say, I suppose he is here?
Mr Black:	Here, sir, My son is very sorry, sir. He did not know he was doing wrong. Only the day before I had been explaining to him how I paid my bills by means of cheques.
Magistrate:	I don't think much of your instruction, Mr Black. You would not make a very good schoolmaster.
Mr Black:	Perhaps you are right, sir, but we were interrupted before I had finished my explanation. Of course, as soon as I heard about the matter I went round to the shop and paid for the boots. I guarantee that he will never do such a thing again, and hope you will let him off this time. He has never been in trouble before, and I know he had no intention of cheating the shop.

Exercise 2

Directions: Listen to the dialogue again and rearrange the sentences below into the correct order.

Section D: A Government Job
Exercise 1

Directions: Listen to the following passage and then try to answer the questions.

Just a century ago, historians say, the way to get a government job was to know someone in the government. That changed in 1883... People who want to work for the government today must show that they are qualified, either by taking an examination or by proving that they have relevant work experience. Qualified applicants then compete with each other for the available positions. The biggest growth of the most positions of the past few years has been the lower levels of the government as federal programs have been shifted to state or local control. Inthe early part of this century, a government job meant security because the civil service offered benefits not available in a private sector. There is no longer that difference, but the civil service is still an attractive career option.

Basically, good government is invisible. It functions in its quiet efficient way. When you turn on the water in the morning, you don't say, "Oh, my, isn't that wonderful. The water is clean." And when you eat your food, you don't say, "Isn't that terrific ? I did not get them poisoning."

You expect these things.

And so, we function that way. And the only time we make the newsmedia is when something goes wrong.

Part Ⅲ: Listening Comprehension Test

Directions: In this part, you will hear three short passages. At the end of each passage, there will be some questions. You will hear both the passages and the questions only once. After each question there will be a pause, you must choose the best answer from the four choices given by marking the corresponding letter (A, B, C, or D).

Passage I

The younger members of most American families don't like foreign food. They like ham-burgers. Their idea of a good meal is a hamburger served with ketchup and French fried pota-toes, which are called French fries. French fries are not considered foreign: most American children and teenagers love to eat them any time of the day or night.

Millions of hamburgers and French fries are eaten every year. Thousands of roadside restaurants prepare and sell them. These are not really restaurants in the usual sense; they often have little space for tables and chairs. Many people buy their hamburgers and take them home to eat, or eat them in their cars.

Sometimes it is not necessary to go inside in order to buy the hamburgers. They are ordered through a window in the restaurant and then are handed out through the window to the waiting customer. Sometimes the customer does not even have to get out of his car.

When an American family travels abroad, this is almost always the custom that the younger members of the family miss most.

1. What are French fries ?
2. Which of the following can't be inferred from the passage?
3. Which of the following is not true?

Passage II

W: Yes, sir. Can I help you ?

M: Yes, I wonder if you could cash some traveler's cheque for me?

W: Of course, sir. How much do you want to change?

M: Well, it depends on the exchange rate really. What is it today in

Swiss francs?

W: Just a moment, sir. Yes, here it is. It's five point eight to the
 pound.

M: Good. In that case, I'd like to cash a hundred, please.

W: Could I have your passport, sir ? And, er, would you just sign
 the traveler's cheques?

M: Sorry ? Where do I sign them ? Here?

W: That's right, sir. Along the top. And I shall need your
 passport.

M: Yes, of course. That's funny. I felt sure I put it in this pocket.
 I wonder what I could have done with it?

W: Did you have it with you when you came out, sir?

M: Yes, I'm positive I did. Either I've dropped it somewhere —
 or — Er — do you really need my passport?

W: I'm afraid we do, sir. It's a rule. I can't possibly cash any
 traveler's cheques without seeing it.

M: Well, I've got some foreign currency I wanted to change as
 well — and a cheque that I received this morning which I want
 to cash. It's most awkward. . .

W: I understand it's inconvenient, sir, but I can't do anything
 about it. Perhaps you'd just have one more look. . .

M: Yes. Just a moment. It doesn't seem to be in any of my jacket
 pockets. And I can't have left it in the hotel, I'm sure. I picked
 up everything as I came out.

W: Perhaps I could serve the next customer while you're looking for
 it, sir.

M: No, no. I've just found it, thank goodness. Strange — I'd put
 it in my overcoat pocket. I've never done that before. Here you

are.

W: Thank you, sir. Mu, mm. Good. Thank you. Now how would you like the money?

M: In pound notes, please. Thank you very much.

4. What is the woman?

5. How much did the man cash?

6. Where did the man find his passport?

Passage Ⅲ

According to a recent survey, a large majority of Americans are in favor of retaining the present 55-mile-an-hour speed limit. This speed limit was imposed in 1973 when fuel shortages became critical. Seventy-five percent of the persons surveyed think the law is a good one. They point to the decrease in the highway death rate or to the saving of fuel as reasons for their opi-nion. Easterners and older people, rather than young adults, are more likely to argue for retaining the law.

Likewise, only 3 percent of the people surveyed favor a higher speed limit for trucks. The trucking industry believes that truck en-gines work more efficiently at higher speeds and that trucks travel-ing at higher speeds reach markets more quickly thereby saving consumers' money.

Some of the persons argue that trucks on certain highways are already involved in a number of fatal highway accidents.

7. What was the principle reason for the original imposition of the 55-mile-per-hour speed limit?

8. Which of the following ARE less likely to favor retaining the 55-mile-per-hour speed limit?

9. How many of the people surveyed believe that the law is a good one?

10. Why do truckers want a higher speed limit for trucks?

Unit Twenty-seven

Part I : Listening Practice

Section A: European Monetary System (1)

Exercise 1

Directions: You will hear an interview between Dennis Rothfield and Jackie Lippleton. Fill in the missing parts of the following outline as you listen to the conversation.

Jackie: Mr Rothfield?

Dennis: You must be Ms Lippleton. Why don't we sit down over here, Ms Lippleton.

Jackie: Thank you very much. This is a beautiful office you have.

Dennis: Yes, it is very nice, but I don't spend much time here. As you probably know, I work more out of the Paris office of the World Bank. I'm only here now because of the conference that the bank is sponsoring here in New York. I've seen you at some of the meetings, I think.

Jackie: I've been attending as many as possible. They have really been informative and helpful. They've also been very good for me because they've brought together many of the leaders in finance in the world which has made it possible for me to interview many more in a short time than I would normally be able to do.

Dennis: And speaking of interviews, what kind of information are you interested in having from me?

Jackie: Well, to begin with, I'd be interested in knowing exactly what your position is and what is it that you are trying to do?

Dennis: Well, obviously, I am an officer of the World Bank. Currently, I am on loan from the Bank to the office of the Organization Economic Cooperation and Development in Paris. I work with the Organization as an advisor to their efforts to set up a European Monetary System. I've been assigned to them for the past two years.

Jackie: What exactly is a monetary system in the sense you use the term and how would this particular system work in Europe?

Dennis: As I am using the term, a monetary system is a system where the rates of exchange for the currencies of the various countries are fixed in relation to each other.

Jackie: Fixed in relation to each other? What does that mean?

Dennis: It means that there are not great changes in the rate of exchange of one currency for another. For example, let's say that the U.S. dollar and the English pound have a fixed relation to one another of, say, $2.25 to every British pound. If the value of the dollar rises, the value of the British pound must rise a nearly equal percentage. The rate of changes should always be approximately two to one no matter how much the value changes.

Jackie: Are you trying to start a European exchange system which allows no change in the rate of exchange between any two currencies?

Dennis: Well, we think that no change would be almost impossible. We are trying to keep the rates of exchange the same so that no change is more than 2.1/2 %.

Jackie: It seems to me that that would be quite difficult to do. What nations will the European Monetary System involve?

Dennis: Most of the nations of the Common Market are involved as well as some others. Germany, France, Denmark, Norway, Austria, Italy, Switzerland, the Netherlands, Belgium, and Great Britain are all involved. Nearly every country in Europe is at least considering getting into the system.

Jackie: It must be a very attractive thing.

Exercise 2

Directions: Listen to the cassette once again. Then answer the following questions.

Section B: European Monetary System (2)
Exercise 1

Directions: You will hear a continued interview between Dennis Rothfield and Jackie Lippleton. Fill in the missing parts of the following outline as you listen to the conversation.

Jackie: Mr Rothfield, speaking of monetary system, what are the advantages of having a monetary system in Europe?

Dennis: The greatest advantage is that such a system brings stability to the exchange rates. It allows smooth and steady adjustments in the rates rather than wide swings. It also prevents some of the stronger currencies such as the German mark or the Swiss franc from rising to exaggerated levels of value.

Jackie: How is having a common monetary system able to prevent the disruptions you mention?

Dennis: Well, a common system allows the European nations to cut the separate links of their currencies to the dollar. With the beginning of the system, any change in the value of the dollar will affect all of the countries equally. This is an advantage because the European countries trade more with each other than with other countries throughout the world.

Jackie: It seems the system really will bring stability to the currencies in Europe. But I'm sure that such a system must have some disadvantages. What are they?

Dennis: Well, the disadvantages that a country sees in the European Monetary System depend on the strength of the economy of the country.

Jackie: What do you mean?

Dennis: Well, the weaker nations have several disadvantages. For one thing, they cannot manipulate the exchange rates or simply follow the market as they have done in the past. Adjustments can be made when the value of a currency really does drop, but, if the system is to work at all, such adjustments must be very small and very infrequent. This means that these nations must work very hard to fight inflation and boost their economies or the fixed rate of exchange will force them to price their manufacturers right out of the market.

Jackie: It sounds like there might be quite a bit of risk for the weaker economies.

Dennis: There definitely is risk. But the benefits outweigh the risks. The biggest benefit is that the inflation will be decreased. Being in the system will help each nation to be able to carry out unpopular measures to stop inflation.

Jackie: What are some of those measures?

Dennis: Well, one measure is the control of wages. A country can moderate its wages because, if it doesn't, it may price itself out of the market. If wages are moderated, prices don't rise and inflation is decreased.

Jackie: What are the disadvantages for the countries with stronger economies?

Dennis: Well, these countries have exactly the opposite problem. They must learn to allow more inflation. Most of the countries with strong economies think that a little inflation is all right, but the final result is stability.

Jackie: That seems like a very desirable result. But how will the European Monetary System affect the rest of the world?

Dennis: There could be some definite effects on the rest of the world. Having the European Monetary System is going to encourage the nations which belong to it to trade more with each other. This might mean that they will trade less with the rest of the world. This could affect the U.S. and Japan both quite a lot because these countries trade with European nations a lot. We don't know if the system will really have that effect, however. We will have to wait and see.

Jackie: Well, Mr Rothfield, I appreciate your time and information very much. I will be looking forward to hearing you speak at the convention later this week.

Dennis: Thank you, Ms Lippleton. I'll look forward to reading what you write about us.

Exercise 2

Directions: Listen to the cassette once again. Then answer the following questions.

Section C: Emerson Books

Exercise 1

Directions: You will hear an interview between Mr Allstrom and Jackie Lippleton. Fill in the missing parts of the following outline as you listen to the conversation.

Jackie: It's so good of you to take some time to talk with me, Mr Allstrom.

Mr Allstrom: No problem. Jackie. I'm glad you have come by because I always like to talk about Emerson Books.

Jackie: I'd like to talk to you about Emerson Books.

Mr Allstrom: Well, actually, Emerson Books has gone through quite a transformation in the past few years. We've gone from a typical old-fashioned bookstore to a modern business that uses modern technology and mass-merchandising techniques to gain success. It takes a lot of know-how and a lot of money to be really successful in bookselling.

254

Jackie: What you said is so interesting. Tell me, what is the difference between an old-fashioned bookstore and the modern, business-oriented bookstores?

Mr Allstrom: In the old days, we would have small stores that carried stocks of books dependent on the manager's whims and the wholesaler's sales pitch. Some books would sell well, some would sell poorly, but we would just order books based on intuition, not based on sales statistics. We had no statistics. Similarly, our window displays were haphazardly designed. Who were we trying to attract into the store with our displays? Readers of popular books? Business people? University students? We didn't know because we had no method, no plan. We are in the retail business, and we must always respond to the whim of the customer.

Jackie: So how have you learned to respond to a customer's interests and desires?

Mr Allstrom: First of all, we wanted to get away from the old image of a dusty, poorly-lit bookstore. In our expansion plans, we called for a standardized architecture for the facade of our stores. Our window displays are now coordinated to match the interests of the local community: in one window we will have new releases and bestsellers, and in the other window we'll have "theme" displays like all books on marketing or anthropology, for example. Our store aisles are wide, not rammed with books, and our lights are bright, very bright. This highlights the colors of the book covers and gives the customers the impression that bookstores are for modern, lively people and not for dusty old university professors.

Jackie: That's still my impression of what a bookstore should be like.

Mr Allstrom: That kind of bookstore exists but it doesn't make a lot of money. Our managers used to scratch their heads when a customer asked for a book, but now they simply have to point to the proper area of the store. If the book isn't there, the store has updated lists of books on microfiche which tell whether the book is available, how much it costs, and when it could arrive from the wholesaler. Now that's service for our customers.

Jackie: What other kinds of technological marvels do you use in your stores besides microfiche?

Mr Allstrom: Our latest improvement has us all excited, Jackie. Each store is getting a computer terminal hooked into a central computer. In fact, the terminal will be a combination of a sales register and an inventory system.

Jackie: I've seen those fancy cash registers at some department stores. They make strange noises, too, when you are checking out. So why do you need an instant inventory system? Computers are expensive — couldn't you just close your doors twice a year and take inventory?

Mr Allstrom: We can't afford to wait six months to find out that we bought too few copies of one book and too many of another book. What happens if a person comes in looking for a certain book and we don't have it because it sold out the day before? That customer will walk out of the door and we will have lost a sale. But with a daily inventory system we will know how many copies of that book we have sold. It will show us a trend so we can anticipate our future needs. This way we can re-order a book before it sells out and for the books we can't sell right away, we can do one of the three things: not re-order the book, send the book back to the wholesaler, or put the book on sale at a reduced price.

Jackie: Now I understand the system and it sounds marvelous. Thanks again for your time, Mr Allstrom.

Mr Allstrom: So long!

Exercise 2

Directions: Listen to the cassette once again. Then answer the following questions.

Section D: Ben and Jerry
Exercise 1

Directions: Listen to the following passage carefully, and then fill in the blanks with the words you have heard from the passage.

Ben and Jerry don't look like owners of a multimillion-dollar business. They don't wear suits. Nor do they have a master's degree in business. What they look like is two hippies from the sixties. They have known each other since they were children. In their twenties, they decided to open an ice-cream business. So they took a five-dollar correspondence course in ice-cream making. After that, they opened their first store in Burlington, Vermont, in 1978. At no time did they realize that their store would grow into a 58-million-dollar business. Their ice cream became famous and so did their business philosophy. It is an unconventional corporation. It pays its suppliers more than market prices and pays its executives less. It issues a social performance report analyzing how well it did in the community.

Basically, Ben and Jerry's philosophy is a business that makes money in a community must give it back to the community. So 7.5 percent of its pretax profits goes automatically to charities. More unusual is that they print political messages, related to peace and environmental issues, on their ice-cream containers. Also, they believe in treating their employees well. Pay must be as equitable as possible between top managers and factory workers. Under no circumstances can anyone earn more than five times the salary earned by the lowest-paid worker. Now they are still working on making their business help the community more.

Exercise 2
Directions: Listen to the cassettes again and then answer the following questions.

Part Ⅲ: Listening Comprehension Test
Directions: In this Part, you will hear 10 short conversations con-

cerning offer and request between two speakers. After you have
heard each conversation, try to choose the best answer.

1. W: Would you tell me how I can get to the National Library?
   M: Sure, Let me give you a hand.
   Q: What's the man doing?

2. M: I can not work out this math problem.
   W: Why not come to me?
   Q: What does the woman mean?

3. W: Oh, I am a bit under the weather.
   M: You'd better go to the school clinic. Can I help you?
   Q: What does the man suggest?

4. M: Would you care for a biscuit?
   W: Not just at the moment, thank you. I'd rather have anoth-
      er piece of cake if I may.
   Q: What does the woman want now?

5. M: Hi, Alice, would you like to go to a movie tonight?
   W: Thanks, I'd love to. I haven't been to a movie for a long
      time.
   Q: What does the woman mean?

6. M: Oh, my boy, the question is too difficult for me. What
      shall I do?
   W: Don't worry. Let's sit down and try to figure it out.
   Q: What does the woman suggest?

7. W: Don't you feel like having a break?
   M: I'd rather we didn't. We have no time to lose.
   Q: What does the man mean?

8. W: Let me get you some drinks. What would you like to have,

tea or coffee?

M: It makes no difference actually, but I'd like to have the latter if you don't mind.

Q: What do we learn from this conversation?

9. M: The weather forecast says there will be rain tomorrow. Our holiday plan is spoiled.

W: Just cheer up! We might as well do something to make it up by having a party at home.

Q: What did the woman suggest?

10. W: Can't you be quiet? The baby is sleeping. You shouldn't have made such a big noise.

M: Then why not take the baby to the next room where it's quiet?

Q: What does the man suggest?

Unit Twenty-eight

Part I : Listening Practice

Section A: Agricultural Report
Exercise 1
Directions: You are going to hear an agricultural report. Listen carefully. Then fill in the form comparing the two plants.

Ducksalad is a water weed also known as duckweed. It grows rapidly and usually kills all the other plants in the same area. However, some people earn money by growing it. Israeli farmers sell duckweed in Europe, where it is used in salad.

When dried, duckweed has a protein content of between 35 and 50 percent. Soybean has about the same amount of protein, but when duckweed is grown at the right temperature it will increase its weight by 100 percent within two to four days. That is ten times faster than soybean. A private international organization has been supporting experiments with duckweed in Bangladesh for the past three years and more and more farmers have become interested in growing it. The reasons for the project are as follows:

First, Bangladesh is the perfect country for a duckweed project. The temperature is right for growth and the country has about 500,000 hectares of small, polluted water holes. That is what the kind of water duckweed needs to survive. Polluted water contains a lot of nitrogen, phosphorus and potassium. About 97 percent of the population in Bangladesh uses deep holes for human waste and much of the water drains into small ponds. The ponds also collect animal wastes and chemical fertilizers flowing from nearby fields.

The second reason is that duckweed grows rapidly, so it can provide very high-quality, low-cost animal feed. Farmers can use it to feed their domestic animals.

The third reason is that the farmers can earn a lot of money by raising duckweed. In addition to feeding their animals, farmers sell it in the market. It sells for about $27 a ton in Bangladesh. One hectare of duckweed is worth about ten times as much as one hectare of rice. In fact, a duckweed farmer in Bangladesh can earn US $2,000 a year, while a traditional farmer earns only about $100 a year.

In addition to providing farmers with a cash crop, duckweed can purify waste water. It takes 20 days to make polluted water Crystal clear and clean enough to drink.

Exercise 2
Directions: Listen to the tape again. Then give the four reasons why more and more Bangladeshi farmers have become interested in growing duckweed.

Section B: Recycling
Exercise 1
Directions: You are going to hear a radio announcement. Listen carefully then fill in the blanks to show how many of these materials

the people in the United States use.

Recycling saves. It saves money, energy, and natural resources. Consider the facts: Aluminum cans are very easy to recycle. But, every three months, we throw away enough aluminum to rebuild all of the commercial airplanes in the country. Yes, every three months, we could take all the aluminum cans we throw away and rebuild all the airplanes for all of the airlines in the country, Please think of that the next time you throw away a soda can.

And each year we throw away enough iron and steel to supply all of our car makers. If we recycled more metal, our automobile makers would never need any new iron and steel.

Every week, more than five hundred thousand trees are used to make newspapers. Imagine five hundred thousand trees. And two-thirds of these newspapers are thrown away.

This year, we'll throw away enough office and writing paper to build a wall twelve feet high that's three and a half meters. And that wall would be so long it would go from Los Angeles to New York. Imagine these papers, one on top of another, stacked twelve feet-three and a half meters — in a wall running all the way across the United States.

Every year, we throw away twenty-four million tons of leaves and grass clippings. Twenty-four million tons. Those leaves and grass take up space. They could be composted, allowed to rot or decay so that they could become fertilizer for soil. Compost helps farmers make soil better and richer.

We throw away enough glass bottles to fill the two tallest buildings in New York City every two weeks. Think of it, New York's tallest buildings, filled up like trash cans, full of glass bottles — every two weeks. These bottles could be recycled.

We throw away two and a half million plastic bottles every hour. Very few plastic bottles are ever recycled. Two and a half million bottles every hour — wasted!

Exercise 2

Directions: Listen to the tape again. Give brief answers to the questions you hear on the tape.

1. Why is recycling advocated by the speaker?
2. According to the speaker how can leaves and grass clippings be recycled?
3. Whom may the radio talk be sponsored by?

Exercise 3

Directions: Listen to the first part of the tape once more. Then write down as much information as you can from what you have heard.

Section C: Library Call Slip
Exercise 1

Directions: Listen to the dialogue carefully. Fill in the call slip with the information you hear on the tape.

M: Excuse me, miss.

F: Yes. May I help you?

M: I'm a new student here in the college. I've just come from China and I've never used a Western Library before. I wonder if you

264

could tell me how to find the book I need.

F: Do you know the title of the book?

M: Yes. It's Modern Europe.

F: Then you just look it up in the card catalog, that's the cards in those small drawers describing every book in our library.

M: I see.

F: If you don't know the title of a book, you can also find the book by looking under the author's name. For example, the author of this book is Paul H. Beik. You look under Beik and then Paul H. to find the book.

M: That sounds easy enough. Then. . .

F: Then you fill out the call slip with the information required. You hand in the call slip to the librarian behind the desk and she will find the book for you.

M: Excuse me. I'm really sorry to bother you again, but I don't know which is the call number of this book and what a call number is for.

F: The call number is the number in the top right corner of the card. It is used as a guide to find the book, as books are arranged numerically in the stacks. The call number of Modern Europe is 932.51.

M: Thank you very much for your help.

F: Not at all. That's what I'm here for. Hope you find what you need.

Exercise 2

Directions: Study the following statements and put them in ccorrect order according to the talk you hear. Put the numbers in the right circles.

Exercise 3

Directions: Listen to the dialogue again. Then give brief answers to the questions you hear on the tape.

1. What is a card catalog?
2. What is a call number for ?
3. How can you find a book if you don't know the book's title?

Section D: Call Number Systems
Exercise 1

Directions: Listen to the talk carefully. Then fill in the form with the information you hear from the talk.

There are two call-number systems in United States libraries, the Dewey decimal system and the Library of Congress system. Both systems break down all knowledge into categories that are then subdivided, so that every book in the world will have its own Dewey decimal call number and its own Library of Congress call number. Knowledge is divided into twenty-one main classes in the Library of Congress system.

The Dewey decimal system is more commonly used. It is divided into ten main classes. The following is its basic structure:

General works include subdivisions such as bibliographies, encyclopedias, periodicals, newspapers, etc. These materials are too general to go under any single subject.

Philosophy covers the subjects of ethics, logic, psychology, etc.

266

Under Religion you can find books on the Bible and the history and theology of Christian and non-Christian religions.

Under social sciences are there books on sociology, economics, education, etc.

Books on English and other languages, such as grammars and dictionaries, can be found in the section called Linguistics.

Pure Science covers the subjects of mathematics, biology, physics and chemistry.

If you are trying to find books on medicine, engineering, agriculture, home economics or business, you can look them up under the main class of Applied Science.

In Arts and Recreation there are books on architecture, painting, music, theater, sports, etc.

Literature covers poetry, drama, novels and essays from all countries and in all languages.

The last main class is History. In this section you can find books on geography, biography and history.

Exercise 2
Directions: Listen to the tape again and answer the following questions.

Exercise 3
Directions: Listen to the tape once more and fill in the subdivisions in each main class.

Part Ⅲ: Listening Comprehension Test
Directions: In this section, you will hear 10 short conversations

about negation. After you have heard each conversation, try to choose the best answer.

1. M: Isn't that a new book you're reading?
   W: This isn't the first time you've seen me with it.
   Q: What does the woman imply?

2. M: I can't believe you have never seen a giraffe.
   W: I haven't been to the zoo or to Africa. It's not surprising I haven't seen one before.
   Q: What would not describe the woman?

3. M: I'm not prepared for the test. Are you nervous?
   W: No, I'm not. I studied.
   Q: Which is true?

4. M: Isn't that the book I loaned you a while ago?
   W: I'm afraid I'm very bad at returning things.
   Q: What describes the woman's emotion?

5. M: I never drink water without ice.
   W: Don't you think that's bad for your stomach?
   Q: What would be the woman's advice?

6. M: You aren't going to sleep, are you?
   W: I've not had a good day. You can't blame me for trying to rest.
   Q: What will the man do next?

7. M: Wasn't that a good way to see the show?
   W: I think we could have had better seats.
   Q: Where were they?

8. M: It's always difficult to decide what not to do, isn't it?
   W: It isn't, if you think of what to do, not what to avoid.

268

Q: What would describe the man?

9. W: I don't believe we've ever met before, have we?

   M: We've been introduced at other parties. Don't you remember?

   Q: What does the man imply?

10. M: The ice is not cold if you fall on a patch covered with snow. Did you know that?

    W: No, but I don't think it makes any difference. If I fall in the snow, I'll be cold.

    Q: Where are they speaking?

Unit Twenty-nine

Part Ⅰ: Listening Practice

Section A: Talk on Creativity
Exercise 1
Directions: Listen carefully and fill in the blanks.

Albert Einstein once attributed the creativity of a famous scientist to the fact that he "never went to school, and therefore preserved the rare gift of thinking freely". There is undoubtedly truth in Einstein's observation; many artists and geniuses seem to view their schooling as a disadvantage. But such a truth is not a criticism of schools. It is the function of schools to civilize, not to train explorers. The explorer is always a lonely individual whether his or her pioneering be in art, music, science, or technology. The creative explorer of unmapped lands shares with the genius what William James described as the "faculty of perceiving in an unhabitual way." Insofar as schools teach perceptual patterns they tend to destroy creativity and genius. But if schools could somehow exist solely to cultivate genius, then society would break down. For the social order demands unity and widespread agreement, both traits that are destructive to creativity. There will always be conflict between the demands of society and the impulses of creativity and genius.

Exercise 2:

Directions: Listen again and then answer the following questions.

Section B: Science Report

Exercise 1

Directions: Listen to the report carefully and then take notes.

Can a machine act intelligently? Can a machine behave creatively? Both questions are impossible to answer since scientists cannot agree on definitions of intelligence and creativity. However, in answer to the question: can computers write poetry or music or play chess? The answer is "yes".

Machines do best in a kind of poetry with strict rules of composition. The Japanese Haiiko is a good example. The Haiiko contains only 17 syllables, and tries to create a mood or an illusion.

Computers have also composed music. One known composition by a computer was called "Eliot Sweet" for string quartette. It was composed using the rules of simple counter points. The piece, however, is not very interesting since musical quality is difficult to measure. Computers are less successful in this field.

Chess playing ability is something that can be measured. Consequently, computers can be programmed to play chess quite well. A computer at Northwestern University in Illinois has consistently won the annual computer chess championship. It also plays better chess than most human chess amateurs.

In 1973, the State Class D (not very good) chess Tournament in Massachusetts was won by a computer. The rule of the tournament did not say the players had to be human.

One expert thinks that some time in the future a computer will defeat the world chess champion.

In spite of numerous successes of computers in human occupations, their performance is merely competent, not outstanding. To say that some day computers will be better than man in thought is only speculation. That has not yet arrived if it arrives at all.

Exercise 2
Directions: Listen again and then fill in the blanks.

Section C: How to Select and Care for a Christmas Tree
Exercise 1
Directions: Listen to the passage and then answer the questions below.

Before they buy a Christmas tree, buyers would first ask, "Where should I get my tree?"

If you live in a large city or in suburbs, you may decide to go to a local Christmas tree store. These are set up for the sale of trees during the November and December period, or you may go directly to a Christmas tree farm to choose one.

Probably the first thing to look for is a tree with good, fresh, green needles that are soft to the touch. The second thing to look for is a tree that has good shape. If the tree is placed in a living room in front of a window, it needs to have a good appearance.

Once you have a tree, shake the tree well to get rid of the dead needles and pieces of grass before taking it into the house. For best results make a fresh cut at the base of your tree, then place the tree in a container of water. This is a good safeguard against the needles' drying out and becoming a fire danger.

Keep in mind that without water they would become dry, brown and dangerous. Some people have suggested putting chemicals into the water to reduce the fire danger. But ordinary water is satisfactory.

Exercise 2

Directions: Listen again and tell if these statements are True (T) or False (F).

Section D: A Visit

Directions: Listen to the following conversation, and then fill in the form with the information you hear from the tape.

A: Hi, Jane. How is your vacation?

B: Terrific! I went to Washington D. C. to visit my cousin. I saw the Jefferson Memorial, the Lincoln Memorial, the Smithsonian Institution, and the White House.

A: I've never been to Washington. What did you like the best?

B: Oh, the White House. Did you know that it's been the official home of our presidents since 1800 ? And every president except George Washington has lived in it.

A: I didn't know it was that old. Is it really as nice as everyone says it is?

B: It's only a two-storey building built of stone. But it's simple and dignified. It used to be called the president's house. But it was named the White House after the British burned it in the War of 1812. It had to be repainted, of course.

A: I remember now. The president then was James Madison. And his wife Dolly ran out of the burning building carrying Guber Sturant's portrait of Washington.

B: Yes, that's right. It's hanging in the East Room now.

A: How big is the White House?

B: It's big. Imagine 132 rooms is the large staff including the gardeners but the 18 acres outside. It has to be painted every four years.

A: How much ever were you allowed to see?

B: Not very much. Only 6 of the rooms are open to the public. It's a popular tour, and there is always a line of people waiting. They want to look at their property, I guess.

A: Their property?

B: Sure. The White House is owned by the people of the United States. We elect the leaders who live in it.

A: But can just anyone go inside?

B: Of course. Anyone can see our president's home.

Part Ⅲ : Listening Comprehension Test

Directions: In this part, you will hear three passages. Some questions will follow each of the first two passages, but no question will be asked at the end of the last passage. The questions and the passages will be read only once. You are to choose the best answer or write down your answer on the space provided below.

Passage Ⅰ

"Fingers were made before forks." When a person gives up good manners, puts aside knife and fork, and dives into his food, someone is likely to repeat that saying.

The fork was an ancient agricultural tool, but for centuries no one thought of eating with it. Not until the eleventh century, when a young lady from Constantinople brought her fork to Italy, did the custom reach Europe.

By the fifteenth century the use of the fork was widespread in Italy. The English explan-ation was that Italians were averse to eating food touched with fingers, "seeing all men's fingers are not alike clean". English travelers kept their friends in stitches while describing this ridiculous Italian custom.

Anyone who used a fork to eat with was laughed at in England for the next hundred years. Men who used forks were thought to be sissies, and women who used them were called show-offs and overnice. Not until the late 1600's did using a fork become a common custom.

1. How was the custom of eating with a fork developed?
2. What did the English travelers think of the use of fork in Italy?
3. When did the use of forks become common in England?

Passage II

The old idea that child prodigies "burn themselves out" or "overtax their brains" in the early years and, therefore, are prey to failure and (at worst) mental illness is just so much myth. As a matter of fact, the outstanding thing that happens to bright kids is that they are very likely to grow into bright adults.

To find this out, 1,500 gifted persons were followed up to their thirty-fifth year with these results:

On adult intelligence tests, they scored as high as they had as children. They were, as a group, in good health, physically and mentally. Eighty-four percent of their group were married and seemed content with their lives.

About 70 percent had graduated from college, though only 30 percent had graduated with honors. A few had even flunked out, but nearly half of these had returned to graduate.

Of the men, 80 percent were in one of the professions or in business-executive or semi-professional jobs. The women who had remained single had office, business, or professional occupations.

The group had published 90 books and 1,500 articles in scientific, scholarly, and literary magazines and had collected more than 100 patents.

In a material way they didn't do badly either. Average income was considerably higher among the gifted people, especially the men, than that for the country as a whole, despite their comparative youth when last surveyed.

In fact, far from being strange, maladjusted people locked in an ivory tower, most of the gifted were turning their early promise into practical reality.

4. Which of the following is discussed by the author?

5. What did intelligence tests show?

6. What can you infer from the passage?

Passage Ⅲ

If you are like most people, your intelligence varies from season to season. You are probably a lot sharper in the spring than you are at any other time of year. A noted scientist, Ellsworth Huntington (1876~1947), concluded from other men's work and his own among peoples in different climates, that climate and temperature have a definite effect on our mental abilities.

He found that cool weather is much more favorable for creative thinking than is summer heat. This does not mean that all people are less intelligent in the summer than they are during the rest of the year. It does mean, however, that the mental abilities of large numbers of people tend to be lowest in the summer.

Spring appears to be the best period of the year for thinking. One reason may be that in the spring man's mental abilities are affected by the same factors that bring about great changes in all nature.

Fall is the next-best season, then winter. As for summer, it seems to be a good time to take a long vacation from thinking!

7. According to the passage, your intelligence probably varies _____

    _____.

8. Ellsworth Huntington decided that climate and temperature have _____

    _____.

9. The two best seasons for thinking seem to be _____

    _____.

10. According to the passage, any vacations from thinking should be taken _____

    _____.

Unit Thirty

Part I : Listening Practice

Section A: Space Shuttle Flight
Exercise 1

Directions: You are going to hear a news report about America's fiftieth space shuttle flight. There were a lot of firsts on this flight. Listen carefully. Then write down the firsts you hear in order.

America's fiftieth space shuttle flight has ended successfully. The Endeavor space shuttle landed Sunday at Kennedy Space Center in Florida. It was Endeavor's second flight, but there were a lot of firsts in its eight-day earth orbit.

The crew included the first Japanese scientist to fly in an American space shuttle, the first black woman astronaut and the first husband and wife team. It was also the first American space shuttle flight concerned mainly with Japanese research.

The crew did forty-four of the experiments inside a science laboratory. Thirty-four of the experiments were provided by Japan. The United States provided seven. Two involved joint research. Most of the experiments dealt with the effect of the lack of gravity on living systems and materials such as crystal. A crew member also studied different kinds of glass, ceramics and metals to learn if they could be improved. Japan wanted to study methods of building these materials in space.

The Endeavor crew did several experiments concerned with life science. They studied how weightlessness affects plant cells and animal cells. They also studied how lack of gravity affects the early development of animals. One such experiment involved frogs. Female frogs were carried on the flight. Some of their eggs were fertilized during the flight, while other eggs were fertilized on the ground before launch. The eggs were permitted to develop into tadpoles, which are the first form of frog life, swimming in water. The Washington Post newspaper reports that the tadpoles from eggs fertilized in space appeared to act nominally. However, the tadpoles from eggs fertilized on the earth swam in strange circles and didn't appear to act normally. The tadpoles will grow into frogs on earth, then scientists will let the frogs reproduce and study the results of space flight on frog development.

Exercise 2
Directions: Listen again. Fill in the form with the information you hear on the tape.

Exercise 3
Directions: Choose A, B, C or D to answer the following questions.
1. What did most of the experiments deal with?
2. What materials did the crew members study?
3. In the experiment with frogs what did not appear to act normally?

Section B: Cold and Flu Fighter
Exercise 1

Directions: You will hear a conversation between two speakers. Listen carefully and then choose the best answers to the questions from the four choices given.

M: How has this winter been for you so far this year, Jane?

W: I'm fine so far. Much better than last winter, though flu and cold viruses are rampant.

M: As a flight attendant, you are exposed to all those people who may be carrying organisms, but how could you keep from being infected?

W: I keep drinking more and more liquids and what I always do under those circumstances — this is another trick I have for flying — is I take vitamin C in a large dose before I fly and another one when I get to where I'm going. Um, vitamin C does not exactly prevent colds. You are — you are just as likely to be infected with or without vitamin C, but it does seem to be able to abort many colds and to shorten the symptoms of many colds. It doesn't work for everybody, and it doesn't work for all colds, but why not take the chance if you can get rid ofthe symptomsfast and fight that thing off ? I think that's the better part of it.

So I take about a thousand milligrams of vitamin C before I fly, and I take another thousand four hours later or when I arrive. And that seems to be helpful to a lot of people. I have a few friends who — in fact the former head of the Federal Aviation Agency — had this problem of getting pneumonia whenever he flew on a long trip, and this was very devastating to him, and my advice about drinking liquids, avoiding alcohol and caffeine, and taking vitamin C before and after he flew has really helped him a great deal.

1. According to the conversation, how was Jane last winter?
2. What does Jane do by profession?
3. What is Jane's advice to fight against colds?

Exercise 2
Directions: Listen to the tape again and fill in the blanks.

Exercise 3
Directions: Listen to the conversation again and then give a brief summary of the last part of the conversation.

Section C: Discoveries of Sigmund Freud (1)
Exercise 1
Directions: Listen to the talk carefully. Then write down the three methods that Freud used to study mental and emotional problems.

Today we are going to talk about the discoveries of Sigmund Freud who was the first person to make a serious study of the human mind. For this he used three methods, hypnosis, long talks with patients and study of dreams in order to learn the cause of mental and emotional problems.

Freud found that the first two or three years of one's life are important to emotional growth. He said that at birth a child knows only its own body. This was the beginning of emotional growth. A newborn baby knowing only body reminded Freud of the ancient Greek story of Narcissus.

Narcissus was a young Greek man who sat by a pool one day. He looked down and saw his face in the clear water. He was so pleased by his beautiful face that he just sat and sat. He sat so long that he grew roots and became a flower, the narcissus.

Freud said children during the first month of life know only themselves. They are like Narcissus. So Freud called the first stage of life narcissism. He said that all children enter this stage at birth, but as they grow older, their emotions develop. They pass through this stage and begin to learn that there are other people around them.

Freud learned that some of his patients never left the stage of narcissism, although they grew up in every other way. They were intelligent and successful, but their emotional growth had been frozen in narcissism. He said this could happen if a child, when small and dependent, is rejected and does not get the warmth, security and love it so urgently needs. The failure to satisfy a child's basic needs can make it remain permanently in the stage of narcissism. The child when grown up still searches for those things he didn't get as a baby.

Freud said that a person can also be frozen in narcissism as a child if he or she is given too much attention, love and warmth. Such children may be over protected. They are not given a chance to reach out and learn for themselves, because their parents quickly satisfy their every need. This prevents them from growing emotionally. They become fixed and frozen in narcissism. Such children, when adults, can't find pleasure in others, only in themselves.

Freud said they were narcissistic.

Exercise 2

Directions: Write down the key words in the story of Narcissus.

Exercise 3

Directions: Listen to the tape again. Then fill in the blanks in note form.

Section D: Discoveries of Sigmund Freud (2)
Exercise 1

Directions: Listen to the tape carefully. Then write down the key words in the story of Oedipus.

Freud said that gradually children grow out of narcissism to begin the next stage of life. This starts when a child learns that there are others besides itself. It offers an early form of love to others. Little boys begin to love their mothers. Little girls start to love their fathers. At this stage another emotion begins to appear, jealousy. A little boy who begins to love his mother learns that someone else loves her — his father. A little girl also learns that she must share her love for her father with her mother. Freud called the second stage of life the Oedipal stage. He named it after Oedipus, an ancient Greek. Oedipus as a child was separated from his parents and as an adult he killed his father and married his own mother, not knowing that they were his parents. When he found out, he put out his eyes to punish himself.

Freud said that children pass through the Oedipal stage with help and understanding from parents. Soon the children turn to other children, boys to boys and girls to girls. They even develop a love for their friends. When they grow older, a young boy may have a girlfriend and a girl, a boyfriend. Freud said this kind of early love is necessary to develop strong feelings of love later in life. He said children express their emotions again and again, like actors learning the parts they are going to play, when the children become adults, they are prepared to love, mate and have children. Freud believed that some children do not successfully pass through this second stage — the Oedipal stage. He saw that this was so in some of his patients and even in himself.

Freud believed that he had been frozen in the Oedipal stage of life. At the age of 40 he still felt the same jealousy of his father that he had had as a child. He also felt the same strong feelings for his mother that he had had as a child. He said he had an Oedipus Complex and he tried to break the bonds that kept him frozen in this early emotional stage of life. This was a painful experience for him, but he worked at it until he succeeded. He searched deeply into his life, his memories and his dreams. He faced his Oedipus complex and found out why he suffered from it. When he understood how it had happened, he became free of it. It was at this time of his life that he wrote to a friend, "To be completely honest with oneself is good but painful. My neurosis has given in at last."

Exercise 2

Directions: Listen to the tape again. Fill in the blanks with the information you get from the talk.

Part Ⅲ: Listening Comprehension Test

Section A

Directions: In this section, you will hear five short conversations between two speakers. At the end of each conversation a question will be asked about what was said. Each conversation and question will be spoken only once. After you have heard each question, try to choose the best answer.

1. W: My English teacher suggested that I come in and borrow a French-English Dictionary.

   M: Of course Miss, you are welcome to use our dictionaries. They cannot be taken out from the library. Wouldn't it be better if you could get one of your own?

   Q: What did the man suggest that the girl do?

2. W: I'm going to change the color of my hair when I am 50 years old.

   M: You are? Well, when I am 50, I'll grow a beard.

   Q: What can we learn in the conversation about the present ages of these people?

3. M: Do you know the people who live in that old house?

   W: There's a professor named Jones living in it now. He used to share it with his sister, a widow. but she's gone to live with her married daughter, I hear.

   Q: What did the woman tell the man about the old house?

4. W: I'm afraid there won't be time to do any more today. I must get to the post office and it's about to close.

   M: All right. We'll find that other cavity tomorrow. Just don't eat anything like steaks for the next few hours.

Q: Where did the above conversation most probably take place?

5. M: Don't you think John and Jim are telling the truth?

   W: It doesn't seem likely, It would be hard to write two compositions so much alike unless one of them was copying from the other.

   Q: What seems to be the woman's opinion?

Section B

Directions: In this section, you will hear three mini-talks. Some questions will follow each of the mini-talks, but no question will be asked at the end of the last talk. The mini-talks, and the questions will be read only once. You are to write down your answer in the space provided below.

Mini-talk One

In an earlier age, there was a great distinction in the public mind between science and engineering. Whereas the scientist was thought of as an intellectual, motivated by a desire for knowledge and order, the engineer was thought of as a busy, practical person, involved in producing something for which the public was willing to pay. The scientist might discover the laws of nature, but the engineer would be the one to exploit them for use and profit.

Historically, however, the distinction has not been valid. In every century, noted theoretical scholars were deeply involved in the practical application of their own work. For example, in the seventeenth century, Christian Huygeness, a Dutch astronomer, mathematician, and physicist who developed theorems on centrifugal force and wave motion also developed the first accurate timepiece. In the eighteenth century, the British mathematician and philosopher Sir Isaac Newton was credited not only with advancing theories of mechanics and optics, but also with inventing the reflecting telescope, a direct application of his theory. In the nineteenth century, the French chemist and bacteriologist Louis Pasteur first proposed theories of disease, and then set about the discovery of vaccines for anthrax and rabies, as well as the process for purification that bears his name to this day.

I propose that the popular detachment of science from engineering has not provided us with a useful model for comparison, and perhaps not even a historically correct one.

6. According to public opinion in the past, how was a scientist different from an engineer?

7. Who was Christian Huygens?

8. What was the lecturer's opinion about science?

Mini-talk Two

Today I want to help you with a study on reading method known as SQ3R. The letters stand for five steps in the reading process: Survey, Question, Read, Review, Recite. Each of the steps should be done carefully and in the order mentioned.

In all study reading, a survey should be the first step. Survey means to look quickly. In study reading you need to look quickly at titles, words in darker or larger print, words with capital letters, illustrations, and charts. Don't stop to read complete sentences. Just look at the important divisions of the material.

The second step is question. Try to form questions based on your survey. Use the question words who, what, when, where, why and how.

Now you are ready for the third step. Read. You will be rereading the titles and important words that you looked at in the survey. But this time you will read the examples and details as well. Sometimes it is useful to take notes while you read. I have had students who preferred to underline important points, and it seemed to be just as useful as note-taking. What you should do, whether you take notes or underline, is to read actively. Think about what you are reading as a series of ideas, not just a sequence of words.

The fourth step is review. Remember the questions that you wrote down before you read the material? You should be able to answer them now. You will notice that some of the questions were treated in more detail in the reading. Concentrate on those. Also review material that you did not consider in your questions.

The last step is recite. Try to put the reading into your own words. Summarize it either in writing or orally.

SQ3R — survey, question, read, review, and recite.

9. What do the letters in the SQ3R method represent?
10. What does the word "survey" mean?
11. What does the lecturer mean by saying "to read actively"?

Mini-talk Three

Security and commodity exchanges are trading posts where people meet who wish to buy or sell. The exchanges themselves do no trading; they merely provide a place where prospective buyers and sellers can meet and conduct their business.

Wall Street, although the best known, is not the only home of exchanges in the United States. There are the cotton exchanges in New Orleans and Chicago; the Mercantile Exchange, which deals in many farm products, in Chicago; and grain exchanges in many of the large cities of the Midwest. Some exchanges, like the Chicago Board of Trade, provide market services for several kinds of products. These trading posts where products may be bought or sold are called commodity exchanges.

The security exchanges, on the other hand, are meeting places where stocks and bonds are traded. Like the commodity exchanges, they help serve the economic life of the country. But when their operations get out of hand, they may become very dangerous. In 1929, the security exchanges, or stock market, contributed to a crash — a sudden, sharp decline in the value of securities. Many people lost fortunes; many corporations were bankrupted; many workers lost their jobs. The Crash of 1929 has been attributed to many causes, among them wild and unwise speculation by many people and dishonest practices on the part of some businessmen and of some members of the exchanges.

Today, however, investing through security exchanges and trading on commodity exchanges have been made safer by regulations set up by the exchanges themselves and by regulations of the United States government. In 1922, the government instituted the Commodity Exchange Commission which operates through the Department of Agriculture; and in 1934, the Securities and Exchange Commission, to protect investors and the public against dishonest practices on the exchanges.

12. Security and commodity exchanges are meeting places for buyers

289

and sellers of _____
_____.

13. A sudden, sharp decline in the value of securities is called _____
_____

14. Among the reasons for the Crash of 1929 were _____
_____

15. You can infer that _____.

Simulated Listening Test 3

Section A

Directions: In this section, you will hear nine short conversations between two speakers. After you have heard each conversation, try to choose the best answer.

1. M: How did you find your job? Was it advertised in the paper?

   W: I looked and looked for months without finding anything. Then a friend told me about this job. So I applied and got it!

   Q: How did the woman learn about the job opening?

2. W: Finding this china cabinet was a real stroke of luck. Because of the scratch on the side, the dealer charged me $50 less than the regular price.

   M: You were lucky, and with a little polish the scratch won't even show.

   Q: Why is the woman pleased?

3. W: Have you seen that huge new building going up near the market?

   M: Yes, I can't figure out what it's going to be. Not an apartment building? Not a hotel? Probably a bank.

   Q: What does the man think the building will be?

4. M: Did you get to the post office before it closed?

   W: Yes. The xerox machine was out of order, but I did buy the

291

postcards you need.

Q: What did the woman do at the post office?

5. W: What time is your mother arriving?

M: She was supposed to catch the noon bus but called to say she missed it. So she plans to take the 3:30 bus which will get her here about dinner time.

Q: When will the man's mother probably arrive?

6. W: Have you read Mario Puzo's lastest bestseller yet?

M: I've read practically all of his novels but haven't seen that one yet.

Q: What are the man and the woman discussing?

7. M: I bought these towels as a gift last week but have just discovered that they are the wrong color. So I want to return them.

W: If you have your receipt, I can give you credit for the purchase. But I can't refund your money.

Q: Where does this conversation take place?

8. W: Why don't you go to bed, Jack? You look so tired.

M: I have to finish this assignment first. It's giving me a hard time.

W: It's not as important as sleep at this hour.

M: All right. I'll go to sleep soon.

Q: Why is Jack up late?

9. M: Well, what did you think of the movie?

W: I don't know why I let you talk me into going. I just don't like violence.

M: I didn't realize there would be quite so much. Despite everything, though, the story was good.

W: Yes, it was very exciting and well written.

Q: Why does the woman object to the movie?

Section B

Directions: In this section, you will hear two short passages. After you have heard the passages and questions, try to choose the best answer from the four choices given by marking the corresponding letter (A, B, C, or D).

Passage I

The Office of Computer Service has been set up to help all members of the university community. Our main activities include implementing student and faculty research and providing instruction in computer and information science. If you are interested in making extensive use of our services which, by the way, are free for full-time students and faculty members, please observe the following procedures.

1. Submit a written summary of your project to us with a detailed description of the computer help you will need.

2. Make an appointment with one of our staff members to discuss your project and set up a work schedule for your project. One staff member will be assigned to your project and work on it with you until completion.

Questions:

10. What does the Office of Computer Service do?

11. How is the cost of using the computer service determined?

12. What can be best said about the procedure described for using the Office of Computer Service?

Passage II

We often hear people talking about the generation gap. The name is new but the idea is old. Young people and their parents don't understand each other. The world keeps changing. There has always been a gap between generations. Old Mr Ellis thinks he understands what has happened:

" When I was a boy, I thought the world was a beautiful place. My life was very pleasant. But when I was older I learned about people who were treated badly, people who didn't have enough to eat. I wanted to help them, and married a girl who wanted to help them too. We went to meetings and talked a lot, but it didn't seem to make much difference."

" Our children grew up in a world at war. They didn't know when the fighting would stop. They wanted their children to have nice clothes and toys. They didn't want to think about the future. They thought nothing could be done about it."

" Now I have grandchildren and they have their own ideas. They are trying to make the world better. They are trying to help other people. They are making people listen to them. I'm proud of their generation."

Questions:

13. What is the passage about?
14. What is Mr Ellis' attitude toward his grandchildren?
15. Which of the following statements is not true according to old Mr Ellis?

Simulated Listening Test 4

Section A

Directions: In this section, you will hear nine short conversations between two speakers. At the end of each conversation, a third voice will ask a question about what was said. Both the conversations and the questions will be spoken only once. After each question there will be a pause, you must choose the best answer from the four choices given by marking the corresponding letter (A, B, C or D).

1. M: Cynthia says that friendship isn't love, but that one cannot exist without the other.

   W: That's an overgeneralization. She should define both concepts first.

   Q: What does the woman think about Cynthia's opinion?

2. M: All you need to open a savings account is $ 20. But in order to earn reasonable interest you should maintain a balance of at least $ 2,000.

   W: I only have $ 200 but I'll open an account anyway.

   Q: What information does the man give the woman?

3. M: The Consul's reception will start at 7: 00, so please be ready at this time when I come to pick you up.

   W: I'm always ready when you come to pick me up. There's no need for you to be so fussy about it.

Q: What does the man's comment imply?

4. W: When does Mary have to hand in her assignment?

   M: Before the end of this quarter. She got an incomplete last quarter and it will become an F if she doesn't make it up on time.

   Q: What will happen if Mary doesn't turn in her assignment on time ?

5. W: Have you ever put one of these together before?

   M: No, never. But I think if we carry out these instructions exactly, we won't have any trouble.

   Q: What is important for them to do?

6. M: If you'd like us to send the packages to you, Miss, they won't take long to arrive.

   W: There is no rush. Could you please have them delivered this week?

   Q: What does the woman mean?

7. M: My typing isn't dark enough and the paper doesn't look good.

   W: Why not change the typewriter ribbon and see if that will help?

   Q: What would the woman do?

8. W: The phone bill was $160 this month. Someone must have made several international calls without keeping me informed.

   M: I'm sorry, Mrs Jones. I forgot to tell you that I called my girlfriend in Italy a couple of times.

   Q: What's the youth supposed to do when he makes a long distance call ?

9. W: Do you like your new room?

   M: It's nice to have enough space for all my things, so I'm glad I moved. But I miss my friends and neighbors and that beautiful view. I especially miss living so close to the school.

   Q: How does the man's new room compare with the room he had before?

Section B

Directions: In this section, you will hear two short passages. At the end of each passage, there will be some questions. You will hear both the passages and the questions only once. After each question there will be a pause. During the pause, you must choose the best answer from the four choices given by marking the corresponding letter (A, B, C or D).

Passage I

The first English dictionary was published in 1604. The dictionary, compiled by Robert Cawdrey, was actually nothing more than a list of about 3, 000 difficult words, each followed by a one-word definition. Dictionaries published during the 1600's followed Cawdrey's lead. Around 1700 one dictionary maker, John Kersey, did define easy words as well as hard ones.

A man named Dr Samuel Johnson changed all this. In 1755 Dr Johnson produced the first modern dictionary. He included in his dictionary all important words, both easy and hard, and he gave good meanings. He also gave good sentences to show how each word was actually used in speech and in writing. By the end of the 1700's most dictionary makers had followed Johnson's lead. Dictionaries were getting better and better.

The 1800's saw the greatest improvement in the quality of dictionaries. In England scholars planned and prepared the Oxford English Dictionary, a twenty-volume work. One of the most interesting features of the Oxford Dictionary is its word histories. It traces the history of each word from its earliest recorded use up to the time of the printing of the dictionary.

Questions 10 to 12 are based on the passage you've just heard.

10. What best describes the first English Dictionary?

11. Who produced the first modern dictionary?

12. What was the most interesting feature of the Oxford Dictionary?

Passage Ⅱ

And now for the consumer information portion of today's show. Here's a letter from a listener in Maytown. She says: "About halfway through tonight's tuna fish casserole, my husband and I were horrified to discover that the tuna had bits of glass in it. This glass was undetectable until eaten. There is absolutely no excuse for such a situation to exist. Such carelessness could be deadly."

Dr Gene Smith, our consumer information specialist here at WKWK radio replies: " During the canning process, the ingredients normally found in sea food sometimes form a clear crystalline substance called Struvite. The Struvite crystals look very much like chips of glass but they are harmless. The U. S. Food and Drug Administration suggests a simple home test for anyone who finds a glass-like particle in canned sea food. Place the particle in warmed vinegar for a few minutes. If it dissolves it is Struvite. If it doesn't dissolve it isn't Struvite. Cooking the food especially carefully or adding more vinegar to it won't work. Serve something else and complain to the canner and the Food and Drug Administration."

Questions 13 to 15 are based on the passage you've just heard.

13. According to Dr Smith, what is Struvite?

14. According to Dr Smith, what should one do if one finds Struvite in canned sea food?

15. If one finds particles in canned sea food which are not struvite, what should one do?

Simulated Listening Test 5

Section A

Directions: In this section, you will hear nine short conversations between two speakers. After you have heard each conversation, try to choose the best answer.

1. W: I met Peter last week in New York. He doesn't know when he is leaving the country.

   M: Oh, he knows now. He called me yesterday and said that he is leaving for Iran next week.

   Q: What news did the woman hear from the man?

2. M: Have you heard whether George will have to have that operation or not?

   W: That's what I called to tell you. When I visited the hospital this noon, I learned they had operated around 9 o'clock. The doctor seems to think that George is going to be all right, now.

   Q: What information did the woman give the man about George?

3. W: I'm sorry I caused your uncle so much trouble.

   M: Don't worry about it. He is the sort of man who is never happy unless he has something to complain about.

   Q: What can we learn about the man's uncle from this conversation?

4. W: Did the movie have a happy ending?

   M: It was impossible to tell whether the girl was going to die in the war or come home and marry her childhood sweetheart.

   Q: What did the man say about the end of the movie?

5. M: Do you need much time at the shopping center?

   W: Not really, I want to buy a pan for my grandmother's birthday and a few things for school. How about you?

   Q: Where is the woman going?

6. W: I was on a No. 7 bus yesterday. Someone stepped on my toe and didn't even bother to apologize.

   M: Young men nowadays have no manners at all.

   Q: What does the man think of young people?

7. M: Miss, could you please tell me if this is where the uptown bus stops?

   W: No, the downtown bus stops here, so I think your bus stops across the street.

   Q: What is the situation?

8. M: Is it possible for you to work late this evening, Miss Frost? I'm afraid there's some work we must finish this evening. I'm sure I can't manage it by myself.

   W: Work late ? I... I suppose so, if you really think it's necessary.

   Q: Who do you think the woman is?

9. W: How do you feel about flying?

   M: I don't mind flying. What I don't like is not being able to keep an eye on my luggage. Whenever the man at the airport takes it away I never expect to see it again.

   Q: What is the man worried about?

Section B

Directions: In this section, you will hear two short passages. After you have heard the passages and questions, try to choose the best answer from the four choices given by marking the corresponding letter (A, B, C or D).

Passage I

Appalachian Airlines will begin passenger service at Charlotte Airport Thursday with morning and afternoon departures daily to Atlanta, and nonstop service to Washington, D. C. , with connections in Washington for Cleveland, New York, and Boston.

Tired of being crowded aboard large airplanes ? Appalachian Airlines will use comfortable Boeing 737 twin jets with a capacity to seat 106 passengers. There is more room for your underseat luggage, and more room for you.

Most flights will include breakfast and lunch catered by Charlotte's finest restaurants and served by one of Appallachian's courteous flight attendants.

Next time you need to travel, be good to yourself. Fly comfortably. Fly Appalachian Airlines. For reservations or more information, call your travel agent, or call the Appalachian Airlines toll-free number: 800-565-7000. That is 800-565-7000 for reservations to Atlanta, Washington, D. C. , Cleveland, New York, or Boston.

Questions 10 to 12 are based on the passage you've just heard.

10. What is an advantage of taking Appalachian Airlines?

11. Where do passengers get a connecting flight for Cleveland?

12. When do flights leave Charlotte for Atlanta?

Passage Ⅱ

In the 19th century it was common to hear people in Europe and America say that the resources of the sea were unlimited. For example, a noted biologist writing in the mid 1800s commented that all of the great sea fisheries are inexhaustible. Today there's evidence that the resources of the sea are as seriously threatened as those of the land and the air and the concern of conservationists now includes herring and cod as well as the African elephant, the Indian tiger and the American eagle. Further, the threat to fish is more alarming in some ways than the threat to birds and land animals because fish are a much needed food resource. Many people throughout the world depend on fish as an important part of their diets and a decline in the fish supply could have extensive effects on hunger and population. Fishermen in the N. Atlantic alone annually harvest 20 billion pounds of fish to satisfy food demands. But it is important to recognize that these practices can not continue without depleting fish resources within the next few years.

Sea resources are rapidly declining in many parts of the world and the problem can not be ignored. It is only with care and planning in this generation that the food supplies of the sea can continue for future generations.

Questions 13 to 15 are based on the passage you've just heard.

13. According to the speaker what was the attitude in the 19th century toward resources of the sea?

14. What does the speaker emphasize as a reason for maintaining sea resources?

15. Which of the following best describe the purpose of the lecture?

Answer Key

Unit One

Part I : Listening Practice

Section A: Taking a Photo

Exercise 1   a4   b5   c2   d6   e3   f1

Exercise 2   6   4   2   3   1   5

Photos, coin, stool, dial, background, flash

Section B: About a Film

Exercise 1   1. A man

2. She forgets to lock the French windows.

3. The phone doesn't work.

4. She rushes up the stairs and locks herself in the bathroom.

Exercise 2   3   1   5   2   6   4

Section C: Inviting Some People

Express Company: 1. B   2. B   3. A   4. C   5. B

Section D: Express Company

1. Prepaid express bag service   major cities $ 10

Buy a bag in advance.

Call for a quick pick up

2. Same day service   Within the city $ 8   They will go
to you.

3. Express road service   Any town   Depends on   For
larger packages

distance and weight

For further details call:

Tel: 33445656

Ask: for the sales department

Part Ⅲ: Listening Comprehension Test

1. C 2. A 3. D 4. C 5. A 6. D 7. D 8. B
9. D 10. C 11. B 12. A 13. A14. C 15. C

Your Notes:

_____

_____

_____

_____

_____

_____

_____

_____

_____

_____

_____

Unit Two

Part Ⅰ: Listening Practice

Section A: Looking for a Flat
1. 34 New Street in Kanden
2. £75 including gas and electricity
3. one bedroom flat, central heating, small kitchen, bathroom, washing machine
4. Mrs. Green
5. 4 o'clock this afternoon

Section B: Finding out the House Rules
    1. Don't allow a cat to go upstairs.
    2. No smoking in a bedroom
    3. Don't stick pictures with sellotape on the wall.
    4. Close the window when you go out.
    5. Don't put the kettle on the chest of drawers.

Section C: Apartments for Rent
Exercise 1
Thomas Street   University Avenue
Taft Road   Metcalf Street
Exercise 2
1. Metcalf Street   3. University Avenue
2. Thomas Street   4. Taft Road

Section D: Completing an Insuranle Form

Home Contents Insurance

Current policy number:	H3067B
Client's name:	Mrs Riley
Adress of property:	No. 15, Cliff Street
Current insurance cover:	$ 50,000
New insurance cover:	$ 80,000
Special items	Value of item
1. A video camera	$ 5,000
2. A portable computer	$ 4,000
3. A diamond ring	$ 20,000

Part Ⅲ Listening Comprehension Test

1. C 2. B 3. C 4. C 5. B 6. B 7. B 8. C

9. C 10. B 11. C 12. C 13. B 14. D 15. C

Your Notes:

_____

_____

_____

_____

_____

_____

_____

_____

_____

Unit Three

Part I : Listening Practice

Section A: Describing Different People
1. Sex: female
   Age: about 35
   Height: about average
   Hair: Long black
   Others: glasses, yellow flower
2. Sex: male
   Age: an older man about seventy
   Height: Rather short, about five feet or five feet two
   Hair: Grey, large mustache
   Others: white flower in jacket
3. Sex: female
   Age: quite young, about thirty
   Height: really tall
   Hair: blond
   Others: carrying red flowers
4. Sex: male
   Age: about forty-five
   Height: very tall
   Hair: very long, dark
   Others: no flower; wearing a T-shirt saying " Bruce Springs Is
           the Boss".

Section B: At the Doctor's
1. A 2. B 3. A 4. A 5. B

Section C: Leaving a Message
Exercise 1 1. Petty 2. Jenny 3. 4
Exercise 2 1. a hairdryer   2. ring
            3. the end of May   4. shoe
Exercise 3 8 5 3 7 2 4 6 9 1

Part Ⅲ: Listening Comprehension Test

1. C 2. D 3. C 4. C 5. B 6. C 7. C 8. D
9. D 10. B

Your Notes:

_____
_____
_____
_____
_____
_____
_____
_____
_____
_____
_____
_____
_____

Unit Four

Part I : Listening Practice

Section A: Telephoning about Jobs

Exercise 1   A. 4   B. 3   C. 1   D. 2

Exercise 2   1. part-time, Saturday and Sunday, eight hours a day

2. full-time, Tuesday through Sunday, from 5 to about 12. Pay is $3. 35 an hour.

3. working nights; five or six days a week

4. a weekend job; three evenings a week, Hours are five to midnight.

Section B: Talking about Jobs

Exercise 1   Diane — waitress   Tracy — typist

Gred — car salesman

Joe — businessman

Exercise 2   1. F   2. T   3. F   4. F   5. F   6. F   7. F

Section C: Same Job or a New Job

1. Liza new job   2. Tom same job

3. Brian new job   4. Kay new job

5. Janice new job

Section D: Interview about a Job

Al Employment Agency

1. Full Name: Jessica Richards

2. Address: 33 Landseer Road, Newtown
3. Tel: _____
4. Date of Birth: Mach 19th, 1980
5. Education: Secondary
6. Examinations passed: English, Chemistry, Maths, French, Physics, and Biology
7. Interests (hobbies & sports): playing the piano, in a jazz band, water-skiing
8. Experience? Previous posts: lab assistant
9. Post or position required: lab assistant
10. Any special requests: no

Part Ⅲ: Listening Comprehension Test

1. C 2. D 3. A 4. C 5. A 6. C 7. D 8. B
9. B 10. D

Your Notes:

_____

_____

_____

_____

_____

_____

_____

_____

_____

Unit Five

Part Ⅰ: Listening Practice

Section A:　Shopping

Exercise 1　gold pen $135　　bracelet $545
　　　　　　ring $1,259　　watch $23.75
　　　　　　calculator $7.85

Exercise 2　1. watch　　　　2. ring
　　　　　　3. pen　　　　　4. bracelet
　　　　　　They are too expensive for her.

Section B: Paying for the Things
　　　　　　1. Personal check　　2. Credit card
　　　　　　3. personal check　　4. Cash
　　　　　　5. traveler's check

Section C: Discussing Plans for the Weekend
　　　　　　1. B　2. C　3. B　4. C　5. A　6. B

Section D: Completing a Complaint Form
　　　　　　Equipment: electric fan
　　　　　　No. BE 42703-02　Size: medium
　　　　　　Color: blue　　　　Made in/date: 1985
　　　　　　Fault: It doesn't work.
　　　　　　Purchaser: Andrew Emmett
　　　　　　Address: 5 Rainbow Terrace West Old-Field Surrey

Phone No. 77480

Part Ⅲ : Listening Comprehension Test

Section A: 1. C 2. C 3. A 4. C 5. A 6. A
7. B 8. D 9. C
Section B: 10. 11. D 12. C 13. D 14. C
15. B

Your Notes:

_____

_____

_____

_____

_____

_____

_____

_____

_____

_____

_____

_____

_____

_____

_____

_____

_____

Unit Six

Part I : Listening Practice

Section A: Talking about One's Family

Exercise 1   A Tim   B David   C Jane   D Mary

Exercise 2   1. Pat   2. Mary's father

3. Diane   4. Susan

Section B: Exam Results

Exercise 1   Maurice Jones A   Laura Drew A

Ales Humphries C   Erica Allen A

Mike Grant D   Edith Graven E

Lisa Andrews F   Oliver Small D

Exercise 2 1. I never understand Italian.

2. I'm not as clever as others

3. You could do better.

4. He thinks it's boring.

Section C: Making Arrangements

Exercise 1   A. 2   B. 4   C. 3   D. 1

Exercise 2   1. bring: records   meet: bus stop

2. bring: sandwiches, fishing rod and drinks

meet: at the river

3. bring: white wine

meet: at Pat's house

4. bring: dessert-chocolate cake and drinks

meet: in front of his house

Section D: Murder in Heasden

1. Age of dead man: in forties
2. Location body: Under the North Circular Road
3. Time dead man left club: 1:30 a.m.
4. Body found by: a member of the club, an employee
5. Cause of death: multiple head injuries
6. Possible witnesses: a drunk man and two women
7. Dead man's clothes: a light colored raincoat, gray trousers, black shoes, pink tie,
8. Color of hair: dark
9. Motive for murder: Not known, but probably not robbery
10. Club closing time: 1: 30

Part Ⅲ: Listening Comprehension Test

1. B   2. D   3. B   4. D   5. B   6. B   7. A   8. B
9. C   10. D   11. A   12. C   13. C   14. D   15. A

Your Notes:

_____

_____

_____

_____

_____

_____

_____

Unit Seven

Part I : Listening Practice

Section A: Announcement
Exercise 1   1. two   2. Town Hall, Toy Museum
Exercise 2   1. F 2. F 3. T 4. F 5. T 6. F 7. T 8. F

Section B: Announcement for the Afternoon's Tour
1. 1241   2. French   3. Norman   4. wall   5. modern
6. flower, two   7. Tuesday
8. the Roman Goddess of Love   9. clear
10. spring in the hills

Section C: Library Regulations
1. identification card   2. 5, 3 weeks
3. renew them   4. by making a telephone call
5. 50p   6. pay for that
7. in the library   8. Two magazines, not newspapers
9. (5, damage   10. charge

Section D: A Dialogue about One's Vacation
Exercise 1
1. an urban holiday... go camping
2. the aquarium... Grouse Mountain... museums... galleries
3. the ride over... the deck... sat inside... read magazines
Exercise 2

316

1. It's cold and miserable.
2. It's such an elegant city with a lot of British influence.
3. A pin with a tiny totem pole on it.

Part Ⅲ : Listening Comprehension Test

1. C   2. C   3. C   4. B   5. B   6. C   7. D   8. A
9. C   10. A   11. C   12. A   13. A   14. C   15. B

Your Notes:

_____

_____

_____

_____

_____

_____

_____

_____

_____

_____

_____

_____

_____

_____

_____

_____

Unit Eight

Part Ⅰ : Listening Practice

Section A: Story

Exercise 1

1. The forty-fifth floor.

2. They want to walk up to their room.

3. Because they left the key to their room in the hall.

Exercise 2

1. came back very late

2. our lifts do not work tonight

3. want to sleep in the hall, walk up to our room

4. tell us a long and interesting story with a sad ending

Exercise 3

1. T 2. F 3. F 4. T 5. F 6. F 7. F

Section B: Owning a Car

Exercise 1

Reasons for owning a car

1. allows a person to move around freely

2. a comfortable way to travel

3. usually safe in a car at night

Reasons against owning a car

1. very expensive

2. cause worry and stress

Exercise 2

1. check a bus schedule... a train
2. warm... dry... cold... wet
3. maintain... repair   4. urban... park
5. on the street... get stolen... something else

Section C: Dialogue
Exercise 1
1. after 4 o'clock on Friday
2. by 10 o'clock on the Monday
3. £29.25   4. first 300 miles
5. $5\frac{1}{2}$ p per mile
Exercise 2
1. F   2. F   3. T   4. T   5. F

Part Ⅲ: Listening Comprehension Test

      1. C   2. D   3. C   4. D   5. C   6. D   7. D   8. A
      9. B   10. C

Your Notes:

_____

_____

_____

_____

_____

_____

Unit Nine

Part I : Listening Practice

Section A: Plans for a Weekend
1. Pat 2. Jill 3. Mary 4. Sam 5. Ted 6. Jane

Section B: An Interview with a Scientist
1. Always 2. Never 3. Sometimes 4. Sometimes
5. Always 6. Never 7. Never

Section C: Talking about What They Like Doing
1. Bill 2. Maggie 3. Bill 4. Bill 5. Maggie
6. Bill 7. Bill, Maggie

Section D: Things They Want to Do for Weekend
Exercise 1
1. Yes, she does. But she's not a workaholic or anything. She really appreciates her time off.
2. No. She usually runs around like crazy trying to get the housework done. Then she lies around and veges to recuperate for Monday.
3. She tries to get most of her chores done on weeknights.
4. (1) Get into a hobby gradually.
   (2) No need to go overboard with fancy gadgets.
   (3) Take a course at the community center.
Exercise 2

Chris' hobbies: (1) painting (doing landscapes)
              (2) squash (3) tennis
Ann's hobbies: (1) playing guitar as a kid
              (2) photography
Greg's hobby: making ceramic pieces

Part Ⅲ: Listening Comprehension Test

Section A: 1. B   2. B   3. D   4. C   5. A   6. C   7. C   8. B
          9. D
Section B: 10. D   11. D   12. C   13. B   14. C   15. D

Your Notes:

_____

_____

_____

_____

_____

_____

_____

_____

_____

_____

_____

_____

_____

Unit Ten

Part Ⅰ : Listening Practice

Section A: About Building a Shopping Centre

Exercise 1   1. T   2. F   3. F   4. F   5. F

Exercise 2

Mr Boulter: A shopping center is a good thing for elderly people.
We can't get to the big shops in the center of the
town. Everything here is expensive.

Mrs Singh: My shop is not expensive. Children often stole things
from my shop.

Middle-aged Woman: We'll lose an open space. Children will have
no place to play around.

Young Lady: Young people need shops, clubs and discos.

Section B: Accepting and Refusing Invitation

Exercise 1   1. No   2. No   3. Yes   4. Yes   5. No
6. No   7. Yes

Exercise 2   1. dinner   much work to do at the office
2. party   go to a movie
3. baseball
4. dinner
5. pizza place   on a diet
6. go out and do something   write a letter
7. football game

Section C: An Invitation to car Racing

1. F   2. F   3. F   4. T   5. T

Section·D: Making Arrangements

1. A quarter past nine at Sue's place
2. Because it's out of his way
3. Phil Stone

Part Ⅲ: Listening Comprehension Test

1. B   2. C   3. B   4. D   5. D   6. D   7. C   8. A
9. C   10. B   11. D   12. C   13. C   14. A   15. C

Your Notes:

_____

_____

_____

_____

_____

_____

_____

_____

_____

_____

_____

_____

_____

Unit Eleven

Part I : Listening Practice

Section A: Making Appointments
Exercise 1
1. Name: Mrs Simpson   2. Name: Mrs Katzen
   Date: 11   Date: 23
   Day: Tuesday   Day: Wednesday
   Time: 10:00 A.M.   Time: 3:30 P.M.
Exercise 2
1. back trouble   2. Child swallowed a coin.

Section B: Making Reservations
Exercise 1
Sacramento: Mon. Wed. Sat. 22
Mexico City: Tue. Thur. Fri. Sun. 15
Montreal: Wed. Sat. 5
Exercise 2
Sacramento: IC35   11:00 A.M.   12:15 P.M.
Mexico City: IC64   12:00 P.M.   4:15 A.M.
Montreal: IC256   6:15 A.M.   3:30 P.M.

Section C: Asking for Information
Exercise 1
1. Monday to Friday   8～2
2. Monday to Friday   10～9:30   Saturday 10～5

3. Monday to Friday   9~5   Sat. to Sun. 9~1

4. Monday to Sunday   9~10

Exercise 2

1. driver's license   2. children's book

3. bring a class   4. sale

Section D: Completing a Questionnaire

1. Mrs Mary Egerton; 2. 12 Holly Crescent, Peterford; 3. over 50; 4. Housewife; 5. cockroaches; 6. about two years; 7. about every six weeks; 8. in the kitchen around the skirting board, under the stove; 9. corner shop; 10. radio advertisement; 11. satisfied.

Part Ⅲ: Listening Comprehension Test

1. C   2. A   3. B   4. B   5. D   6. D   7. A   8. A   9. A

10. D

Your Notes:

_____

_____

_____

_____

_____

_____

_____

_____

Unit Twelve

Part I : Listening Practice

Section A: Safari Tour

Exercise 1

1. You mustn't get off the land-rover without permission.
2. You must all stay close to the guide.
3. You all have to sign these insurance declarations.
4. You mustn't disturb the animals.

Exercise 2

1. land-rover, could be attacked
2. company regulation, sign
3. disturb, wild, tame, zoos
4. 50 miles, 80
5. insect repellent, drinking water, rolls of 35mm film, a packed lunch

Section B: Making a Visit to the Zoo

Exercise 1   1. F   2. F   3. F   4. F   5. F   6. T
Exercise 2   1. C   2. B   3. C   4. B   5. B   6. A   7. B
             8. B

Section C: A Dialogue
1. a   2. d   3. d   4. b   5. b

Section D: Uinfamiliar Objects

1-6 2-3 3-5 4-2 5-7 6-4 7-10 8-9 9-8 10-1

Part Ⅲ: Listening Comprehension Test

1. C 2. D 3. B 4. A 5. A 6. D 7. B 8. A 9. C
10. D

Your Notes:

_____

_____

_____

_____

_____

_____

_____

_____

_____

_____

_____

_____

_____

_____

_____

_____

_____

_____

_____

Unit Thirteen

Part I : Listening Practice

Section A: Making an Order

Order booked:	10/6/93
Date required for meal:	Wednesday, 18th.
Client:	William Martin & Sons
Time:	1:15
Type of meal:	business lunch
No. of people:	27
No. of courses:	three
Extras:	1 for a cup of coffee
Drinks:	red wine
Menu:	Beef Harrison, Ice-cream
Cost per person:	13
Deposit:	50

Section B: Filling in a Timetable

Morning Timetable					
	Monday	Tuesday	Wednesday	Thursday	Friday
9: 30 to 10: 45	Intensive Text Study	Dialogue	Intensive Text Study	Listening Class	Test
10: 45 to 11: 00	Break				

Morning Timetable					
	Monday	Tuesday	Wednesday	Thursday	Friday
11：00 to 12：00	Grammar Practice	Extensive Reading	Intensive Text Study	Grammar Practice	Role Play
12：05 to 13：00	Pronunciation & Spelling Practice	Oral Activity Work	Writing	News Broadcast	Free Oral Activity Work

Section C: A Talk about Earthquakes

Exercise 1

1. Different kinds of waves, or vibrations.

   of these earthquake waves travel through the crust of the earth.

   go through the deeper rocks.

2. the kinds of rocks they go through

   they pass near the center of the earth

Exercise 2

1. The rocks in the earth's crust are under stress like huge bent springs.

2. The pressures may cause great breaks or faults.

3. They may move up, down, or sideways along the breaks, or faults, in the rock.

4. As blocks of rock shift, several kinds of vibrations spread out in all directions. This is an earthquake.

Section D: Filling in a Form

Exercise 1

329

Professor's doubt	The student hadn't done the calculations himself
Student's explanation	One week before the project was due, he was ill, and his roommate helped him with the project.
Professor's decision and his reasons	The student still got "F", for he was given a month to work on the project, and he should do it individually.
Student's remedy	To make an oral presentation about the government's role in running the economy and try to get the extra credit.

Exercise 2

1. grade, project; "F";
2. approach, similar to, seriously doubted, calculations;
3. week before, due, sick, research, the night before, all night, really, own;
4. a month, get a head start, wait, supposed, prepare, individually, remains, the same;
5. the government's role, running the economy, oral presentation, subject, extra credit.

Part Ⅲ: Listening Comprehension Test

1. D 2. B 3. C 4. D 5. B 6. D 7. C 8. B 9. A
10. C

Your Notes:

Unit Fourteen

Part I : Listening Practice

Section A: Farming Methods

Exercise 1 1. F 2. T 3. F 4. F 5. F 6. F 7. T 8. F

Exercise 2

Past

    1. planted the same crops

    2. never gave the land a rest

    3. planted in long, straight rows

    4. never planted trees

Modern

planted different crop each year

gave the land a rest

formed rows in curving lines

plant trees to stop the wind

Section B: About Littering

1. and... street...   litter — garbage

  litter... put...

  It's... to... But...

  city... view

2. Often... they...   fence — wall

  there... garbage.

3. Food... carry...   drop — throw

4. They... they... up...　　spoil — destroy
   is... people... They...
   they...
5. States... and...　　　　dirty — filthy

　　　　　　　　　　　　　punish — fine

　　　　　　　　　　　　　jail — prison

　　　　　　　　　　　　　view — scene

Section C: Noise Pollution

	Factory workers who always hear noise have poorer hearing than other groups.
	around airports or on air routes the noise of airplanes taking off and landing causes the greatest problems.
	Traffic sounds break in on our peace and quiet. Trucks and motorcycles cause the most problems.
	In the city: noise of buildings going up, emergency automobiles; In the suburbs: barking dog, playing children, and lawn mowers.
	Radios, record players, TV, the sounds of plumbing, heating and air conditioning

Answer the questions:

1. At a level of 140 decibels people feel pain in their ears.
2. Automobiles, trucks, buses, motocycles, airplanes, boats, factories, bands — all these things make noise.
3. The noise bothers not only our ears, but our minds and bodies as well.

332

4. One way is to cut down on the amount of noise. The other is to protect ourselves against the noise we can't stop.

Part Ⅲ : Listening Comprehension Test

1. A 2. C 3. A 4. B 5. D 6. A 7. D 8. B 9. C
10. A

Your Notes:

_____

_____

_____

_____

_____

_____

_____

_____

_____

_____

_____

_____

_____

_____

_____

_____

Unit Fifteen

Part I : Listening Practice

Section A: Dreams

Exercice 1

simplest: aware of things missed during the day

dreamed: teeth falling out

means: dental trouble

dreamed: missing an important appointment

means: engagement forgotten to write down

deeper: how we really feel about our relationships

dreamed: bashing her husband over the head with a vacuum cleaner

means: resented him for not allowing her to take an interesting job

Exercise 2

1. It means a dental trouble
2. It hints an engagement fogotten to write down
3. The feeling of resentment towards her husband, for he insists that she should stay home.

Exercise 3

Psychologists, our dreams, interesting information, take the time, seriously, simplest, aware of things, we were too busy to notice them, deeper, how we really feel about

Section B: About Sleep

Exercise 1

Reasons for sleep: the body needs to rest

Functions of sleep:

1. recover: the body recovers from the activities of the previous day

2. prepare: the body prepares itself for the next day

Four levels of sleep:

1. muscles: relax little by little

2. heart: beats more slowly

3. brain: slows down

4. body: shifts back and forth from one level of sleep to another

When dream occurs: eyeballs: begin to move more quickly

eyelids: are closed

REM: rapid eye movement

Overcoming sleeplessness: 1. breathing: very slowly and very deeply

2. drinking: warm milk

3. counting: sheep

Exercise 2

1. F 2. T 3. T 4. F 5. F

Section C: "Why Older Is Better"

1. The knowledge the older people gain improves his intelligence.

2. Psychologically, the older people are tougher.

3. They feel their power.

4. Their love deepens.

5. They become more themselves.

Fill in the blanks:

coping with, healthier, protect, rely far more on, humor, altruism, creativity, fired, gone, divorce, loved, survived, tougher

Part Ⅲ: Listening Comprehension Test

Section A: 1. B 2. D 3. A 4. A 5. D 6. C 7. C 8. D
          9. C
Section B: 10. D 11. C 12. B 13. A 14. D 15. B

Simulated Listening Test 1

Section A: 1. B 2. D 3. C 4. B 5. C 6. C 7. C 8. A
          9. C
Section B: 10. A 11. B 12. B 13. C 14. A 15. D

Simulated Listening Test 2

Section A: 1. B 2. C 3. C 4. B 5. C 6. C 7. B 8. D
          9. C
Section B: 10. A 11. D 12. C 13. B 14. A 15. D

<u>**Your Notes:**</u>

_____

_____

_____

_____

_____

_____

_____

_____

_____

Unit Sixteen

Section A: Listening for Gist
Exercise 1
1. air hostess   2. Teacher   3. Dentist
4. shop assistant   5. tourist guide   6. salesman
7. Disc Jockey   8. traffic warden   9. waiter
10. taxi driver

Exercise 2
1. airways, flight   2. homework
3. open up wide, filling, chipped
4. larger size, fit, stock   5. building, designed
6. buys, products   7. record, radio
8. yellow line, no-parking   9. menu, chef
10. Road, park

Section B: Car Pool
Exercise 1
1. They are in a car near New York.
2. Because of the traffic jam.
3. At tunnels or bridges.
4. In a car with only one person.
5. Park their cars outside the city and pick up public transport.

Exercise 2   1. T   2. F   3. T   4. T   5. T   6. F

337

7. F   8. T

Exercise 3

1. It will be expensive and fewer people would drive alone.
2. It will be free.
3. It will be expensive.
4. It's practical and will save money.

Section C: Energy and Environment

Exercise 1

1. The Energy Minister.   2. At a press conference.
3. To build three more nuclear power stations.
4. Angry, upset, against the idea.

Exercise 2

Second speaker's response

A. Nuclear power is unsafe.
B. A lot of radioactive wastes. No one knows the long-term effects.
C. Other possibilities, e. g. solar energy, wind/ wave power, coal.
D. He doesn't believe this.

Section D: A Conversation between a Man and a Doctor

1. Full name: John MacDonald
2. Address (permanent or temporary): "Seaview" Hotel
3. Duration of stay (if visitor): 4 days
4. Symptoms: bad stomach-ache for two days, and feeling sick and weak
5. Possible Cause: change of diet

338

6. Prescription: medicine
7. To be taken: three times a day, after meals
8. Suggestions: not to eat too much, and drink plenty of orange
   juice and don't go out in the sun

Part Ⅲ: Listening Comprehension Test

1. D 2. B 3. A 4. C 5. C 6. B 7. D 8. B 9. D
10. B

Your Notes:

_____

_____

_____

_____

_____

_____

_____

_____

_____

_____

_____

_____

_____

Unit Seventeen

Part I : Listening Practice

Section A: Guessing about the Situation and Speaker
Exercise 1

1. football match
2. Law court
3. church
4. quiz show
5. airport
6. weather forecast
7. car showroom
8. driving lesson
9. school
10. tour (of London)

Exercise 2

1. football commentator
2. Judge/magistrate
3. vicar /priest /minister
4. T. V. presenter
5. announcer
6. forecaster
7. car salesman
8. dirving instructor
9. head master/principal
10. tour guide

Section B: Taking Messages
Exercise 1

1. Meet Stacey at school at 4:30 . Stacey has told Others. Bring volleyball and Stacey's money.

2. Dinner with Tim on Thursday. Will meet at 7:00 instead of 6:30 . Will pick you up here.

3. Dr White. Dental check-up. Thursday, 2 p.m. Call if not convenient.

4. Diane called. Ruth Lee needs a ride tomorrow. Can you

take her? Call her 547-6892.

5. Car ready next Tuesday. Car needed a lot of work. Replaced battery but still working on starter. Will cost around $350. You need new snow tires.

Section C: What's Happening

Exercise 1

A. 6 B. 5 C. 2 D. 3 E. 4 F. 1

Exercise 2

Picture A: Yes, delicious, like to have some more.

Picture B: Yes, good teacher.

Picture C: Yes, great game. What a Play!

Picture D: No, the service is so slow, expensive.

Picture E: No, boring, terrible, bad.

Picture F: No, awful, too crowded, too loud, terrible.

Part Ⅲ: Listening Comprehension Test

1. C 2. A 3. B 4. C 5. A 6. C 7. A 8. C 9. C
10. A

Your Notes:

_____

_____

_____

_____

_____

Unit Eighteen

Part I : Listening Practice

Section A: Listening for Specific Information
Exercise 1
1. Weight; 13Pounds
2. A car; 650
3. A cash-card; 8976
4. A fax; 593381; Code-440865
5. A bank account; 60917718
6. A foreign-exchange counter; 410,000 pesos
   (Exchange rate; 4,100 to 1)
7. Weather; 83 F
8. Waterloo; 1815

Exercise 2
1. On a diet and doing a keep-fit class
2. Rusty, expensive   3. Yes
4. He'll contact him and talk about the new contract.
5. Probablyina bank   6. For a holiday
7. Because Dave and Jane are there.   8. Quiz

Section B: A Lecture on Bridges
Exercise 1

a. suspension bridge   b. Flat beam bridge
c. Railway arch bridge
Exercise 2

342

1. branch, step   2. Primitive, achievements
3. guided, materials   4. designs, combinations
5. concrete, spans   6. completed, landscape
7. daily, life

Section C: A Lecture on the Educational Systems of the U. S. And
         Great Britain

Exercise 1
    The United States: Local school systems have their own standard
                   exams. There are twelve grades in the U.S.
    Great Britain: There is a nation-wide standard examination.

Exercise 2
1. A 2. B 3. A 4. A 5. B

Exercise 3
1. F 2. T 3. F 4. T 5. F

Section D: An Interview at Scotland Yard
1) Babyface is   A   2) Bad Billy is   C
3) Harry the Horse is   D   4) Mickey Mouse is   B
1. Fill in the information you hear on the lines provided below.
1) The policeman's phone number is 224466.
2) Policewoman's phone number is 224477.

Part Ⅲ: Listening Comprehension Test

    Section A   1. D   2. D   3. A   4. A   5. C
                   6. C   7. B   8. B   9. B
    Section B   10. D   11. C   12. D   13. D   14. B 15. B

Unit   Nineteen

Part I : Listening Practice

Section A: Listening for Main Ideas
Exercise 1

1. Train /British Rail
2. Washing-powder
3. A credit card
4. Shampoo
5. A car
6. Chocolate / Sweets
7. Whiskey / Alcohol
8. A newspaper
9. Soap / Face-cream
10. A bank

Exercise 2

1. British Rail, no delays, take you faster
2. stains, dirt, white
3. Spendcard, accepted, discount
4. hair, greasy, conditioner
5. design, 2-litre, boot
6. nuts, delicious, coconut
7. water, Scottish barley, barrels
8. reporting, current issues, daily
9. looks, skin creamy / complexion
10. invest, interest rates, money

Section B: Radio Announcements
Exercise 1

A. 4. Saturday
B. 2. Friday and Saturday
C. 3. Monday~Sunday
D. 1. Wednesday

Exercise 2

A. 8: 30 free   B. 9:00 pm $ 10
C. 11 am~10 pm $ 2. 50   D. 7:00 pm free

Section C: Sunglow Tours
Exercise 1

Names:	Julia Carter, Mark Carter
Address:	32 Alderley Avenue,
Destination:	Belgrade; Vienna
Transport:	plane; coach
Length of holiday:	15-day
Cost:	£ 166
Includes:	breakfast; evening meal; medical costs

Exercise 2

1. T 2. F 3. F 4. T 5. F 6. T 7. T

Section D: Traveling with Your Pet
Exercise 1

1. 34% of dog owners and 11% of cat owners say they take their vacations with their pets.

2. Before you decide to take your pet on the road, be sure he does not get car sick.

3. Always attach your pet's leash before opening the car door or window because, no matter how well trained, he could get excited in new surroundings and run away.

4. It has your beeper number, cellular phone number or a friend's phone number.

5. To prevent your pet from getting lost.

Exercise 2

toiletries (medications, scooper, paper towels, sandwich bags for dog waste removal, and disposable litter pans for cats),

necessities (leash, bedding, water and food dishes, food, a jug of water, and vaccination records), entertainment (toys and chewies).

Part Ⅲ: Listening Comprehension Test

1. A   2. B   3. B   4. D   5. B   6. D   7. C   8. D   9. B
10. A

Your Notes:

_____

_____

_____

_____

_____

_____

_____

_____

_____

_____

_____

_____

_____

_____

Unit   Twenty

Section A: Gussing the Meaning

Exercise 1

1. a pair of trousers　　2. a return ticket
3. a newspaper and mints/sweets
4. ballet or theatre tickets
5. drinks　　　　　6. tickets for a coach trip
7. a haircut　　　　8. soup and fish
9. a game of squash　　10. throat medicine

Exercise 2

1. in a clothes-shop　2. at the station
3. at a newsagent's　4. at a box-office
5. at a pub　　　　6. in a tourist office /travel agency
7. at a hairdresser's /barber's
8. in a restaurant
9. at a sports club　10. at a chemist's /pharmacy

Section B: News Report

Exercise 1

New York　Value of Dollar Falls but Yen Rises
Washington Better Security on International Flights
Florida　　Space Shuttle Delayed
California　Fire Fighters Try to Save Homes in Forest
New Jersey Teenagers Arrested for Computer Crimes

347

Exercise 2

1. F   2. T   3. T   4. F   5. F   6. T   7. F   8. F
9. T

Section C: Short Speech
Exercise 1
1. sales force, market
2. firm, fifth, sales, outsell, competitors
3. 37, market, leadership, share
Exercise 2
1. It's much better now. In only six years, he has brought the firm from a very low fifth position in regional sales to the point where we now outsell all but one of our competitors.
2. The company has moved Bill to northern California to work his sales magic in one of this company's most competitive regions.
3. His move should be regarded as promotion for him.
4. He is capable of doing business well.
5. The speaker wishes Bill Masters the best of luck in his new job.

Section D: Only 9,900 Shopping Days until Social Security Can't Meet All Its Obligations
Exercise 1
1. steps, solid footing, taxes, benefits, the retirement age, the funds
2. free, (888) 735-2377, World Wide Web
3. a policy, attention, money, future
Exercise 2

1. F   2. T   3. T   4. F   5. T   6. F   7. T

Part Ⅲ : Listening Comprehension Test

1. A 2. A 3. B 4. C 5. C 6. C 7. C 8. B 9. C
10. D

Your Notes:

_____

_____

_____

_____

_____

_____

_____

_____

_____

_____

_____

_____

_____

_____

_____

_____

_____

_____

_____

_____

Unit　Twenty-one

Part Ⅰ : Listening Practice

Section A: Listening for Gist
Exercise 1
1. Garden　　　　2. Vending-machine
3. Microwave oven
4. Computer/Word-processor/Video Game
5. Clothes　　　　6. Hifi /Music system
7. Art　　　　　　8. Concert
9. Tennis　　　　10. Holidays
Exercise 2
  1. lawn, flower beds, fence
  2. button, cold water, hot chocolate
  3. food, be cooked in no time, electricity
  4. switch, disc, programme
  5. fit, tight, shrink, suit
  6. compact, speaker, cassette-player
  7. modern, abstract, colors and forms
  8. singer, guitars, drum, records
  9. player, backhand, score
10. tan, beach, hotel, camping

Section B: Investigation on Damage
Exercise 1
1. Make a damage report.

2. Because of the storm.

3. Because he got house insured and he could get compensation from the insurance company.

Exercise 2

1. Tiles	2. TV aerial
3. bedroom window	4. Chimney
5. bricks have blown off	6. Tree
7. shed roof	8. kitchen window
9. garden wall	

Section C: Stock Report

Exercise 1

1. Mon. Dec. 12   Prices for all the metals were £1. There will be only small fluctuations though there may be increased interest in gold. Silver and tin seem to be good buys.

2. Tue. Dec. 13   Gold £1.40, silver 83p, tin £1.05, platinum 95p, nickel 92p, copper £1, continued increases in gold and tin, the decline in the price of silver is temporary.

3. Wed. Dec. 14   Gold £1.35, silver 79p, tin £1.10, platinum 91p, nickel £1.10, copper 98p, good future for silver; nickel is on the way up.

4. Thu. Dec. 15   Gold £1.30, silver £1.02, tin £1.18, platinum 87p, nickel £1.10, copper 95p, considerable fluctuations in the prices of many metals though silver and gold are the safest investments at pre-sent.

5. Fri. Dec. 16   Gold 81p, silver £1.02, tin £1.15, platinum 87p, nickel £1.60, copper 65p. improved long-term performance for all metals, though there may be a temporary decline in the price of tin.

Exercise 2 (omitted)

Section D: Hot Cake
Exercise 1
1. on July 24th, 1.3 %, in June, in May, 0.9 %
2. to June, 3.3 %, 2.4 %, 1994, half a percentage point
Exercise 2
1F   2T   3F   4F   5T   6T   7F   8T

Part Ⅲ: Listening Comprehension Test

1. C   2. D   3. B   4. A   5. B   6. B   7. D   8. D
9. C   10. B   11. C   12. A   13. B   14. C   15. A

Your Notes:

_____

_____

_____

_____

_____

_____

_____

Unit   Twenty-two

Part I : Listening Practice

Section A: Listening for Descriptions
Exercise 1

    1. a 2. b 3. c 4. c 5. c

Exercise 2

    1. date

    2. big earrings, V-necked sweater, no glasses

    3. zip, a tear

    4. mirror, one flat tyre, bags

    5. stripes on the sleeve and pockets

Section B: Wills
Exercise 1

    1. disposition, property, take effect

    2. disposition, a devise

    3. disposition, a bequest

    4. the testator, testamentary capacity

    5. written / in writing

    6. the contents, within six days

    7. three witnesses

    8. nuncupative will, personal property

    9. handwriting, a holographic will, real or personal property, both

Exercise 2

    1. It is about disposition by an individual of his or her

property, intended to take effect after death.

2. It means being of full age and sound mind and acting without undue influence of others.

3. (1) When a person is at a point of the apparent imminence of death, with no time or opportunity to make a written one.

   (2) The oral will must be declared in the presence of at least three witnesses.

   (3) The contents of the oral will must be reduced to writing form within six days after it was declared.

4. (1) A holographic will is valid only if it complies literally with the controlling statute.

   (2) In some states of the USA, a holographic will is also valid if wholly written, dated and signed by the testator's own hand, though it is without formal exececution or attestation.

Section C: Cryptography
Exercise 1

1. Uses of cryptography.
2. Cryptography is writing in secret codes.
3. That he used cryptography.
4. Smugglers of alcoholic beverages.
5. In the form of cryptographic codes.

Exercise 2

1. hidden, writing
2. 4,000 -year-old
3. use, cryptography, secret

354

4. method, simple, decipher
5. Era, alcoholic, ship, shore, wireless
6. form, codes, information
7. information, banks
8. protect, information
9. ancient art, form, 21st

Section D: Mike and Pat

Exercise 1

1. Husband and wife.
2. Because Mike never wipes his shoes before entering the room and so makes the floor filthy.
3. He feels angry.
4. She strongly objects to it and points out that there's cigarette ash on every carpet in the house and she thinks cigarettes are a waste of money.
5. Their attitudes are quite different. Pat thinks of housework as an important part of her life and works 15 hours a day at home doing housework. But Mike thinks housework is different and implies housework doesn't matter. This makes Pat very angry.

Exercise 2

Whose behaviour?　　Pat: 3　　Mike: 1, 2, 4

Whose opinion?　　　Pat: 1, 5　Mike: 2, 3, 4, 6

Part Ⅲ: Listening Comprehension Test

1. A　2. D　3. C　4. A　5. C　6. C　7. B　8. B　9. D
10. B

Unit Twenty-three

Part I : Listening Practice

Section A: Understanding between Management and Workers
Exercise 1
1. They would think he was annoyed with them.
2. Everybody eats in the firm's canteen.
3. He says some large firms have one canteen for everybody but most large firms have separate canteens.
4. Because it fosters the feeling that there's between "them" and "us".
5. Workers and management are on the same side of the fence.
Exercise 2
1. Workers and management are on two separate sides of the fence.
2. We all sink or swim together.
3. Managers don't care about the workers.
4. Workers are inferior.

Section B: Motivating Employees to Work Harder
Exercise 1
A. salary   B. fringe benefits   C. promotion
A. satisfaction   B. feel proud   C. treat
D. participate, management discussions
Exercise 2
1. Because he has written a book on this subject.
2. No, more money is not enough anymore in motiva-ting workers

356

in modern society.

3. Because they don't want the headaches of being a supervisor or a manager, and they also don't want to leave the town or their friends.

4. A. Higher level of education and much higher standard of living.
   B. Almost everyone can find some kind of job.

5. A. work, vacation   B. discussion, planning
   C. profit-sharing, stock dividend

Section C: Questionnaire and Opinion Surveys

Exercise 1

1. shoe
   A. underpaid (or they were not being paid enough
   B. pay more
   C. out of business

2. A. the possibility (or feasibility) of giving everyone a rise
   B. the cost of producing shoes
   C. the price, U.S. stores   D. Korea

3. impossible, increase salaries

Exercise 2

1. To give workers a chance to express their opinions.

2. If management is not really willing to consider the opinions of the workers, or make changes, workers will feel angry that their opinions are being ignored. Sometimes it's difficult for management to do what the workers want.

3. a. Labor is so expensive in the U.S.
   b. The U.S. shoe industry could not compete with the prices of imported shoes on the market. Workers volunteered to take a

cut in pay.

Section D: Drunk Driving

Exercise 1

1. A. 44,000 people   B. drunk drivers
   C. stricter laws
2. a thirty-year-old, California
   A. four bottles of beer   B. speeding
   C. ran through, crashed
3. A. not the first time he had been arrested for drunk driving
   B. too harshly, planned the accident

Exercise 2

1. Stricter laws have been passed
2. You will be considered a murderer in the eyes of the law
3. At the inrtersection
4. 5 people
5. He was brought to court and sentenced to 77 years in prison

Part Ⅲ: Listening comprehension Test

1. A   2. D   3. C   4. B   5. C   6. A   7. D   8. C   9. D
10. A

Your Notes:

_____

_____

_____

_____

Unit   Twenty-four

Part Ⅰ : Listening Practice

Section A: Civil Service Reform
Exercise 1
    1. F 2. F 3. T 4. T 5. F
Exercise 2
1. Civil service reform, efforts for honest government.
2. He could not win the support of his Republic Party, so he failed to win the Presidential nomination in the Republican Nominating Convention in 1884.

Section B: Electronic Observation
Exercise 1
1. employers using computers, cameras, listening devices and telephones to observe their workers
2. a system for recording messages
3. electronic mail-messages sent between computers
4. the International Labor Organization
Exercise 2
1. Twenty million workers, From Factory workers to highly paid engineers.
2. It is common in telecommunications, insurance and banking.
3. They have major objections to it. They say it violates human rights and destroys the feeling of trust between workers and employers.

Exercise 3

greater power, observe, court orders, suspected criminals, required, phone calls, considering, restrict, work places

Section C: Domestic Violence against Women

Exercise 1

Topic: Domestic violence against women

Facts: Medical experts say: wife-beating is the most serious health threat.

The government says: more young women are injured by men they know than strangers.

Experts say: it takes place in every social, economic, racial and religious group.

A federal crime study says: 4 million women are beaten yearly by husbands or ex-husbands or boyfriends.

In the past: Beaten women: afraid to discuss, refused to take action.

Police: refused to arrest wife beaters.

The court: not take the issue seriously, rarely sent wife beaters to jail.

Progress made: Activists: formed local groups, set up temporary homes.

Justice system: Police and court deal with it seriously. In 26 states they must arrest wife beaters.

Legislation: new crime bill has been signed by the President.

Exercise 2

1. O. J. Simpson's case of being accused of killing his former wife.

2. Because they knew they would face even greater violence if they did.
3. a. Improve law enforcement and training for police and judges.
   b. Set up more temporary housing for beaten women and their children.
   c. Establish a special telephone number to provide information and help.

Section D: Running for Mayor

Exercise 1

1. His loud music and his pink hair.
2. A musician
3. He is running for mayor.

Exercise 2

1. T 2. F 3. F 4. T 5. F 6. F

Exercise 3

" From the concert hall to City Hall, Jerry is with you!"

It shows that Jerry Ward thinks that he knows what people want because rock is the music of the people so he can also be a good mayor of the city.

Part Ⅲ: Listening Comprehension Test

1. B   2. A   3. B   4. B   5. C   6. B   7. A 8. D
9. C   10. D   11. C   12. D   13. B   14. D   15. A

Your Notes:

_____

Unit   Twenty-five

Part Ⅰ: Listening Practice

Section A: Edward Heath
Exercise 1
1. music, politics
2. A. a variety of interests
   B. inward-looking, narrow-minded
   C. come back to, a fresh mind
3. debating
4. tearing itself apart again

Exercise 2
1. He is a politician.
1. Because if you have got various interests, you will become broad-minded, solve the problems with a fresh mind and serve your electors much better than you could otherwise.
3. Probably from a musical family.
4. He became interested in politics at school through a debating society.
5. In order to change European politics.

Section B: A Politician Becomes an Executive
Exercise 1
1. Career in government.
   A. Senate   B. Budget   C. U. N.
   D. chief of staff E. Treasury   F. 1976

362

2. Career in business. January of 1977
3. politics, business.
   A. what business would be like
   B. money
4. government involvement in big business

Exercise 2

1. Because he used to be very successful in politics and the government service.
2. He wanted to show the degree of his commitment.
3. Because his work at Austin and Goodwin's has given him a whole new perspective on both politics and business.
4. He would do his best to fight for less government involvement in big business.

Section C: Differences betcueen Managing in Government and Managing in Business

Exercise 1

Differences between managing in government and managing in business.

1. results, profits
2. appearances, public image
3. government, business

Similarities.

1. planning, budgeting
2. lower levels
   A. press coverage or news media
   B. lunches with employees
3. Uncertain

Exercise 2

1. It depends much more on efforts.

2. Because they are often concealed by the politician who made the mistake.

3. The salesmen's and lab technicians' ideas.

4. Because they are the people who are affected by changes in company policy and direction, and they know better than anyone about what is working out well and what isn't.

Section D: Dropouts

Exercise 1

1. A. West Virginia   B. New Jersey

2. A. pizza parties   B. lotteries

    C. at-risk, after-school jobs and summer jobs

    D. money, incentive

Exercise 2

1. Because they are bored with learning at school.

2. Because he thinks money can be a stimulus to get students to go to school.

3. Because they think the most effective way to solve the problem of dropouts is to get students interested in learning, but not to force them to learn.

Part Ⅲ: Listening Comprehension Test

1. C   2. B   3. D   4. A   5. D   6. A   7. D   8. C   9. D

10. B

Unit   Twenty-six

Part Ⅰ: Listening Practice

Section A: About U. S. Presidents
Exercise 1
1. was the chairman of the Constitutional Convention, but he was elected President principally because he had been the commander-in-chief during the American War of Independence.
2. the 12th man to hold the office of the Presidency, a military hero in war of 1812.
3. the 18th, the commander of the Union armies during the Civil War.
4. the 21st, a famous antislavery lawyer.
5. the 26th, was a cabinet officer in the administration of Theodore Roosevelt and the appointed governor of Philippines and later of Cuba.
6. the 33rd, supreme Allied commander in Europe during World War Ⅱ.

Exercise 2
1. United States, President, native-born citizen, 14, 35
2. Chairman, elected, war, Independence
3. Commander
4. lawyer

Section B: Words that Get You Hired
Exercise 1

questions	you should say or do	don't say or do
1.	talk about your education and work experience	
2.	a simple, straight-forward answer	deceptions
3.	research the company	lack of knowledge about the company and industry
4.	back your assertions with concrete examples from work or school	I can do anything you need
5.	speak of the weakness that is really overuse of a strength	I can't think of any
6.	define an ideal boss	don't knock your last boss
7.	write down what made you proudest in each of the past five years	
8	if pressed, give a range	Don't bring up pay in an initial interview

Exercise 2

1. He/She wants to know "Who are you, really ?"

2. He/She will be alert for deceptions.

3. "Lack of knowledge about the company and industry" ranked with "arrogance/cockiness" and "poor oral communication" and will lead to job-interview turnoffs.

4. Back your assertions with concrete examples from work or school, the interviewer wants more focus. But don't define your scope too narrowly.

366

5. He/She is probing for candor, honesty and good psychological balance.

Section C: Court Case
Exercise 1
1. William Black.
2. The assistant in the Smith's/ shoeshop.
3. Police Constable James Brown.
4. Mr Black — William's father.
5. The Magistrate.
Exercise 2
4—3—2—1—6—5—7

Section D: A Government Job
Exercise 1
1. Only if he had an acquaintance in the government, he could get a government job.
2. He must take an exam or try to prove that they have relevant work experience, so as to show that they are qualified.
3. Because federal programs have been shifted to state or local control, that means the federal administration lets the local governments take more duties.
4. He would feel more secure and gained more profits.
Exercise 2
How does a good government function: good government is invisible. It functions in its quiet efficient way.
Comparison 1: When you turn on the water in the morning, you don't say, "Oh, my, isn't that wonderful. The wa-

ter is clean."

Comparison 2: When you eat your food, you don't say, "Isn't that terrific ? I did not get them poisoning."

When we make the newsmedia: when something goes wrong.

Part Ⅲ : Listening Comprehension Test

1. B 2. C 3. A 4. A 5. B 6. D 7. D 8. B 9. A
10. D

Your Notes:

_____

_____

_____

_____

_____

_____

_____

_____

_____

_____

_____

_____

_____

_____

_____

Unit Twenty-seven

Part Ⅰ : Listening Practice

Section A: European Monetary System (1)

Exercise 1

1. The introduction:
   A. Hilda Rothfield
   B. New York, Paris
   C. World Bank
   D. Organization for Economic Cooperation and Development

2. Monetary Systems (in general):
   A. are kept in a fixed relation to each other.
   B. same rates kept.

3. The European Monetary System:
   A. 2.1/2 %.
   B. Germany, France, Denmark, Norway, Austria, the Netherlands, Italy, Switzerland, Belgium, Great Britain.

Exercise 2

1. Because he is attending the conference sponsored by the World Bank.

2. A. Because they have really been informative and helpful.
   B. And it has been possible for her to interview many more leaders in a short time than she would normally be able to do.

3. He is an officer of the World Bank, and an advisor of the Organization for Economic Cooperation and Development.

4. He has been assigned there to help set up a European Monetary

System.

5. No. No change would be almost impossible.

Section B: European Monetary System (2)

Exercise 1

1. Advantages of the system:
   A. stability, exchange rates
   B. smooth and steady adjustment, rates, wide swings
   C. stronger currencies from being overvalued
   D. links, the dollars, countries equally

2. Disadvantages to weaker nations:
   A. exchange rates
   B. inflation, economies, force them to price their manufactureres
      out of the market

3. Advantages to weaker nations:
   A. inflation
   B. to stop inflation, control of wages

4. Disadvantage to stronger nations:
   inflation

5. Effects on world:
   A. more trade with each other
   B. less trade with Europe
   C. Japan, U. S.

Exercise 2

1. The strength of the economy of the country

2. When the value of a currency really drops

3. Because the inflation will be decreased

4. Because they think a little inflation is all right, and the final re-

sult is stability

5. He is going to make a speech at the convention

Section C: Emerson Books
Exercise 1
1. Background — Description of old bookstores
    A. intuition, statistics
    B. attract into the store
2. New Stores
    A. New Image
    B. facade
    C. a) new releases and bestseller
       b) theme display
    D. wide
    E. very bright
    F. modern, lively people
3. Computer Terminal
    A. an inventory system
    B. Advantages
       a) future needs
       b) book before it sells out
       c) any sales
Exercise 2
1. They carried the stocks of books dependant on manager's whims and the wholesaler's sales pitch.
2. Because they had no method and no plans.
3. Computer terminal.
5. They can't afford to wait six months to find out that they bought

a few copies of one book and too many of another book.

Section D: Ben and Jerry

Exercise 1

1. Personal information about Ben and Jerry:
   A. wear suits, master degree
   B. hippies, sixties
   C. children

2. Information about their business:
   A. Burlington, Vermont
   B. famous, business philosophy
   C. unconventional

Exercise 2

1. They took a corresponding course in ice-cream making.
2. A business that makes money in a community must give back to the community.
3. Very well.
4. Pay must be as equitable as possible between top managers and factory workers.

Part Ⅲ : Listening Comprehension Test

Offer and Request

1. C   2. B   3. D   4. B   5. C   6. C   7. D   8. B   9. D
10. D

Your Notes:

Unit   Twenty-eight

Part I : Listening Practice

Section A: Agricultural Report
Exercise 1

	Amount of Protein %	Weight Increase in 2~4 Days %	Comparison of Growth Rate
Duckweed	35~50%	100%	10 times
Soybean	35~50%	10%	1 time

Exercise 2

1. Bangladesh is a perfect country for duckweed: its temperature and polluted water holes are right for duckweed growth.
2. Duckweed can provide high-quality and low-cost animal feed.
3. Farmers can sell it for $ 27 a ton in the market and earn a lot of money.
4. Duckweed can purify waste water.

Section B: Recycling
Exercise 1

Material	Time	Amount
Aluminum	3 months	enough to build all the commercial airplanes in the country
Iron and steel	each year	enough to supply all the car makers in the US

Material	Time	Amount
Trees	1 week	more than 5,000,000 trees
Paper	this year	to build a wall 12 feet high from L. A. to N. Y.
Leaves and grass clippings	every year	24,000,000 tons
Glass bottles	every two weeks	enough to fill the two tallest buildings in N. Y. City
Plastic bottles	every hour	2,500,000 plastic bottles

Exercise 2

1. Recycling saves money, energy and natural resources.
2. They could be composted, allowed to rot or decay so that they could become fertilizer for soil.
3. The radio talk may be sponsored by the Environmental Concern Fund.

Exercise 3

(See the transcript)

Section C: Library Call Slip

Exercise 1

Print name	Call number: 932. 51
Date	Author or Periodical: Paul H. Beik Book Title: Modern Europe Date or Volume:

Exercise 2

4 1 3 2

Exercise 3

1. Cards in small drawers describing every book in a library.
2. Call number is used as a guide to find the book, as books are arranged numerically in the stacks.
3. You look under the author's name.

Section D: Call Number Systems

Exercise 1

Dewey decimal system   10
Library of Congress system   21

Exercise 2

1. Call number systems break down all knowledge into categories.
2. They are used to classify books in libraries.
3. Dewey decimal system is more commonly used in USA.

Exercise 3

General Works	Bibliographies, encyclopedias, periodicals, newspapers etc. too general to go under any single subject.
Philosophy	Ethics, logic, psychology, etc.
Religion	Bible, history and theology of Christian and non-Christian religions etc.
Social Sciences	Sociology, economics, education, etc.
Linguistics	English and foreign language grammars, dictionaries, etc.
Pure Science	Mathematics, biology, physics, chemistry, etc.
Applied sciences	Medicine, engineering, agriculture, home economics, business, etc.

Arts and Recreation	Architecture, painting, music, theater, sports etc.
Literature	Poetry, drama, novels, essays, etc., (of all countries and in all languages)
History	Geography, biography, history

Part Ⅲ: Listening Comprehension Test

1. A 2. B 3. A 4. D 5. A 6. C 7. D 8. C 9. A
10. C

Your Notes:

_____

_____

_____

_____

_____

_____

_____

_____

_____

_____

_____

_____

_____

_____

_____

Unit   Twenty-nine

Part I : Listening Practice

Section A: Talk on Creativity

Exercise 1

> as, teach, tend to, and, if, could, solely to, would, down, demands, widespread, to, between, and, and.

Exercise 2

1. To the fact that he never went to school, and therefore preserved the rare gift of thinking freely.

2. As a disadvantage.

3. To civilize, not to train explorers.

4. The explorer is always a lonely individual with the faculty of perceiving in an unhabitual way.

5. For the social order demands unity and widespread agreement, both traits are destructive to creati-vity.

Section B: Science Report

Exercise 1: notetaking:

* Topic of the lecture: Machine Intelligence: Can computers write poetry or music or play chess?

* Machines write poetry: Machines do best in poetry with strict rules. eg. Japanese Haiiko.

* Computers compose music: e. g. "Eliot Sweet", but not very interesting since musical quality is difficult to measure. Computers are less successful in this field.

* Chess played by machine: It can be measured. Computers can be programmed to play chess quite well, better than human chess a-mateurs, e. g. in Illinois a computer won the annual com-puter chess championship, e. g. and in Massachusetts, a computer won the Chess Tournament in 1973.
* Conclusion: Computers' performance is merely competent, not outstanding. That computers will be better than man in thought is only speculation.

Exercise 2

ability, measured, computers, programmed, consistently, annual, championship, amateurs

Section C: How to Select and Care for a Christmas Tree

Exercise 1

1. In a local Christmas tree store or on a Christmas tree farm.
2. A tree with good, fresh, green needles that are soft to the touch.
3. A tree that has a good shape.
4. Shake the tree to get rid of the dead needles and pieces of grass.
5. Because this is a good safeguard against the needles' drying out and becoming a fire danger.

Exercise 2

1. F 2. F 3. T 4. T 5. F

Section D: A Visit

1. 1800
2. George Washington
3. two-storey, stone, simple, dignified;
4. the British burned it in the War of 1812, and it had to be re-

378

painted white.

5. The president James Madison's wife Dolly ran out of the burning building carrying Guber Sturant's portrait of Washington.

6. 132, 18, every four years;

7. 6, the public;

8. the people of the United States, property.

Part Ⅲ: Listening Comprehension Test

Passage Ⅰ 1. C 2. D 3. C

Passage Ⅱ 4. D 5. C 6. C

Passage Ⅲ

7. from season to season

8. some effect on most person's intelligence/ a definite effect on our mental abilities

9. spring and fall

10. during the summer

Your Notes:

_____

_____

_____

_____

_____

_____

_____

Unit   Thirty

Part Ⅰ: Listening Practice

Section A: Space Shuttle Flight
Exercise 1
1. The first Japanese scientist to fly in an American space shuttle
2. The first black woman astronaut
3. The first husband and wife team
4. The first American space shuttle flight concerned mainly with Japanese research
Exercise 2

Number of Experiment	Provided by
34	Japan
7	U. S. A
2	joint-research
43	in Total

Exercise 3
1. B   2. C   3. D

Section B: Cold and Flu Fighter
Exercise 1
1. C   2. D   3. B
2.
Exercise 2

    a large dose; does not exactly; with or without; able to abort;
for everybody; for all colds; not take the chance; better part of.

Exercise 3

Jane fights against colds by drinking a lot of liquids and taking a large dose of vitamin C and her advice has helped her friends a great deal.

Section C: Discoveries of Sigmund Freud (1)
Exercise 1
1. hypnosis   2. long talks with patients
3. study of dreams
Exercise 2
young Greek man, sat by pool, looked down and saw his face in water, so pleased by his beautiful face, sat long, grew roots, became flower
Exercise 3
Narcissism: First stage of emotional development
Definition: New born babies knowing and loving only themselves
Causes of people frozen in narcissism:
1. failure to satisfy a child's basic needs (no warmth, security and love)
2. quickly satisfy a child's every need (too much attention, warmth and love)

Section D: Discoveries of Sigmund Freud (Ⅱ)
Exercise 1
as child, separated from parents, as adult, killed his father, married his own mother without knowing, put out eyes to punish himself
Exercise 2
frozen, 40, jealousy, child, feelings, complex, bonds, frozen,

stage, painful, worked, succeeded, memories, complex, suffered, understood, free, honest, good, given

Part Ⅲ : Listening Comprehension Test

1. C 2. D 3. A 4. D 5. D
6. practical
7. a Dutch astronomer, mathematician and physicist.
8. It is related to engineering.
9. The letters stand for five steps in the reading process: Survey, Question, Read, Review, Recite.
10. To look quickly.
11. That one should think about the ideas while reading the words.
12. stocks, securities, bonds, cotton, grain and other commodities.
13. a crash
14. wild and unwise speculation by many people and dishonest practices by some businessmen and some members of exchanges
15. b

Simulated Listening Test 3

Section A 1. C 2. B 3. D 4. B 5. A 6. B 7. C
8. C 9. C
Section B 10. C 11. D 12. A 13. A 14. A 15. C

Simulated Listening Test 4

Section A 1. B 2. D 3. C 4. B 5. D 6. A 7. A 8. A

9. B

Section B   10. B   11. C   12. D   13. D   14. C   15. A

Simulated Listening Test 5

Section A   1. B   2. C   3. A   4. B   5. B   6. B   7. A   8. A
9. C

Section B   10. B   11. A   12. D   13. A   14. D   15. A

<u>**Your Notes:**</u>

_____

_____

_____

_____

_____

_____

_____

_____

_____

_____

_____

_____

_____

_____

_____

_____

_____

图书在版编目（CIP）数据

研究生英语听说教程教师参考书/罗立胜主编. 修订版
北京：中国人民大学出版社，1999
研究生英语系列教材
ISBN 7-300-01886-6

Ⅰ. 研…
Ⅱ. 罗…
Ⅲ. 英语-视听教学-研究生-教学参考资料
Ⅳ. H319.9

中国版本图书馆 CIP 数据核字（1999）第 19695 号

研究生英语系列教材
Postgraduate English Listening and
Speaking (Revised Edition)
研究生英语听说教程（修订版）
Teacher's Book
教师参考书
北京市研究生英语教学研究会
主　编：罗立胜
副主编：祝　扬　任林静
编　写：李光立　彭　漪　王宝娣
　　　　韩丽峰　姜文东　刘　延

出版发行　中国人民大学出版社
社　　址　北京中关村大街31号　　　　　邮政编码　100080
电　　话　010－62511242（总编室）　　010－62511239（出版部）
　　　　　010－82501766（邮购部）　　010－62514148（门市部）
　　　　　010－62515195（发行公司）　010－62515275（盗版举报）
网　　址　http://www.crup.com.cn
　　　　　http://www.ttrnet.com（人大教研网）
经　　销　新华书店
印　　刷　河北涿州星河印刷有限公司
开　　本　850×1168毫米 1/32　　　版　　次　1994年4月第1版
　　　　　　　　　　　　　　　　　　　　　　 1999年5月第2版
印　　张　12.25 插页1　　　　　　　　印　　次　2005年7月第6次印刷
字　　数　305 000　　　　　　　　　　定　　价　25.00元